"If a man could bite the giant hand
That catches and destroys him,
As I was bitten by a rat
While demonstrating my patent trap,
In my hardware store that day.
But a man can never avenge himself
On the monstrous ogre Life.
You enter the room—that's being born;
And then you must live—work out your soul,
Aha! the bait that you crave is in view:
A woman with money you want to marry,
Prestige, place, or power in the world.
But there's work to do and things to conquer—
Oh, yes! the wires that screen the bait.
At last you get in—but you hear a step:
The ogre, Life, comes into the room,
(He was waiting and heard the clang of the spring)
To watch you nibble the wondrous cheese,
And stare with his burning eyes at you,
And scowl and laugh, and mock and curse you,
Running up and down in the trap,
Until your misery bores him."

— EDGAR LEE MASTERS, SPOON
RIVER

CHAPTER ONE

"You got the wrong address, kid. We didn't call an exterminator."

In the crimson nightclub, a haze of gritty cigarette smoke drifted into Cyrus's face as he stared up at a muscled bartender. The guy was straight out of a seventies porno—cigarette hanging from his mouth, bushy hair on his arms, and a brown velour shirt. Cyrus was convinced someone had invented a time machine and stolen him from 1977.

Cyrus became intently aware of the steel sprayer strapped to his back. The forty-pound canister threatened to damn near drag him to the floor. Another reminder of his mission.

"I lugged this equipment all the way over here," Cyrus said, patting the sprayer. "My boss is gonna kill me if I don't use it."

The bartender folded his arms. His giant biceps flexed under his shirt as he scissored his cigarette. "Not my problem," he said, blowing another cloud in Cyrus's direction. Smoking was supposed to be banned in Chicago bars, but paranormal nightclubs didn't have to play by the rules.

The bartender was staring at Cyrus so hard, his eyes might as well have been lasers. Cyrus wondered what type of paranormal the guy was. It was never wise to ask. If Cyrus had to bet, he might have pegged the guy for a werewolf.

"Come on, man, work with me," Cyrus said. He climbed onto a stool at a laminate bar whose surface was styled like a brown agate marble. His wool coat sleeve stuck on something sticky and he pulled it loose with a sound that reminded him of a bandage ripping.

"Ugh," Cyrus said.

The bartender swiped a rag off a nearby tap, slapped it like a jock would slap a towel in a locker room, and tossed it to him. Cyrus's stool squeaked as he reared back to catch it.

"It's just Jack, kid," the bartender said.

Cyrus dabbed his coat gingerly.

Cyrus and the bartender were the only people in the room. With no music playing and the lights at full red brightness, the club felt empty, wooden. Every sound was twice as loud, with a deafening echo.

Places like this looked better in the dark. For one, you didn't have to concern yourself with the rats—because this place had a bunch of them. Second, there were all sorts of stains on the floor…

Cyrus swept his gaze across the neon sign behind the bar that said "JoJo" in bright pink letters, the brass, shimmering stripper pole in the corner of the room, and up the spiral staircase to a back office with black-tinted windows. He needed to get up there, but this bartender was going to be trouble. He noted the long metal VIP balcony over the wood dance floor, full of orange plush couches and skinny bar tables.

He turned to the bartender. "A nightclub like this has to have pests, right?"

The bartender still stared at him, unblinking.

"Even if we did, you think I'm going to hire a kid like you to take care of it?"

Cyrus wanted to punch the guy, but if he did that, he'd get

himself thrown into the mirror behind the wall, or worse, into the street on his ass.

"I'm not a kid."

"Show me your driver's license and I'll reconsider."

"I don't need one," Cyrus said. "I take the L."

He did have a driver's license, but he had purposely left it at home. The last thing he wanted was for this guy to know who he was. Hell, he wasn't even supposed to be at this shady paranormal nightclub. If Desmond and the Regulators found out what he was doing, he'd receive a stern warning.

"I'm with Danzanello Pest Control," Cyrus said. "We've been around for one hundred years. Rats, bed bugs, roaches. You name it, we take care of it."

"We don't have any of those things," the bartender said.

"Like hell you don't," Cyrus said.

Of course the guy was lying. Cyrus had been here an hour earlier as a rat, sniffing around. Not only did the place have a colony of hostile rats in the kitchen subfloor, but it also had spiders, ants, and a particularly bad infestation of German cockroaches behind the refrigerator. If the guy couldn't see the pests, then he needed professional help.

"Tell you what," Cyrus said. "I'll prove to you how good our company is. I'll treat your place for free. If you don't see my traps full of creatures, then you can tell me I'm full of it. If I'm right, then promise me a meeting with your boss so we can talk about a treatment plan."

The bartender puffed. "You're persistent."

"I'm honest," Cyrus said. He patted his sprayer again. "I have to show my boss I'm worth keeping around."

He stuck out his hand.

The bartender glanced at his watch. "We open in one hour. Do your thing and get out. Come back in two days and we'll talk."

Cyrus grinned. "Crazy good pest control, coming right up."

~

It happened that summer. It was a typical Chicago summer. The air sweltered and your sweat clung to your skin. The blue skies reflected in triplicate off the glass panels of the skyscrapers downtown. You were happy to be alive, among the crowds of people and the sunshine and the sudden thunderstorms.

Cyrus was supposed to be getting his life back on track. Dating women. Finding an apartment of his own. He had never wanted to be a rat shifter, but life among the paranormal wasn't so bad after all. He was learning to live again.

But then his sister changed forever.

While he was fighting a nephilim who lost control and threatened to destroy Chicago, his sister Becca was possessed by a demon. In a split second, she was never the same.

The usually snarky Becca had lost her sparkle. Sure, she still bossed him around and made jokes at his expense, and she looked out for him like any big sister should, but she wasn't the same. He couldn't look at her without knowing that a demon had nestled itself inside her mind. It was always talking to her. He could tell by the tortured look in her eyes.

He blamed himself. If he hadn't become a rat shifter, this would've never happened. He would've never put Becca in danger.

The winds of time changed; summer flashed into autumn; autumn decayed into winter. Snow fell from the sky in large drifts. The winds rolling off Lake Michigan made the air ten times colder than the forecast predicted. The streets took on a patina of ice and dirt-colored snow.

This was supposed to be a time of joy leading up to the holidays, the time of year when Cyrus had to think about Christmas presents. When he and Becca would eat holiday dinners at his mom's. It was supposed to be the time of the year when he reflected on his life and looked forward to the coming year.

Now here he was, trying to save his sister. There was only one man in the city who could help him, and he owned this club. He was notoriously hard to get to.

As he stood on the street corner looking up at JoJo's Dive, rubbing his hands together to keep warm, he told himself that if he got Becca into this, then he could get her out of it. He had to.

JoJo's was a rundown, skinny nightclub between two vacant buildings. With so many of the buildings in urban Chicago, you never had any idea what the vacant spaces used to be. The first-floor windows of the vacants were covered with brown paper. That made the neon lights of JoJo's Dive stand out.

An electric hum drew his eyes upward to the second story. A tall neon sign of a woman drinking from a martini glass, all legs and red lipstick, flashed pink on the second and third floors. The exterior of the bar was covered in V-shaped wood bars that reminded Cyrus of a display at a picture frame shop. The building was straight out of the nineteen seventies. Normally, he wouldn't be caught dead in a place like this. He was already on the wrong side of town.

But he had a mission. Becca was depending on him.

A frosty wind tore through him, making him shiver and pull his wool coat closer.

He pulled out the wand from his spray pack and adjusted it to a shower spray, then sprayed the exterior of the first floor where the sidewalk met the foundation. He noticed a long crack in the foundation near the kitchen. He made a mental note and didn't spray the area around the hole.

But he wasn't really spraying. Not in any amount that would deter a real pest. He had filled the pack with water. It was just subterfuge so he could pay attention.

Thank God Fontanelli let him borrow his equipment for

the day. One of the perks of working in pest control was that ol' Font let him treat his mom's and sister's places. He definitely wouldn't have been upset at Cyrus treating this shady nightclub. Font would have seen dollar signs before he even walked in the front door.

But Cyrus couldn't use the Fontanelli name. It would put Font in danger. He came up with the name Danzanello—thoroughly Italian, thoroughly unique, and not likely to raise any suspicion.

Cyrus stopped for a moment at the wooden front door. A quick creak made him jump back just before the door swung open.

A blur of fur click-clacked past him. He smelled her before he saw her—cigarette smoke and roses.

A tall blonde woman in her twenties with hair cut to her shoulders, star-shaped sunglasses, and pink platform shoes. A mink fur draped her frame and hung down to her knees. If she had whiskers and a tail, she could have made for a convincing extra in the *Cats* musical.

Whoever she was, she almost took his face off at the rate she rushed out of the club.

Cyrus kept spraying and kept her in his peripheral vision.

The woman stood on the corner and sighed, walking back and forth. She sighed and let out a quiet grunt of displeasure. Something told Cyrus it wasn't the cold that was bothering her.

A cloud of cigarette smoke drifted into Cyrus's nostrils and he coughed just as a horn blared.

A stretch limousine eased around the corner and slid down the street like it owned it. Looked like an old Lincoln from the seventies, the kind he'd seen in movies. Tinted windows. Gold dollar sign hood ornament. Reflective chrome grill. They sure didn't make limos like that anymore. Around downtown Chicago, it was more common to see stretch Hummers or Cadillacs—not vintage vehicles.

The limo pulled to the side of the road and slowed to a stop in front of the woman, who stood with a hand on a hip, puffing smoke that hung overhead like a thundercloud.

The limo driver, dressed in a black chauffeur uniform, rushed out and opened the rear door.

This was the moment Cyrus had been waiting for. His chance to finally see the elusive JoJo Skaggs, the only man who could help Becca.

Cyrus's jaw dropped as the door opened.

CHAPTER TWO

"You're wasting your time, girl. You'll never get rid of me, so you might as well accept your fate."

Becca pushed the Garamanthus's snarling demon voice out of her mind as she brushed flecks of snow off her cheek. She tightened her knitted scarf and tucked down her chin, bracing for another bitter gust.

The streets in Logan Square were like wind tunnels on cold days like this. It never mattered what she wore—even her warmest duffle coat and beanie didn't do a thing for her. She could have worn two of each and it still would have felt like she was wearing a t-shirt. Her only saving grace was that her hair was tied up in a bandanna under her beanie. Otherwise, the wind would have blown her hair all about. Becca always thought it was some cruel joke that it was colder in Chicago than in states up north.

The wind howled again, and the demon spoke, as if on cue with the cold.

"I'm keeping score. Every step you take against me, I will return against you three-fold. One for you, one for Cyrus, and one for your dear, sweet mother…"

Keep your mind blank, she told herself. *Don't let him get to you.*

Becca squinted as the wind drew out tears. All she could do was put one foot in front of the other. The wind pushed against her like a bouncer at a nightclub trying to stop her from getting in.

"I'll get to you all right," Garamanthus said. "I hear your every thought, remember?"

Becca bumped into something warm. A man in a pea coat and a plaid scarf, standing on the corner holding a paper cup of roasted coffee. The cup lunged forward and he caught it, but not before an arc of liquid spilled onto the quarter panel of a passing car.

"Watch it!" he cried.

"Sorry," Becca said, slipping past.

Since Garamanthus started talking to her on the walk, she had stopped paying attention. She glanced up at the colorful joisted masonry on both sides of the street.

Where was she again?

She stood on a street corner with several people, staring at an orange "do not walk" pedestrian light for several seconds, trying to remember.

How long had she been walking? A few blocks, maybe. She was still in Logan Square, her neighborhood. But she had temporarily forgotten where she was going and why she was walking so quickly. The thought nagged her, like trying to remember the location of a lost item.

"Maybe if you forget where you were going, you'll develop some sense," Garamanthus said. "Trying to accomplish your goal will only increase your score."

Becca shook her head as if the act would shake the demon quiet. She closed her eyes. A black wall of stillness washed over her eyelids. For a moment, everything was quiet. Peaceful.

Then, footsteps all around her. She opened her eyes and crossed the street, still trying to remember where the hell she had been going.

She was walking so fast. She had the sense that she needed to be somewhere, that the destination was in her mind. But the demon was playing with her memories, rearranging them to confuse her. She hated him for it.

Her confusion made her mad. Mad at the demon. Mad at herself for allowing him to possess her.

"Go back to the Wicked Cat," Garamanthus said. "Pour yourself a nice gourmet coffee—you know the one—and give your dear old mother a call. Her voice will make you feel better. Crack jokes with that little shit of a brother you have. Round out this glorious night by chatting with your assistant manager. He's getting quite lonely on account of being so injured and all. Be a good girl for a change, Becca."

The insult made Becca so furious she screamed.

"Stop it!" Becca cried. A few people standing in a doorwell nearby stopped and stared.

"Oh, that's it—I pushed your buttons."

She imagined the demon's face, coal-blue with two mangled, curved cattle horns and gold chipped teeth, settling into a grin that reminded her of a murderous clown. The demon's face expanded across her mind's eye, swirled about like a balloon stuck above a vent—round and round and laughing and laughing.

You have to no right to talk about Cristián, she thought. *Leave him alone.*

"Allow me to leave *you* alone," Garamanthus said quickly. "I won't speak to you for the rest of the night if you turn back now. Turn back, Becca. Turn back before you invite more danger. Turn back—"

A car honked at her.

She was in the middle of another crosswalk. She jumped onto the curb just as a blue minivan sailed past. The demon snickered. Her heart raced.

"Pity," he said. "You would have been more useful flattened on the asphalt. Then I could find another stupid human to possess."

"Stop it, damn it!" Becca cried, putting her hands to her head. She gripped her beanie and closed her eyes.

She had spoken out loud again. Only when the demon's voice disappeared completely did she realize what she had done.

More people on the street were staring at her. The whole city might as well have been staring. Her stomach dropped and she wanted to throw up.

A familiar blinking drew her across the street. The marquee of the historic Logan Theater glittered in the twilight. The theater's majestic, mosaicked half-circle window on the first floor over the marquee burned like fire. An employee was changing the letters on the marquee with a long pole.

Becca found herself stumbling under the marquee, across the black and white checkered tile floor, and to the wall under a glass panel with a movie poster advertising a romantic comedy. She sat down under the poster and closed her eyes.

Since the possession—Cy had aptly called it "moment zero"—she just wasn't herself anymore. She would be humming along at the Wicked Cat, running the coffee shop and bar with no problems. But then Garamanthus would wake up unexpectedly. She never knew when he'd come alive. Suddenly, the demon would carpet-bomb her mind with horrible thoughts. He would attack her and berate her and belittle her. And he would do it in the middle of conversations with customers, to the point where she couldn't hear herself think. Occasionally, he would take over her body.

The takeovers were the worst. She would be doing something, like pouring a cup of coffee, and then the next thing she knew, she was in her apartment, in her bed, huddled between the sheets. To add insult to injury, Garamanthus would pick up his attacks again, telling her how worthless she was and how he could have and should have picked a better host.

The result over the six months was a complete loss of her confidence. Just when she was having a good day, he would appear. If she was having a bad day, he was sure to appear.

How many nights had she cried, wishing for her old self again?

She asked Desmond, the leader of the Regulators, first. She poured him a tall coffee as he sat at the bar, and before he could take a sip, she begged him for an exorcism.

Solemnly, he told her, "Becca, you need more than an exorcism. Demons just don't come out like they do in the movies."

"Then tell me what I have to do," she said. "I don't care what it is."

Desmond had eyed her sadly. "Better to wait it out."

"I'm not waiting," she said.

"Becca, trust me," Desmond said, grabbing her wrist. He patted her hand gently. "I wouldn't steer you wrong. You're in for hell, but it may be over sooner than you think."

She pulled away from him. "You don't know me very well, do you? I don't sit around and wait for anything."

But Desmond, in his usual wisdom, was right. There was no ritual, no supernatural act, no treatment that would rid her of Garamanthus. He was forever nestled inside her mind, and there didn't seem to be anything she could do about it.

Wait it out…No freaking way.

The wind blew again, distracting her from her thoughts. A voice called her.

"Ma'am? Are you okay?"

The theater employee arranging the letters on the marquee had stopped and was staring at her with concern.

"I'm okay," she said. "I just needed to sit down for a minute."

The theater employee took a lingering look at her and shrugged before spearing the next letter with his pole.

She wondered how she must look to that poor guy. She felt so dejected and dark. Maybe the people passing by saw it too.

Something buzzed in her pocket. Her phone. She slipped it out to see a text message from Gilberto Sanchez.

Hey. Just checking in. In case you had an attack, remember that you need to go to 264X Spaulding Ave.

A slight smile crept across her face at the reminder.

Thank God for Gilberto. Somehow, he had known she was going to have an attack. Along with Cyrus, her mom, and Desmond, Gilberto was one of the only ones who knew what she was really going through.

Dancing dots appeared on the screen, followed by another message.

Therapist, remember?

Quickly, Becca found a reply.

I remember. Thanks. But is the address really 264X…?

Gilberto replied almost immediately.

Ye of little faith…

It was the little things that she appreciated now. It was funny how a text message from a friend could lift her up.

Then she remembered Garamanthus. She paused, waiting for him to attack her. But the demon remained quiet.

Becca stood up, smoothed out her duffle coat, and resumed her walk to the therapist's office.

CHAPTER THREE

THE OFFICE WAS in an unmarked greystone partially shrouded by a tall catalpa tree and set off from the street with a tall wrought-iron fence. A soft lamp lit up the first-floor window.

Becca checked her text message to confirm the address—it contained an X just like Gilberto said. Definitely a paranormal address.

She unlatched the wrought-iron gate, walked reluctantly up the steps, and rang a silver-plated doorbell.

Quiet footsteps tracked through the hallway. A curtain in the front door parted.

A middle-aged woman with graying hair in a fringe-cut bob opened the door with a warm smile, enough to turn the wintry day into spring. She wore a purple sweater and cat eyeglasses, and she had an old-fashioned hardcover tome with golden deckled pages tucked under one arm.

"You must be Rebecca Grant," the woman said.

"Becca."

"Very good. Please, come in."

Becca stepped into the vestibule, shivering. The woman helped her out of her coat and hung it on a hook on the wall.

"I'm Carolyn Davidson," the woman said, extending a

perfectly manicured hand with maroon nails. Becca took it. It was warm and soft.

The inside of the house was toasty warm, the kind of warmth that made you wish for Christmas cookies and hot chocolate. This lady had the right idea in reading a book. Becca would have been curled up on the couch reading a book too.

"You're a few minutes early," the woman said. "You won't mind if I finish up a few notes from my last client, will you?"

"Not at all. I'm just glad you squeezed me in on short notice."

Becca followed Carolyn into the parlor. It was like something out of a home magazine: a bookcase full of novels arranged by color, a coffee table with a prim stack of the latest magazines, and a television framed by two large poinsettias.

Becca sniffed and caught the aroma of lavender wafting up from an essential oil diffuser on the bookcase.

Next to the parlor, French doors led into a shadowed office with a Turkish lamp glowing on a neatly organized executive desk.

"Have a seat, and give me a minute. Can I get you a coffee, hon?" Carolyn asked.

Becca declined and sat down on a black leather sectional next to a radiator. Carolyn disappeared into her office and silence settled across the house.

This place didn't look like a therapist's office, but she had never been to therapy let alone a paranormal therapist. She expected the calm sterility of a doctor's office, or a big Georgian manor with wood-paneled walls, like she saw in the movies.

Becca wondered how long this woman had been a therapist. Clearly, the office had just the right touch. What was it like sitting around all day and listening to other people's problems?

Maybe Becca knew a thing or two about therapy too.

Tending bar at the Wicked Cat was like being a therapist in a way. She knew all the regulars and their problems, and she often gave them advice to go with their drinks.

I'm in the hot seat now, she thought. *Geez…*

Footsteps against the hardwood floor stopped her thoughts as Carolyn emerged from the office. "So sorry for the wait," she said, motioning her forward.

The office was fully lit now in a dusky orange glow. Floor-to-ceiling bookcases covered the walls. A single window let in the fading rays of sunlight.

So homey. The only thing missing was a cat.

Carolyn directed Becca to a soft leather couch in the corner. A tissue box sat on the table next to the sofa. The couch nearly swallowed her.

Carolyn sat down on the leather chair facing the couch. She unclipped the pen and began scribbling on a legal pad in her lap. "Normally, I would ask what brings you here, but I already have a good background."

Becca's eyes widened. "You do?"

"Honey, I'm not your average therapist," Carolyn said with a wink. "A gentleman named Gilberto stopped by earlier today and told me about you."

"He...did?"

She didn't know what to think about Gilberto telling her business to this woman. But apparently, he'd seen her too and they knew each other.

"And Desmond stopped by last week to give me a briefing too," Carolyn said. "You've got a lot of people concerned about you, Becca. You should also know that Desmond is paying for your sessions. He said to come as much as you want and not to worry about a thing. And, so you know, everything we talk about is confidential. Desmond and Gilberto may have volunteered information, but I will never do that. You're in a safe space."

If Carolyn was a paranormal, Becca wondered what her

powers were. Desmond told her never to ask, but she became obsessed with the thought. Witch? No, but weren't there things such as white witches?

"I've heard about you, but now I want to know myself," Carolyn said. "Who is Becca Grant?"

Becca settled on the couch. No one had ever asked her a question like that before.

"I don't know who I am anymore," she said after a while.

"Gilberto told me the following things," Carolyn said, consulting her notes. "Entrepreneur. Devoted daughter and sister. I'd say that's a pretty good identity to start with, don't you?"

Becca lowered her eyes to the hardwood floor. "Everything you said would have been a perfect description six months ago. But ever since the demon possessed me, I've questioned everything."

"Like what?"

"I can't do anything anymore without being watched," Becca said. "He's here right now, listening."

She expected Garamanthus to make a witty reply. He did not.

"He talks to me all the time. I can never get a break from him. I have no privacy. He invades my every thought. He knows everything about me. I feel like I've slipped into some alternate timeline and am watching myself spiral into doom."

Carolyn, who had been writing something down, stopped. "What does he say to you?"

Becca recapped their conversation of the last half hour.

Carolyn frowned. "When he starts speaking, what do you do?"

"I tell myself not to listen to him," Becca said. "I tell myself that he's lying. And that nothing he says is true. I tell myself that I love myself and that the only person who decides what happens in my life is me. Not some demon."

"How do you feel that's going?"

A tear jumped into Becca's eye. She let it sit there for a moment.

She told herself, damn it, she wasn't gonna cry to some random stranger she'd never met, but here she was. She swiped the tissue out of the box and dabbed her eye. "I miss my brother. I miss being myself. And even though I tell the demon to get lost, he gets to me every time. I just get so mad at myself. So mad I can't even think."

Carolyn leaned forward. "Becca, for what it's worth, everything you're feeling and experiencing is completely normal. Demon possessions are…tough."

More tears fell down Becca's cheek and she hated herself for it.

"This may sound hard to believe, but you're grieving," Carolyn said.

"Grieving?" she asked. "No one's dead."

The words hit her like a slap.

Carolyn continued. "I've worked with numerous demon possession victims. All of them responded well and are now living meaningful lives."

"Meaningful?" Becca asked. "What's that supposed to mean? Did they get rid of the demons?"

Carolyn shook her head quietly.

"I can help you control it and mitigate it, but—"

The woman hesitated and chose her words carefully.

"Your old self is dead, Becca."

Carolyn's words faded away as Garamanthus came alive, laughing so loudly that Becca couldn't hear the rest of what the woman said.

CHAPTER FOUR

CYRUS EXPECTED JoJo Skaggs to be a gangster. A good-looking guy in a debonair Armani suit and impeccable swirling tie, surrounded by an entourage of muscled men. Who else would own a shady nightclub and ride around in a stretch limousine? Who else could the woman draped in mink at the corner possibly be waiting for?

Instead, a pair of shiny burgundy bluchers stepped out of the limo. Attached to them, brown corduroy pants that flared out at the bottom, covered slightly by an oversized chocolate mink coat that ruffled in the cold wind. Cyrus's eyes rose to a beige turtleneck with a gold chain that reflected off the waning sunlight like ice, and round burnt umber-colored sunglasses.

Cyrus's eyes stopped at the man's head. JoJo Skaggs was a small man. Couldn't have been more than five feet tall. He was built like a turtle, with a short neck and hulking shoulders even though he didn't have much muscle. His chestnut hair—what was left of it—was styled into a neat perm, and he wore a well-trimmed Van Dyke beard. He stood tall out of the limousine and waited as the woman stretched her arms and hugged him. He took the hug like a king took a bow, hardly reciprocating. He gave her a quick peck on the cheek.

"We're gonna be late, baby," the woman said.

"We had a little problem," JoJo said. His voice was cold. "It's good now."

The woman stepped into the limo.

"Are you coming?" she asked.

Cyrus sensed JoJo's eyes on him. He quickly lowered his eyes and resumed spraying. Still, he felt the man's eyes on him, like he was regarding him. JoJo was burning a hole in his back. Cyrus made his way toward the side of the building, but still the hairs on his neck raised.

Finally, JoJo's gaze relented.

"I need to check on something," he said.

"Nuts to that!" the woman said. "You know how Donnie gets when we're late, baby."

"Maybe he'll have to get like that again."

The woman sighed heavily.

"Leave the car running," JoJo said in a sharper tone, probably to the limo driver. "I'll be back in five."

In the corner of his eye, Cyrus watched as JoJo strode across the sidewalk to the front door. The short man paused momentarily before opening the door, like he was keeping an eye on Cyrus.

Suddenly, Cyrus's heart raced. A little voice told him to run, run, run. He was going to get himself killed. He felt that usual pang in his gut of adventure and danger and excitement. Something about this guy chilled him like no others had —not even Murgalen.

In half a second, the side of the building skirted to the right and he was back at the Wicked Cat, sitting in the booth in the corner under a mason jar light, talking to Rocco and Luna. Luna, dressed in her usual pink flannel with the first button undone, long blonde hair and creamy brown eyes, and Rocco in his leather jacket and jet-black moussed hair nursing a glass of scotch that reminded Cyrus of caramel syrup.

"We've been thinking about it, bud," Rocco said, "and the way we see it, Becca is six kinds of screwed."

Luna elbowed him. "Babe, stop!"

"Somebody's gotta level with him," Rocco said. "Desmond isn't being honest with ya. It's been bothering me for a while."

Luna slid Rocco's glass away. "What Mr. Idiot here means to say is that we are here for you, Cy."

Cyrus stared into his glass of strawberry soda. The ice cubes had turned into jagged chips.

"I'm not giving up," he said. "That's not in my blood. It's not in Bec's blood either."

Luna grabbed his hands.

"Cy, I love that about you," she said. "You shouldn't give up. The glass is half full!"

"No, it's not," Rocco said. "It's not even half empty. Dude, you don't even have a glass."

Luna punched him on the shoulder.

"If you were him, you'd want to know," Rocco said under his breath.

Cyrus looked up. "Know what?"

"The reason Desmond keeps telling you there are no options is because there are no *good* options," Rocco said.

"Rocco, stop," Luna said. "Now."

"If you stop, I'll throw my drink in your face," Cyrus said.

Luna glanced nervously between the two of them. "Cy, some things are better left unknown. Mr. Idiot here is about to say something really, really bad."

The trigger on his spray wand clicked.

Crap. He was out of juice.

JoJo, still standing at the front door, finally went in and shut the door behind him.

Cyrus sighed. He checked his watch.

JoJo said he needed five minutes. That meant Cyrus had two minutes to get up to his office.

Cyrus slipped into the alley and offloaded his spray pack. He found the crack in the exterior wall he had noted on his survey of the property.

Safely in the shadows, he focused his energy on the hole as his body shrank down into a rat. His bones reeled down upon themselves as if beckoned by an invisible pulley. His incisors elongated as if out of nowhere, and his tail sprang from his back.

His feet hit the gravelly asphalt. His whiskers caught a universe of city smells like little webs. Cigarette smoke, watery women's perfume, the thick, masculine odor of a men's cologne that was layered on a little too thick…

And the hole. The smell of rotting food drifted out of the fist-sized hole in the foundation between two bricks. Cyrus squeezed himself between the cracks and threw himself into darkness.

CHAPTER FIVE

CYRUS PUSHED THROUGH THE SHADOWS. His whiskers slipped across mud, sediment, and broken chips of wood. He scampered through debris and pitch blackness, his nose low to the ground.

He stopped, sniffed, and caught a skewed whiff of old, evaporating scotch that had lost its astringency.

The scotch evoked Rocco's voice, and he was back at the Wicked Cat again surrounded by the din of clinking glasses, hushed talk, and the Grateful Dead playing a little too loud from the speaker in the corner of the room.

"Suppose you run into money trouble," Rocco said. "What would you do?"

"Huh?" Cyrus asked.

"You have a job, and boom—you don't have a job anymore," Rocco said. "What do you do?"

"Find another job," Cyrus said. "Duh."

Rocco lifted his glass of scotch. "What if there aren't any jobs?"

"It's Chicago, dude."

"Just hear me out," Rocco said.

Cyrus's whiskers brushed against something cold and rigid as a bone.

He stopped. Tensed. Sniffed the air.

There was a sudden rank smell of decaying insect exoskeleton—papery and like saliva. Cyrus's hair stood on end. Something shifted in the darkness and stalked toward him.

He backed away and ran toward the light. His claws scratched the ground as he ran.

"If there weren't any jobs, I'd ask my family for money," Cyrus said.

"Good idea," Rocco said, sipping more scotch and wincing as it went down. "But let's say you don't have any family. Or better yet, they won't give you any money. Then what?"

"You're killing me. I guess I'd rob a bank."

Rocco laughed out loud. "Not bad, bud, but you don't exactly want to go to the slammer for the rest of your life, do you? I mean, you wouldn't have money problems anymore, but you'd have a lot worse problems."

The lightning bolt of light—the alley—loomed near.

But why was he running?

No, he couldn't turn back.

Whatever was behind him was close now.

Becca was depending on him. The clock was running out to catch JoJo. He ignored his rat instinct, dug his claws into the floor, and twisted around.

Six atomic eyes glinted back at Cyrus, followed by two mandibles that clicked against each other.

"You're running out of options," Rocco said. "What do you do?"

Cyrus thought about Rocco's words. "I don't know."

"Suppose you hear about a guy," Rocco said, leaning in, "who has all the money you need."

Cyrus gulped.

"All you have to do is talk to him and he'll give it to you," Rocco said.

Luna hung her head and the color drained from her face and she swallowed hard.

"Babe, seriously, you have to stop," she urged.

Rocco ignored her. "The money's yours, except there's just one condition," he said.

The spider clicked and clacked as it moved, like gears and cogs grinding. It was the size of Cyrus's rat head.

The giant spider struck at Cyrus first, raising up its front legs. The legs flashed in the light, but then disappeared. The spider had the advantage.

Cyrus bared his incisors with a loud hiss. He let his whiskers guide him, and his body sidestepped to the right as the spider chomped at him.

Wham! Cyrus threw his weight into the spider's side, crushing it against the wall.

The spider snapped at him, but he dug a claw into its eyes, smashing in its head.

The arachnid's eyes powered down like a giant mech unplugged. It lilted to the floor, its legs curling upon itself. Its juices leaked onto the ground, mixing in with the mud.

The blackness of the building spread out before him like a velvet curtain, and he charged as fast as he could toward the original scent of alcohol.

Soon, he broke into light. Tile floor. Warmth that radiated around him like air in a blistering desert.

He was in a canyon of stainless steel and cracked tile. Somewhere nearby, a familiar odor licked into the air, and he smelled raw chicken and oil. A fryer.

Cyrus slunk along the bottom of an oven past a volcanic burst of heat. In the distance, his poor eyes made out the faint shape of a swinging door. He ran as fast as he could toward it.

"You've got two options," Rocco said. "Pay the guy back

within a certain amount of time—with serious interest—or do something for him that's equal to the money he's giving you."

"And if you don't?" Cyrus asked.

Rocco made a slicing motion across his neck.

"Jesus, man," Cyrus said.

"I told you he was Mr. Idiot," Luna said. "Now that you believe me, Cy, why don't we change topics?"

Cyrus slipped out of the swinging door and hugged a wooden wall. He was under the bar now.

He stood on his hind legs and sniffed.

No one was in the bar. The bartender had gone.

Still seeking safety, he scurried along the bottom of the bar, toward the spiral staircase that led to JoJo's office.

The steel on the staircase was coarse—textured enough for him to climb easily. He hopped onto the first step and clambered up a baluster shaped like a drill bit. Soon, he was running up the handrail, his tail working overtime behind him and keeping him balanced. He slid up the staircase with the speed of a toy race car.

His whiskers caught a whiff of hard cologne and his instinct jumped him off the railing. He zoomed under a couch just as his eyes detected a man's shadow on the platform.

JoJo was leaning on the railing and looking over the dance floor. He had helped himself to a beer from the tap and drank it like a kid drank their favorite soda on a hot day. The ice jingled in the glass as he glugged the beer down. The hops in the beer were so strong, Cyrus could taste them under the couch.

Cyrus's heart raced as JoJo strode across the platform. His bluchers passed the couch and tracked into his office.

Cyrus crawled out of the shadow of the couch and toward the door to JoJo's office, which was slightly ajar.

"So you're telling me to go to a loan shark?" Cyrus asked Rocco. "I don't need money."

"You don't need money, but you need magic," Rocco said. "And that, Cyrus, is the only difference."

"So there's such a thing as a loan shark for magic?" Cyrus asked. "A magic shark?"

"Wow, that doesn't quite give the image you're looking for," Luna said.

Rocco laughed. "They call him JoJo the Demonsharp, to be exact. He traffics in demons. If there's anyone who can solve Becca's problem, it's him. But he ain't pleasant, bud. I just thought you should know."

"He's bad news, Cyrus," Luna said. "Please stop listening to Rocco and trust me."

"Sorry, Luna," Cyrus said, meeting her eyes. Normally, her big brown eyes could have made him do anything. Luna had a way of mesmerizing him. But the charm wasn't working today. He nodded to her as if to say, "I'll listen to you next time." Then he turned to Rocco.

"Tell me more."

The conversation faded from Cyrus's mind. He tried to ignore his accelerating heartbeat as he zipped into the crack of the door jamb just before it clicked shut.

JoJo chuckled. "Give me a good reason I should put it down."

Barry turned his head. "Because I'm not stealing anything."

"That's what a thief would say."

Barry gulped.

JoJo nudged the gun further into Barry's back.

"I was trying to get a reference on what we should pay for pest control," Barry said.

"You're a pest."

"Maybe. But a kid came in here saying he could get us a good deal. Offered to treat the place for free to start," Barry said.

"The hell do I care about a roach or two?"

"Your girl cares."

JoJo grunted.

Barry gulped again. The guy had clearly never been at gunpoint much. He was sweating like it was a summer day.

After a few seconds, Barry clarified, "Your girl Simone. But I'll bet you the others wouldn't be too happy to see the creepy crawlies we've got around here."

"The lights are always off and the people are always high," JoJo said.

"What else do I have to do to get you to drop the gun?" Barry asked.

Barry's arms were sweating through his velour shirt. Time must have been slowing down for him. Seconds into minutes and minutes into hours.

JoJo stared at him and ran the conversation through his head again, forward and backward, stopping on a key word.

"All right, I'll buy it," JoJo said, lowering his gun. Barry sighed with relief and turned around.

"One of these days, you're going to learn to keep your head on a swivel," JoJo said.

He slipped his gun back into his mink coat. "If you want to age a man quick, keep him under the barrel of a gun."

"That's rich, JoJo."

Barry folded his arms and sat on the corner of the desk. "So, are we a go tonight?"

Barry pulled at his shirt, revealing the top of a rune tattoo. "I'm itching to let this thing out for a little while."

"It's a demon feeding, not an orgy," JoJo said. "Keep your shirt on."

Barry frowned. "You know what I meant."

"You're not up tonight," JoJo said. "I need you here."

"Damn it."

Barry probably wouldn't have minded an orgy. Only small-minded men asked for them, and if you looked up "small-minded" in the dictionary, you'd see Barry at the bar, sour-faced and pouring a drink. Still, he was easing into this new life nicely. He'd come to JoJo a few months ago asking for a favor—his girlfriend or whoever had some kind of disease. Barry wanted it gone.

JoJo almost couldn't have been bothered with such a simple ask. His menagerie of demons didn't like small favors, but he sensed something in Barry, something that told him the guy would be a good one to keep around. JoJo always followed his gut.

Curing Barry's girl was no big thing. By the end of the week, she was doing backflips or whatever. Completely healed. Word on the street was that she landed some neato executive gig and made more money than she and Barry knew what to do with.

JoJo imagined the confused look on her face the morning she woke up cocooned in a bed sheet feeling the usual warm spot next to her and finding it cold because Barry was gone. Forever.

Oops. A man couldn't exactly get what he wanted the way he wanted it. Too bad Barry belonged to him now, infested with some godforsaken demon that JoJo had picked up in Chinatown or somewhere. That demon had been a pain in JoJo's ass and he wanted the damn thing out. That tinny voice wheeled around in your mind like a hamster in a wheel, talking and talking and talking so you couldn't hear yourself think or take a piss. Of all the demons JoJo had known, he hated the talky ones—demon trash, not any different than human trash. Somehow, he'd taught Barry to mute the damned thing. Better Barry than him.

With a new demon in his body and plenty of havoc that needed to be done, it was better for Barry to be a child of the darkness. If he ever tried to leave, the demon would explode out of his chest and end his misery.

JoJo grinned as he walked over to a rotary phone on the desk. He picked it up and cradled the receiver to his ear. He dialed with the crook of his index finger, dragging the ring seven half revolutions until he got a dial tone.

A sleepy woman's voice answered. Dominica Parva, his newest obsession, and he didn't mean her body. Her mind. Came to him six months ago wanting to get in on the action, wanting a demon for herself to love and hold and raise hell with. That was the kind of woman he craved.

"Hey, baby," JoJo said.

The woman purred with pleasure. "I thought you'd never call."

"Be at the Montclair Building, fortieth floor," he said. "Thirty minutes. Wear something nice."

"A date," she said distastefully. "You spent last night with me. I didn't answer the phone for a date."

"It's not a date."

Her voice brightened. "Is it time?"

"Good news and bad news," JoJo said. "Good news is you're right. Bad news is there are a few others who want in too. Might be ugly."

"I can handle ugly," she said.

JoJo puffed and hung up.

Barry was staring at him, shaking his head.

"That's not the one who's into tarot, is it?" he asked.

"What if it is?"

"They're the worst," Barry said.

"What's worse," JoJo said coolly, "is little kids around here." He recalled the kid on the curb spraying pesticide. "We don't need any pest control. Tell that kid to beat it."

"You got it. Sorry for the trouble."

Something crawled up JoJo's leg. Searing pain erupted in his ankle.

"Ow!" he said.

He shook his leg and a brown rat fell out. JoJo cursed and jumped into the air as the rat raced out of the office.

"How'd that thing get in here?" he asked.

Barry grabbed a broom and chased the rat onto the platform.

JoJo grabbed his gun and followed.

Outside, the rat was nowhere to be found.

"Where'd it go?" JoJo asked.

Barry stalked toward the nearest couch. Quickly, he threw it aside.

Nothing.

"It just disappeared," Barry said, shrugging.

JoJo bent down and rubbed his leg. Two bite marks dripped blood, leaking onto his bluchers. He cursed and rubbed fresh blood between his fingertips.

"Sure you want me to get rid of that kid?" Barry asked.

JoJo swept across the platform, looking for any trace of the damned rat. Then he looked out across the dance floor shot through with pink and purple spotlights.

"Do it or don't do it," JoJo said. "I've gotta jet."

He jogged down the spiral staircase and stopped at the bottom, taking another look around the bar. The bite mark on his ankle burned like a sun.

Ignoring the pain, he strutted outside to his limo, into the smoke-wreathed leather interior, into the mink-covered arms of his girl who told him how much she loved him. As the limo pulled away, he caught a shape in the corner of his eye—the kid from earlier, walking up the alley, hopping onto an electric skateboard, and rolling away.

JoJo stared after him until the limo turned at a light. Then Simone handed him a joint. One puff later, the tall glass and brick buildings outside lost their edges, and a wave of calm spread through him. A hand slipped into his mink coat and ran fingers along his shirt, and he forgot all about that kid.

CHAPTER SEVEN

CYRUS'S HEART didn't stop pounding until he made it to the nearest bus station.

The taste of JoJo's blood was still on his tongue. The man's flesh had ripped like cheap paper, followed by a rush of warm, viscous blood tinged with iron and a million other sensations that his rat tastebuds couldn't place. JoJo's blood was an incendiary bomb in his rat brain.

His heart raced as he kept replaying the conversation in his mind.

"Tell that kid to beat it," JoJo had said.

If Barry had made it down to the alley before Cyrus and saw Cyrus's pile of things in the alley—but not Cyrus—it would have raised suspicions. JoJo might have told Barry to kill Cyrus. JoJo might have pulled a gun on Cyrus himself.

His only choice was to bite and cause chaos.

Thank God he'd surveyed the place earlier. He had slipped between the gap in the top step and jumped all the way to the bottom of the spiral staircase. His tail had served as a rudder midair and helped him land on his feet. By the time JoJo and Barry could figure out what was going on, Cyrus was back in the kitchen, back in the hole in the foundation, back into the alley.

His electric board carried him fast across the streets of the River North neighborhood. The glass and granite buildings, bars, nightclubs, and hotels passed by as Cyrus took in deep breaths and kept looking over his shoulder to make sure the limo hadn't followed him.

As he bent his knees, swerved past a pothole, and leaned into a turn, he wondered what kind of people visited JoJo's Dive. From the look of it, it had to be the down-and-outs, the serial poor decision makers. But maybe not. After all, *he* had visited JoJo, and he didn't fall into any of those categories. Yet. Sometimes he wondered, though. If he described the place to someone and said a rat shifter frequented there, Cyrus doubted the other person would have blinked.

What the hell was JoJo talking about on the phone? The guy couldn't speak full sentences to save his life.

"JoJo respects crazy," Rocco had said. "Catch his attention and you'll capture his imagination. Your best bet is to get an audience with him, but you can't do that unless you do something crazy."

In a few days, he'd find out if Rocco's advice was right.

He shook the strange man out of his mind for now. There'd be plenty of time to talk to him.

The bus station was eerily empty for a Saturday night. The only other person around was an old woman in gray rags begging for change on a nearby bench. Her eyes zeroed in on him as he passed.

"Could you spare some change, dear?" the woman asked in a thick Great Lakes accent. "I'm down on my luck, hey."

Cyrus avoided eye contact. He had nothing to give her. He wished he did, though, he really did. As he climbed onto the bus, he could still see her face in his mind, wrinkled and weathered from years of living on the streets. Cold frost-colored eyes, a kind grin, and liver-spotted hands.

As the bus rode through the streets, a drizzle of snow fell from the sky, danced in the undersides of the orange streetlights, and peppered the bus's big rectangular windows. The last flames of evening fire against the glass panels of the city's tallest buildings smoldered out as night seized the city with a blackened, starry grip.

The bus dropped him off at a Blue Line L station. Suffering a new assault of wind and snow and the intense weight of his board and the spray pack, he took the covered stairway to the raised platform two steps at a time and slipped into a stainless steel L car just as it departed.

He threw himself down on a rock-hard seat next to a window as the train rumbled alive and screeched down the tracks.

The car was only a quarter full, and most of the people on it looked just as tired and cold as him. A few of them stared at him, and he wondered what they were thinking.

The train clattered along the tracks, through a brown tunnel, and out into the city streets. The snow was falling harder now, big flakes that turned the world outside into a winter wonderland. Christmas lights twinkled in the windows of high-rise apartments, and Cyrus couldn't help but feel a twinge of sadness when he thought about how he would be spending Christmas this year.

Alone. Again.

Dating just didn't feel right with Becca suffering the way she was. If he found someone nice, he'd never be able to take her to meet Becca. Any respectable woman would take off running if, after a few months of dating, he said, "This is my sister, and she's possessed by a demon. Oh, and by the way, I can turn into a rat. Wanna see?"

Plus, he had to keep a watchful eye on his sister. He just didn't have the energy for dating. He had been trying so hard to find a cure for Becca that it was only during times like this that he realized he was neglecting himself. He tried to push the thoughts out of his mind as he watched the city go by outside the window.

His phone buzzed. His mom. He slipped in his earbuds.

"Hi, Mom."

"Hi, honey. I was going to stop by after Becca's therapy session, but she isn't answering."

Logan Square wasn't completely out of the way of her house near the University of Illinois Chicago, but the proximity to the Blue Line was a perfect excuse to drop in every now and again.

"I'm on my way home," he said.

"Were you working today?"

"Yep."

"For Fontanelli or as a Regulator?"

Cyrus froze. He couldn't exactly lie to her like he did in the past. His mom had been standing right next to Becca when she got possessed. His mom knew about all things paranormal now. It unleashed her inner helicopter parent. In fact, he was pretty sure she had invited Desmond over to her house for dinner at least once to pump him for information. She and Desmond were on a first-name basis. Ever since her unwanted initiation into the paranormal world, she'd made sure to drop in on him and Becca a lot more often. Especially Becca.

"Regulator work," Cyrus said finally, sheepishly.

"What did Desmond have you doing this time?"

"Not Desmond. Rocco and Luna."

"Oh."

His mom's disapproval was so strong, it could have traveled through the phone, grabbed him by the collar, and shook him.

"Desmond's jobs are better. He will keep you safe," she said. "He promised me that—"

"I know, Mom. But seriously, I'm fine."

The train zipped into an underground tunnel. Darkness fell across the car like a shroud for a moment before orange subterranean lights blazed by like the flame from a blowtorch. The train jostled on the tracks as it took a hard curve, and the wheels screamed like buzzsaws.

His mom said something else, but a gray blur caught his eye.

A gray, torn work smock covered in dirt and grime. Sitting across from him, staring right at him, was the woman who had begged him for change at the bus station.

She sat, whistling. Her ruddy cheeks were red from the biting wind. Her square face was grandmotherly, set off with a protruding jaw. Her piercing eyes were so blue, they could have been shot through with frost. She smelled of fresh earth and ozone after a thunderstorm. She stopped her whistling and smiled at him, revealing a missing lower tooth.

Cyrus's heart raced again. It wasn't a coincidence that this woman was here. She hadn't been on the bus, and there was no way in hell she could have miraculously ended up on the same train as him.

If she wanted to kill him, it'd be like shooting a rat in a barrel. He tried to think of a plan.

"Cyrus? Are you there?" his mom asked.

"Sorry. Tunnel," he said, not taking his eyes off the woman. The woman continued her whistling and pulled out a coin purse. She slipped out several coins from her smock and counted them one by one before placing them delicately into the purse.

"Anyway, I'll be there in about an hour," his mom said before they said goodbye.

Cyrus glanced around the car. No one else seemed to be paying attention to the woman. The woman's whistling trailed off, as if she were inviting him to escalate the encounter.

"You're following me," he said quietly.

The woman cocked her head to the side, as if she was trying to understand him.

"Come again, dear?"

"You're following me," Cyrus said louder and more confidently.

Then she grinned, her eyes twinkling.

"Yes," she said finally. "Of course I am."

"I don't have any money," Cyrus said, making sure everyone on the train heard him.

The woman held up a ragged, dirt-stained fingernail to her lips as the train approached an underground station. "There's no need for that. Humor an old woman, will you?"

Cyrus wanted to get up and flee as soon as the doors opened. As soon as he could, he'd bolt and leave this woman far behind. He'd make sure she didn't follow him this time by slipping into a sewer.

"You can go," she said softly. "I wouldn't blame you. I also don't blame you for your suspicion. Last time you got surprised on a train like this, it didn't go so well, did it now?"

The train slowed as Cyrus remembered his fight on a train with two evil fae. To say it didn't go well was an under-statement.

"How did you know that?" he asked.

The old woman gave him a prim smile. "Stick with me until the next stop and I'll explain everything."

She gestured to the doors as the pillars of a station flew by.

"Or, you may get off," she said. "I really wouldn't blame you, dear. If you go, I won't follow you, and you'll never see me again. You have my word."

The intercom system beeped and the train conductor came on in true Chicago, staticky glory. The conductor had an even stronger Great Lakes accent than the old woman.

"Sorry, folks, but we have a problem with this train. It is officially out of service. We'll have to ask you to get off and wait for the next train, which will be here in a few minutes."

Several people groaned.

The train jerked to a stop. The doors opened with a loud

shish. All the passengers rose and streamed off the car until only Cyrus and the woman remained.

"And if I stay?" Cyrus asked.

"I'll have you back to your wonderful mother in an hour," she said, winking. "I don't want her to worry."

Cyrus glanced between the woman and the doors.

This was his last chance. Yet something told him to stay.

The doors closed.

The woman clapped her hands with excitement. "What an honor! You've made my day, Mr. Grant."

Cyrus's eyes widened. "How…how do you know my name?"

"Everyone knows your name," the woman said. "You just sit tight and we'll be able to talk soon."

The train rolled away from the station. As it left the platform, Cyrus wondered if he was making a gigantic mistake.

The intercom blanketed the car in a staticky wash again.

"Pleased to have you aboard, Mr. Grant! How the heck are you this fine day?"

The conductor began whistling a happy, carefree tune that reminded him of a cartoon.

"Hang on to that pole over by there, dear," the woman said. "And don't worry too much. It'll be over before you know it."

The woman grabbed on to the nearest metal pole and joined in on the whistling.

"What will be over?" Cyrus asked.

He had barely finished the sentence when the train roared forward like a rollercoaster.

His stomach clawed up into his throat and he instinctively reached for the nearest metal pole. He caught the cold, round tube just in time.

The next thing he knew, the train screeched into a ninety-degree drop. He found himself screaming.

The last time he felt like this, he had been on a rollercoaster at Six Flags amusement park. In a split second, he was back on the Goliath again—front car, leading the way, clenching his lap bar with white-hot knuckles as the car nose-dived at the ground like a hungry falcon.

The wind had lashed his face with invisible whips. Everyone was screaming around him like they were being murdered by ghouls and loving every minute of it. Then, the coaster launched into the marigold evening sky dotted with cirrostratus clouds that looked like fingers massaging the sky. Before he could catch his breath, the car swirled down into a vicious, stomach-busting corkscrew, up and to the side and upside-down and around and round and round…

"This part's brutal!" the conductor said in a splotchy burst of static, ripping him from the memory. "Are you hanging on, Mr. Grant?"

Cyrus couldn't breathe.

The metal pole rattled as the train rolled into what he swore was an inversion loop. He was upside-freaking-down on an L train!

"What the hell is going on?" he cried.

The old woman was hanging too, her rags trailing about her.

"It's why I told you to hang on, dear," the woman said, as if this was the most normal thing in the world.

The train rotated into another corkscrew, this time like a drill boring into the earth. Waves of dirt smeared the window as dirt blew around the car at hurricane force. Cyrus's skull banged around in his head and he couldn't think anymore.

The train shook so fiercely it was a miracle it didn't break apart. Cyrus held on tight as the train flew faster down into the bowels of the earth.

CHAPTER EIGHT

Becca lay on Carolyn's couch, staring up at a copper tin ceiling.

"Tell me how you're feeling right now," Carolyn said.

A pen scratched on paper. Becca wondered what she was writing down.

"I feel…so frustrated," Becca said. She took in a deep breath.

"Why?" Carolyn asked.

How long had she been here? Through the single octagon stained-glass window, the last rays of the evening were long gone, replaced with wintry starlight.

"I'm frustrated at myself for not being stronger," Becca said. She focused on a tile on the ceiling whose ornate texture reminded her of the ridges on a metal picture frame. "I'm supposed to be strong. I've lived my whole life independently. I don't like to rely on anyone for anything. I'm supposed to be tough-as-nails Becca. People rely on *me*. I'm the person people come to with *their* problems. And now, who am I?"

She turned to Carolyn, who was watching her and hanging on every word, leaning forward. The woman nodded, mirroring empathy and understanding. It made Becca feel so at home.

"I don't know who I am anymore."

"Though you've changed, deep down, you're still the Rebecca Grant everybody knows and loves," Carolyn said. "I assure you of that. You never lost that."

Becca resumed her glance at the ceiling. "But you said the old me is dead."

"Becca, when was the last time you experienced something traumatic in your life?" Carolyn asked.

Becca dug deep. She was back at Dad's funeral, standing beside his coffin. The blue walls of the funeral home reminded her of a blue sky over a cemetery. There were more plants and flowers than people. The scent of woody candles danced in the air. It was the third time in her entire life that she'd ever worn a dress and she hated every minute of the flowing black monstrosity.

Her dad's cold dead body slept among all the noise and the crying and the chattering and the condolences. She asked herself how even the dead could sleep among all this freaking noise. Dad wore his black glasses and a polka-dotted tie that she had bought him as a gag Christmas gift one year. Tears in her eyes, she leaned down and adjusted the knot on his tie one last time.

"You loved your father," Carolyn said. "What did it feel like when they closed the lid on the casket?"

"It felt like me, my brother, and my mom were all alone. No one to help us. It felt like…a new chapter in our lives, and I had to keep on living with half a heart, because the other half of my heart was locked in that coffin with Dad and I would never get it back."

She was numb inside.

"That's very good," Carolyn said. "I want you to think about your demon possession in the same way that you think about your father's death. Even though the circumstances are completely different, have you considered that they both represent new chapters in your life?"

Becca sighed. "I guess not. But maybe you're right."

Carolyn scribbled something on her notepad. Becca would have paid a thousand dollars and a lifetime's worth of coffees at the Wicked Cat to know what she was writing. Maybe Carolyn was recommending her for the psych ward. Or maybe her smile was just a facade for "You're really messed up. Of course I can't help you. No one can help you. You're positively and totally screwed, Becca."

"Earlier, you said that other people had successful outcomes," Becca said. "What does that mean exactly?"

Carolyn set aside her notepad and pen. She clasped her hands together. "It means that they learned to tame the demons within," she said. "I gave them tools to use every time the demon launched a verbal assault. Speaking of tools, I want to share the first tool with you. Would you like to learn it?"

Becca rolled up, shaking off sleepiness. She rubbed her eyes and nodded. "Give me *all* of your tools."

"We'll start with one," Carolyn said. "It's very simple. Whenever—"

Garamanthus came alive in Becca's mind and snarled, "You silly girl! Don't listen to her. If you do, I will increase your score!"

Becca closed her eyes and winced. "No!"

She felt a hand on hers. She opened her eyes to see Carolyn staring back at her, inches from her face. "Stay with me," she said calmly, with the patience and understanding of a nurse. Something told Becca she had seen this before. Many times.

"This woman is an imbecile!" Garamanthus cried. "I will make sure you hear nothing else, and you will pay for this!"

"Shut up," Becca said.

Carolyn patted her hand. "Becca, look me in the eyes and concentrate only on me."

The demon uttered a curse in that harsh syllabic tongue that she didn't understand. She lifted her eyes and stared into Carolyn's brown eyes. She squeezed the woman's hands. "Help," she said.

"Let him finish," Carolyn said. "He can't talk forever. When he runs out of breath, I want you to think the following phrase. Say it out loud if you have to, hon: I don't have to believe anything you say. Shut up and go to hell."

A wry smile spread across Carolyn's face.

Garamanthus took the words personally.

"You can go to hell, you hussy——"

Are you finished? Becca thought.

Garamanthus fell silent.

Good, because I have something to say. I'll take it one step further. I don't have to believe anything you say. So shut the hell up and go to hell.

Garamanthus puffed. "This isn't over." His voice blew away like a dandelion on the wind, then all was quiet and still in her mind.

"That was wonderful," Carolyn said.

"No," Becca said, shaking her head incredulously. "That was…awesome."

In all these six months, the demon had never obeyed her like that. She had simply told him what to do, and he did it. Why hadn't she thought of it? It was her body, after all. At the realization, she swelled with pride, but then realized, *Oh my God, it took me six months to realize this? What is wrong with me?*

Carolyn squeezed her hand gently.

"Becca, because you did so well today, I'll give you another tool. Don't speak to the demon with your thoughts. Speak to him like you're speaking to me. It'll make you sound like a crazy person, but it will help you release your pent-up emotions. Can you do that?"

"I think so," Becca said.

"I want you to think about our discussion today. Come back and see me in a few days, okay?"

Becca stood under the starry night, staring up at the heavens. Little snowflakes whirled down in irregular columns. The sidewalk was covered with a glistening sheen of white.

She hadn't known what to expect from this session, but she felt light. Like herself again. Like she had just emerged from a confessional. The stars were a little brighter, the sky just a little bit more navy, the sounds of the city around her just a little more vibrant.

God, she missed her old self. For a second—just a second, she felt like her old self again.

She walked to the street, unlatched the wrought-iron gate, and let it clang behind her. As she made it to the sidewalk, she realized that the date and time she had given Carolyn for her next appointment wouldn't work.

She turned around to run back to Carolyn's and stopped in her tracks. The wrought-iron fence was gone. So was the postage stamp lawn with a fresh layer of snow. Instead of the stately greystone, another home—of brick and timber—stretched into the sky. Through the front window, a family of four ate dinner at a neatly decorated table.

Her heart sank. Carolyn's voice echoed through her mind. "Honey, I'm not your average therapist."

She would have to call Carolyn in the morning.

Becca trudged through the snow back to the Wicked Cat, lost in her thoughts.

CHAPTER NINE

A few blocks away, on another residential street, she heard footsteps crunch in the snow behind her.

She turned and only saw the trees swaying with their empty branches pointed at the moon as if giving an offering.

She glanced across the sparkling snow, darkened cars, and hearth-lit windows, but saw no one. She jammed her fists into her coat and kept walking.

Garamanthus came alive in her mind, laughing.

"It was the ancient Greeks who first said that your senses will fool you," he said.

Becca ignored him.

"You were right to look behind you," Garamanthus said. "You're in danger."

Becca froze. A cold wind cut through her. Somewhere, more footsteps crunched in the snow.

She reached into her coat for her pepper spray. She never left home without it. Chicago wasn't exactly the safest city in the world, even when you factored out the supernatural. She wrapped her fingers around the leather holster.

"That's a knife in a nuclear weapon fight," Garamanthus

said distastefully. "It won't help you any if it's who I think it is."

"Who is it?" Becca asked. She couldn't believe she was using her own words to talk to the demon in her head now.

Silence.

"Who is it?" Becca asked sharply.

"After how you treated me earlier, why should I tell you anything?" Garamanthus asked.

"Just answer me!" Becca said.

The demon laughed. His tone was full of malice, condescending.

"You don't get it, do you?" he asked. "If you die, I fail to accomplish my purpose. Therefore, it's in both our interests to keep you alive."

Becca gripped the pepper spray canister harder. Maybe he was playing a trick on her. Maybe this was payback for the therapy session.

"Why should I believe you?" Becca asked.

"Believe me or not," Garamanthus said. "It doesn't change the truth."

More silence.

"It's possible that my enemies of old have found me," Garamanthus said. "I have a lot of enemies, Rebecca."

Becca's mind raced.

"What have you done?" she asked.

"I suppose I did *something*," the demon said playfully. "And if you're not careful, you might die. Oh, the fun!"

Becca wheeled around. The postage stamp front yards were still empty. The hair on the back of her neck rose.

Suddenly, she was warm with fear. Somewhere, someone laid on their horn and it blared into nothingness as the sound passed over the street.

A branch cracked.

"You'll find that I can be a friend to you," Garamanthus

said. "Especially in a time like this. Well, let's keep you alive, shall we? Check your six."

Becca turned around and saw the same old trees wavering in the wind. In a nearby ash tree, she saw the man's feet first. A shadowed man in a hoodie pulled close over his head. He wore a silver cross around his neck.

She staggered back as the man jumped out of the tree and landed on one knee.

"You're a smart cookie," Garamanthus said. "Just repeat after me."

"You've run for a long time," the man said.

Becca staggered back. Her fingers trembled on the pepper spray.

"Leave me alone," she said.

The man took several steps toward her.

Garamanthus spoke and she repeated after him.

"I don't have time for you," she said.

The man growled angrily. "Possessing a new human won't work. You can't hide behind her. I've got orders to bring you in."

"I'm not going to be part of your schemes," Becca said to Garamanthus.

"Schemes?" the man asked curiously.

"Now is not the time for verbal mix-ups," Garamanthus said. "Stay focused! Repeat after me."

"You'll have to kill this girl if you want me," Becca said. Then she realized what she had said. "Wait, what?"

"Deal," the man said.

The man charged her.

Becca jumped out of the way and into the street.

"Back off!" she shouted. "Somebody, help!"

But the street remained silent.

"Calling for help won't work," Garamanthus said.

The man took several steps toward her and she raised her pepper spray and depressed the button. A triangle of wet, acrid spray hit him right in the eyes from five feet away. The man recoiled instantly and dropped to the street, writhing and coughing.

"Stay back!" Becca cried. The wind blew and she coughed and covered her mouth with her sleeve. Her eyes watered.

Something told her to run, but more footsteps surrounded her.

More men in black hoodies and silver crosses.

She cursed.

"As I said, you brought a knife to a nuclear attack," Garamanthus said. "There is only one answer if you want to survive."

The men closed in on Becca.

"Allow me to take over," Garamanthus said.

"What? No!"

"Then die."

"I don't want to die," Becca said.

"Your indecision is tiring," Garamanthus said.

Suddenly, Becca couldn't feel her arms anymore. Panic spread across her body. She was losing herself. The demon was taking over. She struggled to move, but she felt as if she were in a dream where she could see and hear and feel, but she couldn't move her arms and legs.

"No!"

"Can't be helped," Garamanthus said. "You'll owe me big after this. Besides, you'll benefit from the muscle memory."

Becca's arms moved of their own accord, closing into fists. Next, her legs bent as she assumed a fight stance. She kept her center of gravity low.

Becca screamed inside her mind as Garamanthus opened her mouth and let out a guttural cry. Then, her body launched into the air as the men charged.

CHAPTER TEN

THE FIGHT—IF you could call it that—only lasted for a few seconds. Becca lost all sense of time.

Her forearm struck one of the men's throats. The shockwave was intense and immediate. Her other fist flipped up into the underside of the man's chin, and her left leg scuffed the street as it hooked up into a roundhouse kick into the man behind her.

The second man staggered backward, and Becca used his weakened body like a springboard, kicking off his chest and jumping into a kick that landed square in the first man's nose. He fell like a woodblock tower. The second man wobbled and fell to his knees in surrender.

Suddenly, two hands grabbed her from behind and she was in a half Nelson. A rough, hairy elbow pushed into her windpipe. She gasped.

I'm going to die, she thought.

But Garamanthus knew what he was doing because she reached both hands back in an awkward grapple and seized her fingers into the third man's eye socket. After a ragged spiral throw, he was on the ground, grabbing at his eye.

She stood in the center of the three men, fists up to her face and ready for more. But there was no more.

"I'll be benevolent and give you your body back this time," Garamanthus said. "If you know what's good for you, I highly suggest that you run."

Becca felt her arms and legs again. Her legs tingled. She had used muscles she didn't even know she had.

But she had her body back.

She ran.

The bright lights of North Milwaukee Boulevard were a welcome sight. She was back in the heart of Logan Square. She slipped out of an alleyway and into a stream of people, where she felt safe. Her heart was still beating like a mad hammer, and she had barely caught her breath.

Who were those men? she thought, then remembered that she needed to speak, not think.

"Old enemies," Garamanthus said.

Becca was keenly aware of the other people around her. If someone heard her, it would be awkward. She didn't feel like dealing with stares right now.

"I have enemies everywhere," Garamanthus said. "That's what happens when you live for several hundred years and inhabit countless hosts. I believe a certain Kirk MacLeod encountered them on one of his last missions before I left his body. Now *there* was a hospitable host."

Kirk MacLeod. The man responsible for her possession. She didn't know if she could hate anyone more. The necromancer's calm sunglassed face hovered in her mind's eye. She remembered how he had opened his mouth like a snake shedding its skin and breathed Garamanthus into her, all while maintaining a death grip on her arm as he swapped blood with her against her will.

"Why can't you see this for what it is? An exciting start to a dangerous new adventure?" Garamanthus asked.

"I don't have time for adventures," she muttered as she jaywalked across the street.

"But it appears that adventures have time for you," Garamanthus said. "Aren't you going to say thank you for saving your life? I didn't have to do that. It was only my survival instinct that prompted my benevolence."

"If you want to do something nice, leave my body."

"Not on your life, and not any time soon, Rebecca."

"Then shut up and go to hell," Becca said.

She entered a greenspace surrounded by a cluster of bare trees. Logan Square Park. The park's eagle monument stretched into the sky on a Greek pillar. Behind the statue, the warm lights of the Wicked Cat flickered between the tree branches.

She walked into that familiar wall of warmth in the Wicked Cat, wishing that the fight had never happened. But the demon's words kept repeating in her head.

There was only one man responsible for her current situation: Kirk MacLeod.

CHAPTER ELEVEN

KIRK MACLEOD HAD NEVER BEEN to the shores of Mexico, but as he lay on a tanning chair, with his arms behind his head and his eyes trained at the big Caribbean sky painted with a thousand cumulus clouds speckled with stars, he thought—a guy could get used to this place.

The resort—a cliffside mecca that was all balconies, palm trees, and Adirondack chairs—was the closest thing to heaven this side of the living.

He'd only been here a week, but he'd already taken advantage of the pool, five-star restaurants, and a Jeep tour of the nearby community. The bartender knew him by name and had a martini on the rocks ready for him every day at 5:00. He spent his days and nights shirtless and in swimming trunks.

He'd watched the sunset. Of all the things he could have done in his life, he'd never thought of something as simple and quaint as watching the sun die. He had lain in the chair under a palm tree strung with fairy lights, with the rhythm of the ocean rushing nearby, and he had watched the sun sizzle into the horizon.

The act aroused a feeling in his chest that he'd never felt

before. The feeling had bothered him for several minutes until he could describe it.

It was...beautiful.

The word disturbed him. What need did a necromancer have for beauty? If his brother were alive to hear him thinking about beauty, he would have snapped him back into reality. There were too many dead who needed tending and demons who needed dirty work done to worry about beauty.

Beauty was what you enjoyed when you went to the great beyond. Just like his brother Aidan and his father Bruce. They knew beauty. They had told him all about the beautiful cascades of the great beyond, the arresting stillness and assault of colors against your eyes, the serenity of it all that just hummed through your soul and made you vibrate at the same frequency of the universe. That was a beauty he could believe in.

But he couldn't shake the feeling. That feeling of beauty in the here and now. The way he smiled when the last rays of sunlight gave way to the night.

He shifted, and sand in the chair chafed his back. He remembered the reason he had come to lie in this chair in the first place. The novel he'd been reading. Well, pretending to read.

He scooped the weather-beaten mass market paperback off the sandy ground. The same old paperback he'd pretended to read on every mission—the one with a spaceship and an exploding planet on the cover. This thing was destined for the garbage after this trip.

He was proud of himself. He had finally made it to page seven. The hero of the story, a stranded special agent in the middle of an intergalactic conspiracy, was trapped on a jungle planet after her spaceship crashed in the trees. On page seven—which Kirk still couldn't believe he'd arrived at after all these years—the hero seeks refuge in the hull of her crashed ship in the middle of the jungle. Then, she hears assassins coming for her. The same bastards that shot her out of space.

Kirk thought the hero was going to get all kinds of dead, but if that happened, the book wouldn't have been worth reading. The poor hero had to escape from this predicament somehow. But by the time Kirk turned to page eight, movement at the pool nearby broke his concentration.

His mark jumped into the pool, the man he'd been hired to travel all the way to sunny Mexico to kill.

The man was unremarkable. Late fifties. Lots of chest hair, balding at the top, and a paunch that indicated a heart attack in the near future. Mousy as hell. Always looking over his shoulder, even when relaxing in the pool. Exactly the kind of man that flees to Mexico when he's done wrong.

Kirk didn't ask too many questions of the woman who sent him here. The woman was a witch—or at least, she acted like one. Long, flowing dress, runes on her nails, and an aura of skin-tingling palpable energy about her.

Didn't matter. He assumed the guy was a cheating lover. It wouldn't have been the first time.

Fifty thousand bucks said he didn't have to ask any questions. All he had to do was complete the job.

He'd had to talk to six different spirits to track this guy down. That pissed Kirk off. Every time he made a deal to get access to the spirit world, he lost a few days of his life. Shortening his life expectancy ensured that this guy had to go. Kirk literally would never be able to get those days back.

It's nothing personal, Kirk told himself, studying page eight and rereading the description of the assassins outside. This was a space opera book for crying out loud, and there hadn't been any aliens yet.

He wondered what the aliens would look like when they showed up. Maybe he'd get to page nine sometime in the next few years.

His mark sat in the pool, sipping a glass of dark bourbon.

The man, hairy-chested and wan-faced, sipped as if every bit of the liquor gave him an understanding of the world. A child dog-paddled past him, throwing up a spray of mist into the man's bourbon. He frowned and motioned to the bartender for a new glass.

"We're out, señor," the bartender said, shrugging. The man, eyeing the kid who had ruined his poolside reverie, jammed his glass on the side of the pool and climbed out. Pool water dripped from his gray swimming trunks like rain.

Footsteps sounded next to Kirk. An olive-skinned woman in a red two-piece bikini. Her curly russet hair was wet and her arms and legs were covered in blotches of sand.

"Nice book," she said, smiling at him and raising an eyebrow.

Kirk nodded, flabbergasted. The woman gave him a lingering, flirty glance, and his eyes followed her as she walked back toward the lobby of the hotel.

Suddenly, a voice spoke next to Kirk.

"I love Mexico."

A hazy, colorless human silhouette with no arms, legs, or feet hovered next to Kirk. It danced in place like static on an old television. Kirk knew the voice as Aidan, his brother. Six months ago, he took a knife to the neck in a theater—freak accident if you ask Kirk—and he loved haunting Kirk every moment he got. If he were at the resort in person, he'd be shirtless and showing off his six-pack with his shoulder-length hair in a ponytail, or worse—a man bun.

Kirk made a deal with a demon to let Aidan come and go from the great beyond to visit him from time to time. This was one of those times.

"You can't flirt to save your life," Aidan said.

"I'm on a mission, remember?"

"It's not like the guy's going anywhere," Aidan said. "Fifty pesos says he's going to his room to lie on his bed and watch TV for the rest of the night. He'll be back tomorrow. Why not treat yourself to a little human interaction for a change? Hey, she's using the outdoor shower—now's your chance to grab her a towel and a drink, brother!"

Kirk couldn't help himself. The woman in the red bikini was running her hands through her hair as the shower poured down on her. She tilted her head back and sputtered out water, then scrubbed sand off her arms with her palms.

"You can't stop looking," Aidan said. "If you're gonna look, why not talk to her?"

Kirk snapped out of it and concentrated on page eight again. "Maybe next time."

"It's like Dad said," Aidan said, "you always were the better-looking one, but I had the game."

"It's not game if women run screaming every time they see your face," Kirk said. "How's your game working out in the afterlife?"

"That's cold and you know it," Aidan said.

Kirk puffed. Over the rim of the book, the mark walked over to a towel basket, but there weren't any towels. He cursed.

It was all part of the plan—Kirk had thrown the fresh towels into the dirty towel bin on purpose a few minutes earlier.

After a while, Aidan said, "I taught you nothing when I was alive. You're a disappointment."

The woman in the red bikini cut off the shower and looked for a fresh towel. Finding none, she shivered, crossed her arms, and called out something in Spanish to a nearby employee who was sweeping sand off the ground.

"You're unbelievable, do you know that?" Aidan asked.

"Yeah, yeah. Whaddaya got for me?"

"Right, the guy's room," Aidan said. "I put Dad on that."

Kirk sighed. "Let me guess. You were busy gawking at the beach."

"Not exactly. I was looking out for you."

"For what?"

"There are fresh wards around the perimeter of the hotel," Aidan said. "Another paranormal has set up camp here. Thought you'd like to know."

"Damn it," Kirk said under his breath. "What else?"

"I can't see a damn thing," Aidan said. "The wards are good. I can't go anywhere near them."

Kirk cycled through potential saboteurs. Maybe someone else was after his mark. If that was the case, then this guy needed to go...expeditiously.

But what if it wasn't a fellow assassin?

"Look alive, brother," Aidan said. "I'm thinking we do the accidental autumn trick. You know, the one where you stick your leg out and be a real nice guy for a few seconds. Might win you brownie points with the lady."

"I'm already ahead of you," Kirk whispered. "Except for the lady part."

"Good. Pay day coming your way in three, two..."

Kirk sat up on the tanning chair, gave a loud pretend yawn, stretched his arms to the sky, and stuck out his feet just as the mark walked by. Kirk's legs were like tree trunks and the man flew forward like Superman before crashing into the cement.

"Ah!"

"I'm so sorry," Kirk said, springing out of the chair. "I didn't see you there, sir."

"Hey, what the hell is your problem?" the man cried. He nursed a skinned knee. "Watch where the hell you're going!" he cried with angry eyes.

"Let me get you a towel," Kirk said, swiping a towel from a nearby chair. It was the towel he'd conveniently placed there and laced with nerve poison. He draped it around the man's knee and rubbed it.

"You can't just rub the blood away!"

"It'll help stop the bleeding," Kirk said, wrapping the

towel around the man's knee like a tourniquet.

The man pushed Kirk aside, called him an asshole, and stomped off. Kirk watched after him. Before he reached the lobby, he pulled the towel off his knee and chucked it in a towel hamper.

"Well done," Aidan said. "The poison'll take a few minutes to kick in."

"And I'll be at the airport," Kirk said, gathering up his book. "Unless Dad wants to take his sweet time."

"All I'm saying," Aidan said, flying next to Kirk as he passed the woman, who was now toweling herself off with a fresh new white towel, "is that it wouldn't hurt you to have another person in your life."

The woman eyed Kirk again. He nodded to her and told her to have a good night. She smiled politely, eyeing him up and down. When he was out of earshot, he said, "I've got you and Dad. That's all the company I need."

Aidan laughed as Kirk entered the open-air lobby with colonial-style Mexican arches with baskets of pink bougainvillea hanging down like vines, scenting the air with its honeysuckle-like smell. Yellow diamond designs on the orange tile pointed inward toward the elevators.

Then, someone screamed like they were being stabbed. Seconds later, several members of the hotel staff ran past.

"The criminal always returns to the scene of the crime," Aidan said, circling Kirk.

"We get a bad rap for that," Kirk said. "People forget the human urge to see their handiwork in action."

"Serial killer, shoplifter, or a graffiti artist," Aidan said in a singsongy rhythm. "To commit crimes is human."

Kirk swung into the hallway that led to the elevator bay. His mark lay convulsing on the floor, surrounded by hotel employees speaking frantic Spanish.

"That is a piece of beauty," Aidan said. "How long do you think it'll take until they put it all together?"

"I'll be long gone before they do," Kirk said, taking a quick photo of the scene with his cell phone. "Guess we ought to take the stairs, brother." As he climbed a nearby stairwell, he sent the photo to his employer. He'd have to remember to chuck the phone in the sea before he left. It was a burner Mexican phone anyway.

A full-throated, cantankerous laugh carried down from the ceiling toward them. Kirk's father, Bruce MacLeod, shot down like a bottle rocket and whistled around.

"Hell of a job, son!" Bruce said.

Kirk grinned at his father's compliment. The old man didn't give out compliments that easily. As a master necromancer, he was usually telling his sons just how wrong they did things. Something about how the new generations and necromancers today having no work ethic.

"Speaking of jobs," Kirk whispered. "Tell me some good news, Dad."

"The man's room is as empty as a rotten bone," Bruce said. "Unless you count the suitcase under the bed guarded by a ward."

"Ward?" Kirk asked. He rubbed his chin. "Hmm. The witch didn't say anything about a ward."

"Who?" Bruce asked.

"The woman who hired me. She said the guy didn't know magic."

"Boy, was she wrong," Bruce said. "That ward was pretty sophisticated if you ask me. Touch that suitcase and you'll go boom."

"Dad, can you believe that Kirk is a celibate?" Aidan asked, changing the subject.

"Not a surprise," Bruce said wanly. "Let me guess, flirty gal at the pool?"

"Bingo," Aidan said.

"Will you both stop?" Kirk asked, stopping on a landing. Through an open-air window that overlooked across the street, a primary-colored swirl of siren lights washed across the street.

"What are the chances I can get into the guy's room?" Kirk asked.

"Less than zero," Bruce said. "It's going to be swarming with authorities. Plus, even if you could get in, you can't do anything about that suitcase. That's going to require some serious magic."

"Maybe you're right," Kirk said. He glanced out at the street, thinking. If he knew what was good for him, he needed to be on the next plane to the States. Something didn't feel right.

Seconds later, he received a text message thumbs-up emoji from his employer and he knew the job was complete. He made a mental note to ask her about the suitcase at the next rendezvous.

"Brother, stay sharp. Someone's in your room," Aidan said as Kirk tapped his keycard against his room door.

His boss had paid for a presidential suite. Built-in alcohol dispensers with enough tequila to make a liquor store jealous. Two-person Jacuzzi. A maid and a personal butler whenever he wanted, with a turndown service. He even had his own kitchenette that went criminally unused except for eggs in the morning. The balcony, with its eye-popping views of the clear blue Caribbean waters and the resort's palapas that stretched across the beach like straw carpet, also went unused.

The only amenities Kirk had used were the California king bed with mahogany bed posts, whose sheets looked as if a twister had passed over them…and the luggage tray next to the door, which was overturned. His suitcase lay face-down on the floor and its contents formed a stepping stone trail to the bed.

Kirk reached down, unsnapped his thigh pocket on his swim trunks, and pulled out his pocket pistol, barely the size of his palm, but powerful enough to do some damage in a pinch.

He cut to the side of the yellow entrance corridor of the suite. A leopard print travel suitcase sat against the wall. He cocked his head at it.

"The hell?" he said quietly, studying the luggage.

His bare feet passed soundlessly over the cold marble floor. He hugged the corner, pointing his gun ahead of him.

The ocean waves reverberated throughout the room. The balcony French doors were open, and the sheer curtains billowed quietly in the warm breeze.

The moonlight framed his intruder in a pale glow, sitting in the rattan egg chair next to the balcony.

Kirk saw her bare feet with grains of sand sparkling in the moonlight, slender legs crossed, foot tapping impatiently. A sleek silver pistol pointed at him.

The woman in the red bikini. A white towel was wrapped around her waist. Her wet hair clumped on her shoulders. She smirked. In her other hand, she held a skull with swirling runes all over it. Green fire glowed in the skull's eye sockets. The skull belonged to Kirk.

"A quiet man reading at a beach resort is a better look on you than an evil necromancer," she said.

"For the record, I wasn't even remotely interested when you gave me the sexy eye," Kirk said.

"I'm way, way out of your league anyway," she said.

"Good. Then we understand each other."

They aimed their guns at each other, the moonlight cutting a wicked slant between them.

"Let me guess," Bruce said, exasperated. "She's the one you were going ga-ga over, Aidan."

If Aidan were alive, he'd be gulping right now.

"I take back everything I said earlier," Aidan said.

CHAPTER TWELVE

THE L TRAIN whistled to a stop. The screeching and the banging and the rattling was over in an instant, but Cyrus's ears still rang like hit gongs.

He opened his eyes. The windows of the car were smudged with dirt. His reflection showed his hair standing on his head like he'd stuck his finger in an electrical socket.

The lights flickered off and on as if taking inspiration from a horror flick. His vision shook from the wild ride.

Somehow, Cyrus had managed to hold on to the metal pole. Somehow, his spray pack and board were still on his back.

His heart pounded at a million times per minute and he struggled to breathe.

"What…what…the…ever-loving f—"

"It's over now, dear," a female voice said. The old woman was seated across from him. "That wasn't so bad now, was it?"

Cyrus stared at her. This woman was either crazy or delusional, and he couldn't decide which one yet.

The doors opened with a pneumatic hiss. A loamy, sandy smell rushed into the car. Dark and pungent, it reminded him of the potting soil his mom used in the garden back home, like blueberries, rotting leaves, and mud after a long, soaking rain.

The old woman gave him a big smile as she gestured to the door. "Be our guest, Mr. Grant."

Cyrus stood and, reluctantly, he wobbled out of the car into a wisp of smoke and the smell of scorching hot metal.

He was in a tunnel. But this tunnel, unlike the typical subterranean tunnels of the Chicago Transit Authority, was braced at the top and sides with octagon-shaped mine timbers. The timbers weren't perfectly aligned and were skewed like off-kilter picture frames deeper in the tunnel.

The earthy walls were lit up with magical yellow torches whose flames burned just as bright as the light boxes he was used to.

A dirt-grimed, leathery hand grabbed Cyrus's hand.

"It is truly an honor!"

It was the woman. Cyrus looked next to him where the woman should have been, but he saw only the dull stainless steel of the L car.

Then he looked down and saw the woman looking up at him, with admiration bright like a child looking up at their idol.

The woman didn't even reach Cyrus's hips. She couldn't have been more than three-and-a-half feet tall. He hadn't noticed her height because she had scared the bejesus out of him.

The woman pumped his hand and dragged him toward the front of the train, where the tunnel opened up.

The door on the front car slid open and a little man wearing brown rags and goggles atop unruly blackish gray hair popped out of the train like Super Mario—with a fist to the sky and a loud yell of happiness. The only thing missing was the pixelated sound effect. He had an inverted triangle of a beard, and it went down to the center of his chest, each hair having a mind of its own.

"Ta-dah! Heh heh."

The little man stooped to inspect the front of the train, which had a giant cylindrical drill the size of a truck attached to the front. Steam rose from the drill's sharp edges.

His eyes widened upon seeing Cyrus and the woman approaching. Then he knelt.

"Pleased to know ya, Mr. Grant! We are eternally in your debt."

Cyrus's head pounded. "How do you know me? Who are you?"

"My name is Bartholomew Ground Claw Ehrgeist the Fourth Redux," the man said, rising proudly. "Call me Bart. As King of the Midwest Gnome Clan, it is my honor to welcome you to our land."

"And I am Gwendalyn Fair Pick Sandstone-Ehrgeist, the Second Child of Magdalyn," the woman said. "I'm the Queen, dear, but you can call me Wendy."

The words hit Cyrus like darts. "You're…g-g-gnomes? Like the ones in a garden?"

"Dose guys are our distant cousins," Bart said. "They're shorter and a little bit impish. Big difference is that we don't wear pointy hats and we prefer to stay out of sight."

He held out his earth-stained palms. Cyrus wondered if the dirt would ever come off. "We're guardians of the lower earth. Thanks to you, we got our lives back."

"Thanks to me?" Cyrus asked.

Wendy tugged his hand and the three of them walked toward a long stairwell with steps cut from smooth earth. A pinwheel of blue light glowed at the top of the stairs.

"For the last hundred years, we were forced to serve the faeries," Wendy said.

"They were a little different," Bart said, nudging Cyrus. Cyrus got the sense that the little man meant the word as an insult.

"Murgalen was a harsh mistress," Wendy said.

"The worst!" Bart said. "She enslaved us and gave us no choice in the matter."

"Then Oleandra came along," Wendy said. "And she was worse. It's not befitting of a queen for me to say that we were relieved when they were both…extinguished, but—"

"We were happier than earthworms in a rainstorm, Mr. Grant!" Bart said. "I do ten cartwheels every day and drink a flask of sandy beer just to celebrate my freedom. And that's before I even get started in the morning!"

A blue light shone at the top of the tunnel, and it grew brighter the higher they rose on the steps.

"Why did Murgalen enslave you?" Cyrus asked.

"You could say that we gnomes know a thing or two about everything," Wendy said. "But what the fae really wanted was our treasure."

They reached the top step. The blue light washed over Cyrus. Ahead stretched an enormous underground chamber with a barrel ceiling at least sixty feet high. The room was the size of several football fields, flush with rolling hills of earth.

But on the ceiling was...a blue sky. With lazy clouds drifting across. The clouds had squiggly faces drawn with a black marker, and they were snoring, little bubbles of saliva drifting down from their mouths like cartoon characters.

A gentle whistle hummed across the room—the sun. A bouncing, hand-drawn yellow sun blazed in the middle of the sky. The corners of its mouth pulled into a carefree whistle, and its eyes were squinched closed in delight as it bounced across the sky.

"Magical illusion," Bart said. "We do our best work when night falls. When the real big guy goes down, we bring ours up. You ought to see our moon. She sings opera some days."

"Whoa," Cyrus said, staring up at the artificial sky. It was the realest fakest thing he ever saw. He dropped his gaze to the room itself with rolling hills. Narrow gauge wooden rail tracks crisscrossed the room. Here and there, metal mine carts carrying dirt zipped by from arched tunnels that fed into the room, pushed by little people whistling and dancing to the song that the sun was singing.

Cyrus squinted harder at the hills. A mish-mash of things stuck out of the dirt. Jewelry. Coins. Bones. Dead cell phones from the nineties. In other places, the treasure was laid out on metal planks where gnomes rinsed them off with water spells.

"Most people think of the ocean as the greatest holder of things," Wendy said. "But you'd be surprised at what the earth swallows. Of course, we sometimes find unpleasant things down here, but that's life, dear."

Bart ambled over to a cart and picked out a Gameboy.

"This is an original," he said. "A little bit of TLC and this guy'll be back to new."

"You and electronics," Wendy said, clucking her tongue. She led Cyrus to another cart and pulled out a pearl necklace. "This would make a fine gift for your dear old mom. I'm sure we can find a jewelry case around here somewhere."

Cyrus studied the necklace. The pearls glistened in Wendy's hands. He wondered how long they'd been in the ground before the gnomes found them.

"Murgalen wanted to claim all the treasures of the earth for herself," Wendy said. "She really was a selfish woman. The fae are the most unkind beings we've ever met."

Bart hooked two fingers in his mouth and let out a loud, piercing whistle. The mine carts around the room stopped. The gnomes stood at attention. Cyrus noticed that they all were different races—white, black, Asian—a microcosm of the city of Chicago. They wore goggles and rags, and were all barefoot.

"Everybody, Cyrus Grant is among us!" Bart hollered.

An uproar of applause boomed through the room.

"Three cheers for Cyrus!" Bart cried.

"Hip hip hooray! Hip hip hooray! Hip hip heeeeeeeey!"

Before he knew it, he was surrounded by hundreds of

gnomes, and they lifted him into the air like a crowd surfer at a concert. Dozens of little hands supported him.

"Whoa, hey—"

A sea of toothy, shouting faces began to chant.

"Cyrus! Cyrus! Cyrus!"

Above, the clouds blinked awake. Seeing Cyrus, they began to sing.

"La la la...la la laa laa..."

The gnomes sang and whistled as they marched Cyrus across the earthy plains. He jostled back and forth across a carpet of dirt-smeared hands, feeling like a king being carried by his loyal subjects.

The entourage reached the peak of the highest hill in the middle of the room where two pewter thrones sat crooked on the dirt. Bart and Wendy did a super leap over the gnomes and landed on their thrones as the gnomes set Cyrus on the dirt in front of them.

The little hands sat Cyrus down. Then he was surrounded by questions.

"What's it like to turn into a rat?"

"How cold is it up there, bud?"

"Want a flask of sandy beer to keep you warm?"

"You're even more handsome than we thought!"

"Does your mother know you're down here? Somebody tell his mother where he is!"

"Can you turn into a rat for us?"

"Hey, watch me dance!"

One by one, the gnomes started showing off before Cyrus, vying for his attention.

Cyrus couldn't focus. It was like being in a bazaar where everyone was calling your name, trying to sell you something.

Another whistle cut through the crowd, silencing everyone. It was Bart.

"Now, now, everyone, we don't want to scare Mr. Grant away," he said.

The gnomes plopped down cross-legged around Cyrus.

"We ought to get down to business," Wendy said. "Mr. Grant has somewhere to be."

"Uh," Cyrus said, rubbing his head and remembering his mom. "Right."

"Now, dear," Wendy said. "We had to express our admiration. We really are happy to see you. Forgive me for being nosy, but I must know: what on earth were you doing at JoJo's Dive?"

Cyrus's eyes widened. "How did you—"

"We've been keeping an eye on you," Wendy said. "Just waiting for the right time to say hello."

Her face turned concerned. She knew something he didn't.

"I have my reasons," Cyrus said.

"There's no reason good enough in the world to get tangled up with JoJo Skaggs," Bart said. "He and dose demons he hangs out with are bad news."

"How do you know about JoJo?"

"We know every paranormal in Chicago," Bart said. "Our tunnels go under every street. We may never meet many of the city's supernatural, but we know them by what they leave behind."

"And JoJo's deposited a lot of bones into the earth," Wendy said. "He's on our top offender list."

"His demons spit bones down here by the truckload," Bart said. "We're a happy-go-lucky clan. We don't like to be undertakers."

"Makes us plumb mad to dig down bones!" a woman cried.

"Yeah, it's the pits!" another cried.

A furor of noise and complaining erupted among the gnomes. Bart whistled and silenced them.

Bart and Wendy eyed Cyrus for an answer. Somehow, they knew about his antics, but he didn't exactly feel like explaining himself. Yet, he felt comfortable among the gnomes.

"My sister is in serious danger, okay?" he asked. "She's been possessed by a demon. JoJo is the only one who can extract the demon from her. But he's not an easy guy to approach, so I have to get his attention."

"A deal with the devil," Wendy said. "That's no good at all."

"I don't have a choice," Cyrus said. "I won't give up until Becca is safe. This is all my fault."

"It's Murgalen's fault originally," Wendy said, leaning her head on a fist. "I can only imagine the agony your dear sister is going through. She must really be suffering."

"That's an understatement," Cyrus said.

"It's a pretty tough thing to get a demon out of somebody," Wendy said. "They have their own agenda, and they like to stay in people where they can feed off them and spread misery around. But JoJo isn't a man you want to deal with. He's cruel."

Bart leaned over and whispered something in her ear. She swatted at him.

"Oh, Bart!"

Bart whispered something else. Then she grinned.

"Now you're talking," she said.

"Very well!" Bart said. "Mr. Grant, as repayment for your help in freeing us, we will help you. What do you say, gnomes?"

The gnomes pumped their fists in the air.

"Help Cyrus! Hooray!"

"Thanks for your help," Cyrus said. "But what can you offer me?"

The gnomes shifted on the ground, looking at Bart.

Bart pulled at his beard. "We're not exactly a military force, Cyrus. You're talking about a powerful demonsharp. But we can help you track JoJo down. If you ever need us, just call us."

Bart produced a pewter whistle and tossed it to Cyrus. The smooth silver whistle was cold in Cyrus's hands.

"You have our word that we will do everything we can to help you and Becca," Bart said. "Just stand on any L station platform and blow that whistle three times. We'll come right up to getcha."

"Thanks," Cyrus said.

"It's time to get you home, dear," Wendy said. She stood tall and belted at the top of her lungs, "Gnomes, let's get Mr. Grant home!"

Hands lifted Cyrus into the air again. Suddenly, the crowd of gnomes dashed down a rolling hill and into the tunnel. They deposited him into the L car and waved goodbye.

He had barely had time to process what was going on, and he gave them a slow wave as Bart came on the speaker and told him to get ready.

He held on tight as the train rocketed back down the tunnel.

CHAPTER THIRTEEN

IT WASN'T every day that a beautiful woman broke into your room and held you at gunpoint.

Kirk trained his eyes and gun on the woman sitting on the rattan chair, and she did the same to him. A long, uncomfortable silence passed before the woman spoke.

"Aren't you going to ask me why I'm here?" she asked.

"I thought maybe you were going to ask me what I wanted on my tombstone," Kirk said.

"There'll be plenty of time for that," she said, rising. She cradled the skull against her hip like a football.

"You're the one who laid the wards around the hotel," Kirk said.

The woman took a step to the side, keeping Kirk in her sights. "Very observant. I couldn't believe what that guy had in his suitcase. I mean, holy cow."

Kirk narrowed his eyes at her.

"Whoever hired you will definitely want to know what that pig was carrying," the woman said. "It might even net you a nice bonus for good behavior for warning them. Nothing magical. Just sadistic. I just warded the suitcase to keep Dad busy."

"Insolent woman!" Bruce cried.

"Tell me what you want," Kirk said.

"You being dead would be a great start," the woman said.

"Then you shoot first and let's see what happens," Kirk said.

"All those demons you're carrying is a sin against humanity," the woman said. "Dispersing them would help everyone out. But tonight's your lucky night because I'm only looking to destroy one demon. You know him better than anyone else."

Kirk had dozens of demons nestled within him. They were all mostly dormant because he maintained control of his mind and didn't let them in. But they came out from time to time when they wanted something. He sure wished one would come out now.

"He's known in some circles as Fire Eyes," the woman said. "Born in France in 1300, responsible for the deaths of a thousand believers. He's left a telltale mark throughout history —hosts who have gone insane because of his constant banter. His real name is Garamanthus. Our last report detected him in England. His host was an African American male. Handsome, with a fetish for sunglasses, denim jackets, and paperback novels."

Kirk cursed. Before Garamanthus took the stage, he'd traveled to London for an assassination. He thought he had erased his tracks.

The woman held up the skull and uttered something in Latin.

"What's she doing, brother?" Aidan asked.

The green fire in the skull's eyes blazed into pinwheels. The jaws opened and a sucking sound filled the room like a vacuum.

"Kirk!" Bruce cried. "It's a detention curse!"

Kirk could only watch as Aidan and Bruce streamed toward the skull, elongated like spaghetti. Both men cried out in agony as the skull sucked them in.

"Kirk! This is bad!" Bruce cried. The jaws chomped shut, cutting off his dad's voice.

The woman said something in Latin again, and the skull glowed with silver light as it swelled to twice its size. The woman, confident and crazed in the silver, didn't take an eye off Kirk.

Aidan and Bruce screamed as the skull exploded with a bang. A silent shimmer swept across the room, and a silver necklace floated down and clasped itself around the woman's neck. A necklace with a silver skull with emerald eyes, as elegant as fine jewelry.

"What have you done?" Kirk asked.

"Just a little transmogrification topped off with a ward," the woman said.

Kirk's mind raced at her words. He had to rescue his brother and father, but this woman didn't strike him as a liar.

She lowered her gun. "Now we can talk on equal ground."

Kirk lowered his gun too. "You're looking for Garamanthus. I don't host him anymore."

"That's why you're going to help me track down his new host," the woman said. "I'm going to settle old scores, and you're going to take me to him. If not..."

She fingered the necklace. "Kiss your family goodbye."

She strode past him and gestured to the room. "This place is a pig sty. Clean up and pack your bags."

"You made this mess. *You* clean it up."

"You seem like the kind of man who likes his things packed a certain way," she said. "Besides, I've got to change because our flight leaves in two hours."

She grabbed the leopard print suitcase and unzipped it, rifling through neatly folded clothing.

"Flight?" Kirk asked.

"You're stuck with me," she said, standing in front of the mirror and adjusting her hair. "I can't risk you running off and doing a deal with a demon to kill me."

"That's exactly what I would do," Kirk said.

"If you care about your dad and brother, you'll stop thinking heroic thoughts like that," the woman said. "Now for heaven's sake, put some real clothes on. My name's Catalina, by the way. We're headed to Chicago, Kirk MacLeod."

CHAPTER FOURTEEN

ONLY WHEN CYRUS unlocked the door to Becca's apartment, threw his backpack, sprayer, and board on the floor, and walked into the bathroom to wash up did he realize that he was covered in soil. His wool coat was brown with it. A tribal-like smear ran from one cheek to his ear. He looked like he had just finished digging a grave.

He washed his face and tossed an earth-stained rag into the hamper. He had left a trail of muddy shoe prints to the bathroom. Seeing them, he sighed and grabbed the mop. The old Becca would have murdered him for messing up her hardwood floor; the new Becca would have just seen it, shrugged, told him to clean it up or die in a tone that barely had any teeth to it, and wandered off.

He mopped the floor. Soon, the apartment smelled of wood-cleaning soap and Cyrus swept an old mop in a quick arcs as he made his way from the bathroom to the front door.

He wasn't even supposed to be living with Becca anymore. He had been looking for a place of his own and would have found one if it hadn't been for the possession. Bitterness caught in his throat as he remembered his sister sitting at the kitchen table, giving him an ultimatum: *I love you, but get a job, get an apartment of your own, and get out, please.* But when Garamanthus possessed her, he couldn't move out. Becca couldn't live by herself. Not with a demon in her mind.

Cyrus worked with Desmond to time his Regulator gigs around the Wicked Cat's operating hours. He was never too far from Becca when night fell. If it hadn't been for his meeting with the gnomes, he would have been home by sundown.

If he could find a cure for Becca, he'd be able to move into an apartment of his own. A proper bachelor pad. He loved Becca's loft, but it had its downsides. The floors were thin and he heard the late-night rowdiness from the Wicked Cat downstairs when patrons got loud, which sucked when he wanted to get a good night's sleep. Plus, sleeping on his sister's couch wasn't the greatest on his back.

He leaned on the handle of the mop for a moment, daydreaming about a loft of his own. He'd string anime posters up on the walls and keep the fridge stocked with strawberry soda and the pantry with cereal. He'd throw cool parties and play video games into the darkest hours of the night. Hell, he didn't care how small the place was. All that mattered was that it would be his.

His wallet cried when he thought about the reality of the daydream. But you had to start somewhere.

He thought of the gnomes. Their singing and cheers still rang in his head. He still tasted JoJo's coppery blood on his tongue, and his heart leaped as he remembered the encounter with the elusive demonsharp.

The mop banged against the apartment door. He had finished the job. The floor was so shiny and clean, it would have made his mother proud.

His mom…Crap!

He surveyed his t-shirt—it had smudges of dirt on it too. The thought occurred to him to change his shirt when the deadbolt to the apartment door switched over.

Becca rushed in and shut the door quickly behind her. Panting, she rested her back against the door.

"Did you rob a bank or something?" Cyrus asked, cracking a grin.

Becca took a moment to catch her breath. Her knitted beanie fell silently onto the floor. Her starry night bandanna was askew on her head, and long frizzy strands of blonde hair hung out. Then she glanced up at him with troubled eyes.

"I just got jumped," she said.

"Jumped!" Cyrus cried. He ran to Becca and put a hand on her shoulders and inspected her for damage. "What the hell happened? I'll call the cops."

She shook her head. "Not a good idea."

They stared at each other for a moment.

"Paranormal?" he asked.

She exhaled, nodding.

"I was coming home from therapy. I noticed someone was following me."

Cyrus balled his fists. Whoever had tried to hurt Becca, he wanted to destroy them. His sister was going through too much already. His heart swelled with anger and he felt himself getting warm.

"It was a group of guys," Becca said. "They wore silver crosses and they were super creepy. But they weren't looking for me, Cy."

Becca unzipped her duffel coat, unwrapped her knitted scarf, and threw them on a coat hook. "They were looking for Garamanthus."

"Why?"

Becca slid into a chair at the kitchen table. She shook her head.

Cyrus quickly walked into the kitchen and measured out some coffee in a filter. Soon, he had Becca's kitchen percolator humming. The smell of fresh roasted coffee grounds filled the apartment.

"How'd you get away?" Cyrus asked.

Becca stared into space. "He took control."

"Great," Cyrus muttered. "I thought those days were behind you. He hasn't done that in forty-five days."

Becca stared at him, slack-jawed. "You were counting?"

"C'mon, you know you are too," Cyrus said.

"Cy, he kicked those guys' asses," Becca said. "I mean, *I* did. I literally beat the crap out of them. Like anime movie style."

Cyrus folded his arms. "No way."

"If I had to guess, they're still lying in the street," Becca said, sounding worried.

A knock on the door made both of them startle.

Cyrus glanced at Becca. He wished they had a gun. With Becca's possession, it was too dangerous to leave weapons in the apartment. He cursed.

"Do you think it's the guys that attacked you?" Cyrus asked.

The old sarcastic sparkle flashed back to Becca's eyes, just for a split second.

"If they followed me, do you think they would knock, doofus?" she asked.

Cyrus crept to the door and glanced through the peephole. Relief swept over him as he saw his mom in the fish-eyed lens.

"It's Mom," he said.

Becca adjusted her bandanna and motioned for him to open the door.

"You're both home," Aurora Grant said as Cyrus kissed her on the cheek. "It's a minor miracle."

Aurora Grant was dressed in a red duffel coat like Becca's, with a hood and fur collar. The coat was a splash of arterial red that quickly faded to a thin, watery blue along the edges of the sleeves. The snow fell off the collar in thick flakes. Shaking off her coat, she smiled and surveyed the apartment with surprise. Her shoulder-length almond hair was pulled into a low bun.

Her smile faded as she looked Cyrus up and down, eyes zeroing in on the dirt stains on his shirt. Then she tilted her head at Becca, studying her intently.

"You know," Aurora said, "before all of this paranormal stuff started, I would have said something like, is everything okay? Because that's what moms do."

She paused and looked back and forth between Cyrus and Becca's faces. Becca looked guilty; Cyrus imagined his face couldn't have looked much different.

"But now, I know a thing or two about the seedy underbelly you two are involved in," Aurora said. "Moms have supernatural senses, too, you know."

Damn, his mom was good. Now that his mom knew all about the paranormal, if he lied, he'd suffer a fate worse than if JoJo got his hands on him…

Cyrus hooked an arm around his mom as they walked toward the kitchen table. "Mom, we agreed we wouldn't hide anything from you anymore. Isn't that right, Bec?"

Becca ran a hand over her bandanna, straightening it. Before she could reply, Cyrus said, "Mom, quite frankly, I'm shocked. Your guess couldn't have been further from the truth."

Aurora narrowed her eyes at him.

"Aside from getting jumped by a group of paranormal goons, living to talk about it because she went Jackie Chan on them, and a heart-pounding run home, Bec's night is going just fine."

Aurora gasped.

"You're so eloquent when you want to be," Becca said under her breath.

"Becca, you were jumped?" Aurora asked. "Oh my God, are you okay?"

"Just a few scratches," Becca said.

Aurora reached out to Becca, but Becca's hand stopped in midair.

"I'm fine, Mom."

Aurora rose. "Well, it's settled," she said.

"What's settled?" Cyrus asked.

"I'm not leaving until Becca's attackers are behind bars or evaporated to dust," Aurora said.

Cyrus and Becca stole a glance at each other. Cyrus gulped.

"Mom, that's not a good idea," Becca protested.

"Too bad," Aurora said, slipping out her phone. "If you don't mind, I've got Desmond on speed dial."

Cyrus hung his head.

"Nothing buzzkills an adventure like having your mom tagging along," he said, throwing himself in the chair next to Becca.

"Tell me about it," Becca said.

She elbowed him. "What's up with you? Why do you have dirt all over you?"

"Rocco put me on a gig," Cyrus said. "No biggie. Kinda boring, actually. Singing gnomes."

"Gnomes? Like garden gnomes?"

"No, those are distant cousins," Cyrus said. He remembered Bart's speech fondly. "These guys are happy-go-lucky miners."

"Oh." Confusion lined Becca's face.

"I'll get your coffee."

As Cyrus poured Becca's coffee, Aurora got Desmond on the phone. On second thought, he poured himself a mug.

"This is going to be one long night," he muttered.

CHAPTER FIFTEEN

"THEY WERE BEGINNING to think you had abandoned them," a sunglasses-wearing doorman said, opening the door to JoJo's limo and gesturing him out. "I've been answering a lot of impatient questions on whether you have arrived yet, sir."

JoJo straightened his sunglasses, inhaled, and let his marijuana-induced reality spin around him.

The Montclair Building, a sixty-story wonder of steel and glass in the upscale River North neighborhood, rose high into the wintry sky like a jagged, shining claw. The edges of the building sizzled as if the snowfall was setting off a violent chemical reaction. A long red canopy stretched from the street to an automatic revolving door.

JoJo puffed a final cloud of smoke from the joint he and Simone had been sharing in the limo. The snowflakes falling from the sky shimmered under the streetlights. A breeze blew, and the sounds of the cars passing by and the doorman saying good evening to Simone and the limo engine running like velvet and his footsteps in the crunchy snow all blended together into an intense *whoa* that hit him as he stood on the corner. Even the limo door slamming had the intensity of an earthquake.

He adjusted the sleeves on his mink coat. If it was cold outside, he couldn't tell. He could have thrown open his coat and the warmth radiating out would have turned this damn street into summer. People on the street would have been thanking him. Shit, the power companies could have learned a thing or two from him.

Simone sidled up to him and hooked her arm under his. He smelled the rose undertones in her perfume mixed with the candied lemon sweetness of skin lotion. On a night like this when everything was more vivid and intense, it was good to have Simone on his arm.

She giggled. "Is the edge off, baby?"

"What edge?" he asked.

Simone giggled again as they passed under the canopy. The underside of the canopy was supported by steel lattices. JoJo glanced up and studied them for longer than any other man would have.

What was life but a lattice anyway? Human and demon and paranormal and all sorts of problems all mixed together…

The subtle, telltale feeling of enlightenment crept into his mind. This was the kind of thinking the world needed. Men who viewed life as a lattice.

"Baby?" Simone asked.

JoJo stared into his girlfriend's gradated sunglasses. Beyond, he knew her eyes were bloodshot to hell.

"That's my lesson tonight," he said, looking up again.

"What?" she asked.

"Tonight is a latticework of steel," he said.

Simone puffed and rolled her eyes, suddenly sober. "Why is everything about symbols when we do this?"

"Everything is about symbols," he grunted. "You just haven't been paying attention."

"Okay, okay," she said, urging him forward. "Speaking of

symbols, what's the symbol for angry? That's what Donnie is gonna be."

JoJo grunted again. "I can handle Donnie, don't worry."

Simone stared at him for a moment, then burst into another giggle.

"You and the giggles," JoJo said.

"If you didn't keep me high on a night like this, I'd lose my freaking mind."

"Giggle on, then, baby."

Talk about truth. He needed extra weed on a night like tonight.

The doorman nodded to them as he stood watch next to the revolving door. JoJo's steps felt heavy as they passed through the door and into a Greek-inspired lobby with Jurassic-sized ficuses and golden meandros cut into a gray marble floor.

A middle-aged black woman sat behind the security desk, her face lit up by several security screens. Upon seeing them, she held up a hand to wave. JoJo gave her a slow nod.

The Montclair Building had one elevator bay. Two types of people used them. The first were commoners. The executives coming in and out of work at all hours of the night, plebes living in the condos in the middle stratum of the building, and other various, faceless people that infested a skyscraper like this.

The second type were the minor gods, champions of the paranormal, and the men and women to whom the city owed blood. Men like JoJo and whoever happened to be hanging on his arm. All the real champions needed to access the upper echelons was a keycard, which JoJo grabbed from one of the paper-faced goons standing watch at the elevator. JoJo had hired this guy from a rent-a-cop company. Some guy hard on his luck looking for relief. JoJo made his luck easier, but it involved a hard demon. JoJo made him a new man, and he wore a white uniform, a service cap with a fake badge, and giant Coke bottle glasses that were straight out of 1970. He stood guard at the elevators.

"You're the last one, boss," the guard said.

"Just how I like it," JoJo said. "Imagine being first."

A slow smile spread across the guard's face. "You make a good point."

Soon, JoJo and Simone stood in a glass elevator as it whirred up a shaft. The LED panel above the door dinged past the tenth floor.

Then, the demons in JoJo came alive. Loud cackles banged in his head, a mesh of evil voices thin and deep who laughed as if they were recording a laugh track for a bad sitcom.

JoJo folded his arms and tapped his toes impatiently.

"If only the world could hear you," he said out loud. "You sound like a bunch of goddamned fools."

In all the years he'd had demons in his mind, he learned it was better to talk to them out loud. It may have made him sound nuts, but speaking was a release valve that ensured that his inhabitants wouldn't drive *him* nuts.

Simone tilted her head at him. Then understanding flashed on her face. "Oh, it's them." She patted his arm. "What are they saying, baby? Have they mentioned me?"

JoJo winced and ignored her.

The demons settled down. One of the voices rose to prominence, but he felt the others alongside him, listening. The lead demon finally spoke in a frail, elderly, but sinister voice.

"May the blind see, the lame walk, and the money-loving fools be blessed with nothing," the demon said.

JoJo laughed quietly. "That sounds like a good summary of the people we're meeting tonight."

"Whom do we have to regard?" the demon asked.

"Just one host," JoJo said. "This is a sham, remember?"

"Sham," the demon said. "Interesting way to put it."

"I'll do anything to shut you guys up for a while," JoJo said.

"Just one host?" the demon said. "As we thought. You could have had two."

JoJo furrowed his brow. "Two?"

The demons laughed like jackals. Their grating laughter made him want to punch something. Even the old one was laughing uncontrollably.

"You ought to be grateful I'm carrying you," he said.

The old demon gasped for air and let out a whimper of laughter as if to say, "Stop! Stop! You're killing me! Ha ha ha!"

And then he said, "Your soul isn't a uterus."

"Given what's going to happen in a few minutes, you don't honestly believe that, do you?" JoJo asked.

The demon harrumphed.

Above, the door dinged again and the cables whining in the shaft began to quiet.

"What do you mean I could have had two new hosts tonight?" JoJo asked.

"You were so high out of your mind that you couldn't see a damn thing in front of you," the demon said.

"That's why I have you," JoJo said.

"If we came alive at the height of your high, we'd be committing suicide," the demon said. "You know how we hate that state of mind."

"You try holding a colony of demons in your mind and living like a pilgrim," JoJo said.

"How's your ankle?" the demon asked.

JoJo regarded the statement. He became aware of the bite on his ankle for the first time since he left the nightclub. The wound seared with pain.

"What about it?" he asked.

The demons might as well have been falling over each other laughing.

The elevator doors opened. A distant murmur of cocktail glasses clinking, soft conversation, and a quiet grand piano washed into the car.

An oak-paneled hallway with globe lights hanging from the ceiling waited for them. A latticework of brown triangles was etched into the golden-colored marble floor. JoJo's chest swelled with pride as he spotted another sign of his prediction coming true.

The demons clicked off. JoJo frowned as Simone pulled him out of the car.

"What did they say?" Simone asked.

"Cryptic, as usual," JoJo said.

They walked down the hallway. JoJo couldn't shake the pain in his ankle now. He couldn't get the demon's words out of his head. Somehow, he knew that was just where the old demon wanted him.

On the other end of the hallway, a short man in a tuxedo stood in front of two swinging double doors with large diamonds painted on both doors. Seeing them, he ran to them.

"You're late," he said.

"I told him," Simone said, giving JoJo the side-eye.

"That's why I pay you to keep them entertained," JoJo said. "Ever heard of a cocktail, Donnie?"

The insult bristled Donnie. The frown on his face might as well have been permanent. JoJo didn't know why because he'd gone easy on Donnie. Whatever sad excuse for a demon that was nestled inside him, it couldn't even practice basic mind control. Any discomfort Donnie felt was of his own damn doing.

"They're under control, but *she's* like poison," he said. "She's impatient. She keeps sizing up the others. At this point, she knows everything about everyone. If she isn't chosen, she has enough to raise some hell and blackmail."

"That's great because I've already chosen her," JoJo said.

"So you have nothing to worry about, Donnie. You need a nap."

"It sets a bad example," Donnie said. "No other potential has acted like that."

"She's not any potential host."

"Who the hell are you talking about?" Simone asked. Then her eyes widened. "JoJo, you didn't——"

"I don't discriminate in who asks for my help," JoJo said.

Simone stammered. "It's not…it's not…another——"

"Elephant?" JoJo asked. "No, baby, it's not an elephant. Yeah, sure, it's another girl, but there's no reason to give her hairy eyeballs."

He leaned in and kissed her on the cheek. "You're still my lady."

Simone turned away from him.

"Come on now," JoJo said. "How many of the soul killers did I give you?"

"Fifteen," she said.

"How many does Donnie-O here have?"

"One," she said reluctantly.

"One more than he can handle," JoJo said, grinning. "You still got the keys to my kingdom, baby. A little old demon exchange don't change that none."

JoJo kissed her on the cheek again and whispered a nothing in her ear. She giggled again and gave him a long hug.

Were things copacetic between them? No. But hey, that was the game.

The demons came alive again, laughing.

The three of them stood at the door. The piano player finished a tune and applause spread across the room.

"Let's find out who wants some demons," JoJo said.

CHAPTER SIXTEEN

KIRK HAD SEEN some pretty awful things in his life.

Demon summonings gone wrong. Grisly murder scenes. The faces of wicked strangers burned into his mind. His brother and father being sucked into a skull necklace by a mysterious woman.

But at the moment, the winner of the worst-thing-he-ever-saw contest was the words "Flight Canceled" blinking in red on the departure screens at the Hartsfield-Jackson Atlanta International Airport. Going through customs was bad enough.

Nearby, a group of passengers cursed. "How are we ever going to get home?" someone asked.

As passengers ran to their flights in the long hallway next to him and someone somewhere yelled at a flight agent, Kirk shouldered his leather travel bag, staring at the screen and hoping it was a mistake. All he wanted was to get home to Chicago so he could figure out how to rescue his brother and dad. He felt like he was stuck in an evil version of a Holly-wood movie where the main character was trying to get home to his family…except in his case, his family was dead and he wasn't going home to a Christmas-light-covered house in a cul-de-sac with a turkey dinner on the table waiting for him.

What *was* waiting for him was blood. Lots of blood. If he was lucky, he wouldn't lose any of his own.

"Might as well get a bite to eat," a female voice said next to him.

Catalina, dressed in a red sundress, denim jacket, floppy straw hat, and leather Greek sandals, applied lip balm as she stared up at the screen. She stood a little too close to him, and he smelled the sunflower perfume he'd had to deal with on the entire two-and-a-half-hour flight from Cancún. If there was a hell, and if that hell required you to relive a day from your life that you never wanted to think about until hell itself froze over, he'd be forced to sit next to Catalina on a plane and inhale her cloying perfume.

"Two terrible airports in one day," she said wistfully. "You're my bad luck charm."

He stared at her, slack-jawed.

"Where do you get off saying that?" he asked.

Catalina shrugged. "The flight attendant told me that there is a terrible blizzard in Chicago tonight. O'Hare and Midway canceled all flights in and out. The storm is expected to ease up later tonight, and I sweet-talked the front desk lady to make us first on standby. In the meantime, you're buying dinner."

He kept staring, incredulous.

He still didn't even know who the hell this woman was. She held him up at gunpoint in his suite, sucked his brother and dad into the glittering skull necklace, and she even had the gall to take a shower, hog his bathroom, and make him carry her luggage when they arrived at the airport.

On the flight from Cancún to Atlanta, she booked tickets so that they sat next to each other. She started the flight by giving him a stern warning. If he tried to escape, he'd never see his brother and dad again. If he tried any funny business, like summoning a demon in the bathroom, goodbye Aidan and Bruce. If he even thought about venturing more than fifteen feet away from her at any time, she might take it personally and, well—goodbye Aidan and Bruce. Then, she asked if he minded if she put down the arm rest between them.

She had the audacity to stick him in the aisle seat while she enjoyed a meal and magazine in the window seat with his credit card! It was a credit card with an assumed identity, but it still ticked him off. He had used that assumed credit card for a lot of things, but grapes, cracker tapas, and red wine weren't on his list.

The flight attendant, seeing them together, assumed that they were husband and wife. "Does your wife want another wine?" he asked while Catalina was in the bathroom.

"Do you see a wedding ring, bro?" Kirk asked.

The words hit the flight attendant like darts and he realized his mistake.

"I'm sorry, sir."

"Yeah, you are sorry," he said. He stared at him uncomfortably until he walked away.

And that wasn't the half of it. They flew the whole way from Cancún to Atlanta with her making little remarks to him as if she were his wife.

"Want some gum?"

"Would you mind turning off your air vent?"

"Give my trash to the flight attendant, will you?"

She even asked if he wanted to split a pair of cheap airplane earbuds while she watched a sitcom on the in-flight entertainment system. He wished there were words in the English language stronger than "Hell no."

"Your loss," she said, plugging her ears with the buds.

He spent the entire flight more confused than when he was staring at the barrel of her gun in his hotel room.

They spent two miserable hours in customs together

waiting for a sleepy-faced official to welcome them back to America. He prayed they wouldn't catch his false passport and arrest his ass. That might have been better than realizing they only had ten minutes left to catch their flight and running through his least favorite airport on Earth only to find out that the flight was canceled. Now here he was, at some dead-end gate in a stuffy corner of the airport, wondering when he'd ever get back to Chicago.

He followed Catalina to a restaurant parked in the middle of one of the busiest corridors in the airport. A rectangular island of booths and high-backed chairs where you had to order from tablets. Catalina wanted barbecue.

As the server delivered red wine, cornbread, and rib tips, Kirk thought to himself, *I need somebody to confirm that I haven't died. This is some sick joke.*

He settled on Catalina, who was tearing into her rib tips as if she hadn't already eaten on the plane.

He had to figure out what the hell was going on. His sanity depended on it.

"We're going to have a chat," he said.

"About what?" she asked. She glanced at an elderly couple sitting next to them. "You know I told you at the Cancún airport and on the plane that—"

"Yeah," Kirk said. "I remember."

He remembered. While they sat in the Cancún airport waiting to board, she had pulled him in for a whisper. "Let's get a few things straight. If you mention anything out loud about demons, the occult, or anything that even has a whiff of paranormal to it, say goodbye to your brother and father. If you do anything that makes me look like a looney, they're toast. You and I have parts to play. We are coming back from vacation. In case anyone asks, you're going to tell them that you're going back home to work in a corporate job that sucked your soul away ten years ago, and I am going back to my accounting practice. I hope you have a good memory."

Kirk grabbed the basket of rib tips and slid it aside. "How could I forget what you told me? But here's the thing: I've been thinking about this on the flight over here, and I realized that I'm an idiot."

"It took you your whole life to understand that?" she asked.

"Nice one," he said, leaning in. "So what if you tenderize my brother and father. All I've got to do is some deals with...you know… and I can get them back. I'll steal them back right out from under you, and then that fancy little necklace there won't mean a thing."

Catalina settled back in her seat. "Is that right? Tell me more."

"That's all there is to it," Kirk said. "So I'm done playing your little game."

"This is hardly a game," she said. "This is about life and death and good and evil and right and wrong. What if I told you that you would never see your... you know—again? That your plan is harebrained?"

"I'd say you were full of it."

"Maybe," she said. She took another glance at the elderly couple. They weren't paying attention. "Since we've got time to kill, I'll make you a deal. I'll tell you two things about myself."

"What's the catch?" Kirk asked.

"You have to tell me two things about yourself."

"You came all this way to hold me at gunpoint and put me through all of this and you don't know a thing about me?"

"I know more about you than you know about yourself," she said. "I just want to confirm it."

He didn't know why, but he hadn't seen that coming. He couldn't see *anything* coming with this woman.

"Deal," he said, holding out his hand. She shook it and swiped the basket of rib tips back.

"Thing number one: I haven't been back to Chicago in over ten years."

"That's hardly a fact," he said. "Why? Where have you been living?"

"You could call me a free spirit," she said. "But I haven't been back to the city because it hasn't exactly been safe for my kind."

"So you're an alien. That would explain a lot."

Catalina smiled sarcastically. "Just for that, I'm not telling you anything more about thing number one. Your turn, except I don't want any facts. I want to know something that's been bothering me for a long time, Kirk MacLeod. What's the one thing you regret most in your life?"

"Not knowing you were going to be in my hotel room earlier today."

She laughed out loud. So loud, the couple nearby stared at her for a moment before resuming their meal. He got the feeling she did that on purpose.

"Living a life of debauchery and doing things that not even the devil himself would approve of," she said. "There's got to be something, just one thing that you wish you never did. What is it?"

Kirk thought about it for a moment. His mind was just as blank as when he read the first few pages of that damned space opera novel. He couldn't even think of anything to lie about.

"Really?" she asked. "You couldn't save your brother in his last few hours. You don't regret even that?"

Kirk narrowed his eyes. "How did you know that?"

Catalina wiped barbecue sauce off her hands and smirked. "By not answering my question, you confirmed what I believed. Okay. I'll tell you something else about myself. Where I come from, I believe the things you do in this life come back to haunt you. I also believe that there is no such thing as a bad deed going unpunished. Maybe not in this life, but the universe always equals out."

"What are you, into some crackpot metaphysical shit?"

"If I'm wrong, then why is your family trapped?" she asked.

"Because you got lucky."

The tablet on the table beeped. A message popped up asking if Kirk needed any more food. That was the airport's way of saying to get the hell out once you were finished eating. He swiped the message away.

"Second thing I want to know," Catalina said. "What would you be willing to do to get your family back?"

Kirk didn't answer. He thought about the question long and hard. He didn't want to say anything and hoped she would keep talking.

"Because you're in a conundrum," Catalina said. "You can't exactly do something heroic and give up your life, can you? I've just shaken your confidence about getting them back with your usual clandestine methods. What will you do, Kirk?"

"Once I figure it out, you'll be the first to know," he said. "But I get the feeling you aren't going to like the answer because—"

Catalina slung her purse over her shoulder. "You and your bravado. It's so entertaining. Be a good little play-husband and pick up the tab. I've gotta freshen up."

She left him at the table with an empty basket of rib tips and half a glass of wine. He stared at the bill, seeing it and not seeing it and wondering what the hell she meant with her questions.

CHAPTER SEVENTEEN

Becca poured several glasses of beer at the bar of the Wicked Cat. The long draws of amber took her mind off the men who were after her. Nearby, someone laughed at the top of their lungs. She smiled; it was nice to hear *someone* laughing for a change.

She handed the jostling beers to a series of patrons sitting at the bar and wished them well.

The usual crowd had sauntered in for her winter specials —50 percent off select beer whenever it was snowing. The coffee business usually boomed in the winter, but the bar clientele thinned out for not wanting to go drinking in the winter. Her marketing helped keep people coming in the door after dinner.

The snow was still coming down outside, much harder now. It formed a thin layer on the roofs of cars parked on the street. Every time someone opened the door, a curlicue of snow and frost blew into the bar. Even the knitted sweater she wore wasn't enough to completely protect her from the biting cold.

She took an elderly couple's order in a booth near the

kitchen, gave it to the cook, and walked back out onto the floor, where a flash of green caught her eye.

Gilberto Sanchez was sitting in one of the booths, studying a menu. He wore a trim goatee, a puffy green winter coat, and a Cubs stocking cap. He blew into his hands to warm them up.

"Can't heal cold hands?" Becca asked, putting a hand on her hip.

"Ha *ha*," Gilberto said. "That's why I come here, remember?"

"I'll get you a hot chocolate," Becca said. She slid into the booth. "It's on me for reminding me about my appointment."

She rested her head on her fist. "You're a lifesaver, do you know that?"

Gilberto grinned. "Literally or figuratively?"

"I was in the middle of an attack," Becca said. "I was like one of those old people in a parking lot who couldn't find their car. And then my phone buzzed and you reminded me where I needed to be."

"I know demons' games," Gilberto said. "We've just got to stay ahead of the bastard, that's all."

Ever since Becca's possession, she had been going to church with Gilberto. He said it would be good for her spiritual health. The small congregation took her in and prayed for her regularly, even though they didn't know the whole story. Gilberto told them that she had demons in her life, and that was enough. Gilberto himself prayed with Becca at least once a week. It kept Garamanthus away…for a while. But mostly, she just wanted to spend time with Gilberto. He was a good guy to have around.

"How'd therapy go?" he asked.

Becca sighed. "I lay on a couch for an hour, stared at the ceiling, and told her about my mother."

"Seriously?" Gilberto asked.

"I lied about the mom part," Becca said, smirking. "But no, I really did lie on a couch and stare at the ceiling."

"But what did you talk about?" Gilberto asked. "If you don't mind me asking, that is. You can tell me to screw off if you—"

Becca gave Gilberto a quick smile. "Gilberto, if I didn't feel comfortable sharing with you, I would have told you to screw off a long time ago."

The healer sighed with relief. "Ah, okay. It's just that I'm a little skittish with all this. I mean, I can't imagine what you're going through even though you tell me about it."

"She gave me some tips to quiet the demon," Becca said with a comfortable tone that eased Gilberto's awkwardness.

"Did they work?"

"Kind of," Becca said. "I was trying them out when I got attacked by a group of men while walking home."

Gilberto's eyes widened.

Nearby, one of the patrons nursed an almost-empty glass of beer. From the rosiness in his cheeks and the way he was looking around, he needed another one.

"I'll be back," Becca said.

"You can't leave me hanging like that," Gilberto said.

"Give me a minute," Becca said.

A waitress passed by. Becca called her and told her to get Gilberto a hot chocolate.

She grabbed the patron's glass and asked him if he wanted another one. Of course he did. She poured him a fresh glass of dark, chocolate stout and told him to holler if he needed anything else. As she grabbed a rag and cleaned up a nearby spill, she found herself looking up at Rocco and Luna. Tonight, they were all leather, flannel, and zippers—sometimes Becca wondered if they planned their wardrobe together. She could have sworn that she had seen Luna's leather jacket on a magazine cover.

"Hey, Becca," Rocco said. "How'd the meeting with the supplier go?"

Becca stared at him.

Rocco glanced across the bar, then he lowered his voice. "You know, the therapist."

"We're so proud of you for going," Luna said.

Becca raised an eyebrow. They weren't supposed to know. Whoever told them was going to feel her wrath. She didn't feel like talking about her therapy with Rocco and Luna.

"It went just fine," Becca said. "I lay on a couch for an hour and talked about my mother."

"Really?" Luna asked, eyes wide.

"Nothing remarkable," Becca said, drifting away, pretending to be interested in a nearby couple finishing up a bowl of pretzels. After making sure they were okay, another table got up and started to leave and she used that as an excuse to get the hell away from the bar, waving and telling them goodbye.

The chime over the door opened and Aurora and Cyrus walked in, shivering from the cold. Aurora spotted Becca and motioned her over.

"Desmond will be here soon," Aurora said. "Stop working for a few minutes and tell me about your appointment, honey."

"Later," Becca said. Cyrus glanced at her and she gave him a look that said, "I don't feel like talking to anyone right now," and he understood it. He flashed her a look that seemed to say "Okay, but you'll owe me for this one."

Lately, their ESP had been working perfectly. Cyrus said something to his mom and distracted her while Becca stole into the kitchen. A wall of warm air surrounded her, followed by the smell of pretzels and cheesy mushrooms—the bar's most popular appetizers. Her employees rushed around filling food orders for the night.

In her little office behind the kitchen, her assistant

manager, Cristián, sat at her desk, browsing through some paperwork. He was a skeleton of his former self. The old Cristián was thin and made the girls swoon; this Cristián was flesh on bone in a dress shirt and trousers. With no fat, his jaws were angular and his eyes were big orbs in sockets with dark rings that suggested poor sleep and blood circulation.

Kirk MacLeod had been infested with Garamanthus when he shot Cristián in the abdomen. Gilberto brought him back from the brink of death. Several weeks in the hospital and three surgeries later, he lived to talk about it. Becca didn't even want to think about the medical bills the workers compensation had paid for his treatment so far. He had been on the job when he was shot.

Yet, Cristián came back to work at the Wicked Cat. When Becca asked him why, he said, "Because I love this place and I don't blame you." She'd hugged him and wept, though she still felt responsible. So responsible.

She hadn't yet forgiven herself for his injury, and she swore that she'd avenge him. Garamanthus always found amusement in her vows for justice ("See, there's that dark side to you, girl…").

"Hey," Becca said.

"Hey," Cristián said. "I'm just taking a break."

"Funny. Me too."

Becca sat down in the lone chair in front of her desk.

"I'll make you a deal," she said. "If you don't ask me about my therapy session today, then I won't scream."

"Ah, you had your appointment today," Cristián said. "I won't ask you about it, then. But hopefully, it went well."

Becca closed her eyes and rocked back in the chair.

"Sorry, just one question," he said.

She opened her eyes, incredulous.

"Will you go back?" he asked.

Becca thought about it. Memories of Carolyn Davidson's cozy office came back to her. Suddenly, she wished she were lying on the comfy leather couch with slanted rays of twilight coloring the room through the octagon stained-glass window as Carolyn leaned in, listening and smiling.

"I think so," she said finally.

"Good," Cristián said. "Whatever she told you, however you felt, however skeptical you were, promise me you'll go back." He stood and stretched, grimacing. "The guy I'm seeing for my PTSD—I thought he was a jackass at first. It took a few weeks for me to realize that he was right."

"Right about what?" Becca asked.

Cristián gave her a devilish grin. "I thought we weren't supposed to be talking about this. Anyway, I have to check on the Guinness couple."

"They're set for another round," Becca said. "You can't walk away yet. Don't make me grab you and detain you in my office. I'm not above it."

Cristián stretched his arms and found a little relief. One of his arms popped.

"I'll make you a deal," he said. "I'll tell you my secret if you tell me how your appointment went. But I thought you didn't want to scream, remember?"

Becca started to give him a witty reply when someone opened the door slightly and a dark hand knocked on the frame. Desmond Lovelace peered in with concerned eyes and a freshly trimmed beard. His leather trench made him a formidable tower in the doorway. He studied Becca with calm but scrutinizing eyes. Seeing him meant that any peace she'd had in the last hour was over.

"Hope your business can wait," he said.

"We were just finishing up," Cristián said, saluting Becca. "Stay sane, will you?"

"I'll try."

Desmond said a few words to Cristián and then waited until the assistant manager was in the kitchen, out of earshot. He studied Becca with concerned eyes.

"Usually, it's your brother who gets everyone riled up," Desmond said.

"I don't know if that's a compliment or an insult," Becca said.

"It's a fact."

Desmond folded his arms and leaned in the doorway. "How are you, Becca?"

Becca knew Desmond well enough to know that he wasn't making a platitude.

"I've been better. Relatively speaking."

"We're trying to learn more about who these men who attacked you are, but we're having a tough time," Desmond said. "Did Garamanthus give any clues?"

The demon came alive in Becca's mind, clicking his tongue. She had forgotten him until now.

"I told you that I don't know them," the demon said. "Why don't you ask Kirk MacLeod? This is most definitely the previous host's problem."

Shut up, Becca thought. She found herself looking away from Desmond, wincing as she dealt with the demon.

"I'll take that as a no," Desmond said. "I didn't mean to disturb him."

"He's only been disturbing me all evening," Becca said. "What's another few minutes?"

Garamanthus laughed. She tried to ignore his tinny, wicked laugh.

"We're going to put together a plan," Desmond said. "You'll be safe with the Regulators. If we encounter the men again, we can fight back and maybe capture one of them."

"Ah, the big werehyena man and his plans again," Garamanthus said. "I'll give you a tip, dear, but you'll have to repay it. These don't seem like the kind of men who like to walk around the city. Gallivanting around tonight will accomplish nothing. However, if you happen to bait them with your presence and risk your pretty little life…"

"Shut up!" Becca cried.

A few seconds set in before she realized she had said it out loud.

"Not you," she said quickly. "He says to use me as bait."

The comment took Desmond off-guard. "That's not… what I had in mind."

Becca rose and placed a hand on his shoulder. "Desmond, I didn't have getting possessed by a crazy demon in mind either. I don't think he's trying to mislead me this time. At least, not after therapy today."

Desmond regarded her statement. "I was going to ask you," he said. "How'd it go?"

"I lay on a couch for an hour and told her about my mother," Becca said, walking away. "Let's get this planning over with."

CHAPTER EIGHTEEN

"Your sister is avoiding me, and you're running cover for her."

Cyrus sipped a strawberry soda in a booth as his mom stared at him unflinchingly. The Wicked Cat buzzed around them—patrons laughing and chatting. The door kept opening and making him shiver.

"She's not avoiding you," Cyrus said. "She just needed some time alone."

The moment his mom called Desmond, Becca pretended to receive a phone call herself. She slipped out of the apartment, and Cyrus knew she needed to clear her mind. For Becca, that meant getting lost in her work.

Cyrus was, as usual, caught between his mom and sister. His mom's fear was palpable. Her emotional hackles were up. She hadn't taken her coat off and had refused a drink.

"She can't evade me forever," Aurora said.

"She won't," Cyrus said.

Desmond popped between the swinging doors to the kitchen. He made eye contact with Cyrus and motioned for him to come.

"That's our cue," he said.

Aurora grabbed her purse and joined Cyrus as they walked quickly to the kitchen. Rocco, Luna, and Gilberto met them at the door.

"Man, when Desmond mounts up the Regulators, he mounts them up," Gilberto said, fist-bumping Cyrus.

Desmond and Becca had made space in the back of the kitchen by clearing away some shelves so that everyone could fit. Despite the space, everyone still rubbed shoulders. Cristián sent the kitchen employees on break and filled the current kitchen orders by himself—he was Desmond's protected eyes and ears for the meeting.

Cyrus, Becca, Aurora, Desmond, Gilberto, Rocco, and Luna gathered in a circle.

"Let's go over the basics of what we know," Desmond said. "Two hours ago, Becca was walking home when she was attacked by several men who she said wore silver crosses. Fortunately for Becca, her demon host kicked in and fought the guys off. If the demon knows anything, he's not telling us." Desmond turned to Becca with a sympathetic eye. "Did I get it all correct?"

Becca nodded.

"Don't forget about Becca's new anime martial arts skills," Cyrus said, raising his hand.

"Ah, that," Desmond said. "I believe you, but I'll really believe it when I see it with my own eyes."

"Amen," Cyrus said. "I'm going to film her doing backflips and roundhouse kicks."

Becca punched him on the meat of his shoulder. Hard.

"Ow," he said, rubbing it gingerly.

"Does anyone have any updates?" Desmond asked.

Silence set in across the kitchen aside from Cristián plating an order.

"None of our contacts have any information," Rocco said. "We're in the dark, Desmond."

"Then here's the deal," Desmond said. "Whoever those

men were, they'll be back for a second round. That means until we apprehend them, you can't afford to be alone anymore, Becca."

Cyrus knew what was coming…the wrath and fury of Becca. No one was going to stop his independent sister from being independent. On cue, Becca jumped in with an extra snarky tone.

"Between me and Garamanthus, I have those guys covered," Becca said.

"They'll be smarter next time," Desmond said. "It would be a mistake to assume that you have anything covered. No offense."

Becca started to reply, but Desmond pretended as if she didn't. "From one private person to another, I get it," Desmond said. "I wouldn't want to be followed around every day either, but this is life or death, Becca. I intend to keep you alive."

Cyrus leaned in toward Becca. "He's right. The sooner we find those guys, the sooner we can go back to normal."

"Last I checked, I didn't exactly have a normal life, remember?" Becca said under her breath.

Cyrus shrugged. "You know what I meant."

"This is going to require teamwork," Desmond said. "Rocco, Luna—you both are our eyes and ears in the sky. Both of you are going to take turns guarding the Wicked Cat. I want a report of any and every supernatural patron that walks through the door."

"Does guard duty come with free drinks?" Rocco asked, grinning.

Becca folded her arms. "If by free, you mean that Desmond is paying for it, then absolutely. You two are going to drink me out of house and home."

"See? I told you to pay for drinks last night," Luna said to Rocco.

"Just last night?" Becca asked, irritated.

"Enough," Desmond said. "Rocco and Luna, drink water for a change. It'll keep you sharper. Cyrus—I want you to stay around Becca. She'll be fine here at the Wicked Cat, but any time she leaves, you or Gilberto need to go with her. Both of you need to be with her at night. If we get caught off-guard, Gilberto's healing powers will be more important than ever."

Cyrus and Gilberto high-fived.

"Done!" Cyrus said.

"And Becca, I know this is an intrusion on your privacy, but when this is all over, hopefully, you'll thank me."

"Hopefully," Becca said.

"That's part one of the plan," Desmond said. "We're likely to be pretty safe for the next few days. Those men will obviously know that we are on high alert. Three days from now, we'll pretend that we're letting our guard down. According to Garamanthus, we are to use Becca as bait. We'll make it look like Cyrus and Gilberto leave her alone while walking home one night. The men may strike. And when they do, we will be ready. Any objections?"

Cyrus didn't dare speak up. Rocco and Luna looked content. His mom was nervous. Gilberto looked hungry. Becca was annoyed.

"Let's execute, folks," Desmond said. "The plan begins now. I want things to be extra boring for the next three days, got it?"

"The therapy session sounded productive," Aurora said.

Cyrus glanced at the clock—it was already well past midnight.

Back at Becca's apartment, Cyrus, Becca, Aurora, and Gilberto sat around Becca's kitchen table as she finished telling them about Carolyn Davidson. Downstairs, the Wicked Cat quieted down as patrons dwindled. Cyrus suppressed a yawn and turned his face to hide it from his sister. Not even the fresh cup of coffee he made fought off the sleep. Somehow, the roasted smell made him even *more* tired. A warm, drift-off-and-blink-your-eyes-and-then-you're-awake-eight-hours-later kind of sleep was waiting for him.

"So the demon really shut up when you told him to?" Cyrus asked. "Why didn't we think of that earlier?"

"So far, it works fifty percent of the time," Becca said.

"Fifty percent is better than zero," Gilberto said. He scarfed down the last of the bar pretzels that Becca had brought up from the Wicked Cat, then yawned and stretched. "Well, I got a church thing tomorrow. Cyrus, let's take turns mid-morning. Call me if anything comes up. And I don't want to hear anything tomorrow about my choice in movies while I pass the time."

Gilberto tapped Becca on the shoulder and she patted his hand.

"You can watch all the cheesy action movies you want," Becca said.

"With the hilarious Spanish dubs," Cyrus said, grinning. A few weeks ago, Cyrus and Becca had watched *Die Hard* at Gilberto's house—in Spanish. Cyrus had seen the movie a million times, but watching it with dubs was an entirely new experience.

"See ya," he said. He nodded especially to Aurora and said, "Good night, Mrs. Grant."

Cyrus sat like a swaying cobra in the chair, staring at the wall. His eyelids were heavy. Very heavy.

"Cy, go to bed," Becca said sternly.

"I'm fine," he said, jolting himself awake. "I probably oughta make sure Mom gets home."

"You two are stuck with me for the next three days," Aurora said as she closed the door behind Gilberto. "Minimum."

Together, Cyrus and Becca let out a collective groan.

"Mom, you don't have any superpowers," Cyrus said. "You could get hurt."

"What Cy said," Becca said.

"If it weren't for me, you both might have been dead at that theater, remember?" Aurora asked.

When Cyrus and Becca were fighting a tree nymph, Aurora threw a fryer of hot oil in the nymph's mouth, killing her. She definitely saved the day.

"That was different, Mom," Cyrus said. "Now we're up against assassins."

"I fail to see the difference," Aurora said. "Besides, it's too late for me to go home tonight anyway. I'll go home and get a change of clothes in the morning when Gilberto comes."

Cyrus sleep-walked into the hallway closet and pulled out a blanket, pillow, and sleeping bag. "I'll take the floor."

He tossed the blanket to Becca, and she made up the couch.

Cyrus unfurled the sleeping bag. Becca and Aurora continued a conversation. Cyrus had no idea what they said because he soon drifted off into sweet sleep.

CHAPTER NINETEEN

JoJo entered a ballroom of twenty people. Twenty impatient people who couldn't wait to see him.

A tuxedo-wearing pianist with muttonchops played classical music at a grand piano in the corner of the sumptuous room replete with a glossy checkered floor, a million-dollar chandelier that reminded JoJo of a web, and heavy golden curtains with skinny windows overlooking the city encrusted with snow.

And his potential clients—they were dressed in tuxedos, and ball gowns with plunging necklines and gaudy jewels. The place smelled like money. It wouldn't have surprised him if some of these people had henchmen in the parking garage with literal suitcases full of money, waiting to pay up.

Normally, folks met him in the back alley behind his bar if they wanted demons. But this clientele...they wanted something purer, something more powerful. The one-hundred-proof demons that could make things happen in their lives beyond their wildest dreams, not some street demon that came with baggage and a penchant for death. The kind of demons that went in smooth and stayed in smooth, the kind that slowly siphoned your soul and made you look like a ghoul later in life, worse than any cosmetic surgery.

At least that was the lie JoJo sold. The truth was that all demons were the same except for a few minor differences. The lie made the demons feel self-important, and that was the point. It still shocked JoJo that no one else had ever thought to suck up a few demons, keep them contained, and charge big money to let them out. Best business strategy of the century.

There was just one problem. These people weren't here for the demons. The demons were here for them. They just didn't know it yet. Any two-bit chump with even a third of a brain cell would have known that demons don't cost a thing. Just some blood and intent. Like JoJo always believed, money made these people blind.

Except for one.

In the corner of the room, next to the piano, he saw her.

She was a woman of class. A lady of poise and grace, honey-skinned and effortlessly elegant in her black silk cocktail dress and matching heels. Her black hair was pulled into a tight bun. She was the first person in the room to see him.

He'd shared a bed with her the night before. Dominica... She was what you could call demon-crazy. Couldn't stop asking him questions about the demons nestled in his mind. She even knew their origins. His kind of woman.

She held up a glass of red wine. He nodded at her slowly.

Next to him, Simone bristled.

A quiet applause broke out when the crowd saw him. He entered, hands waving, like a king accepting tribute from his subjects.

Donnie, who followed behind JoJo and Simone, motioned to the pianist and made a slicing motion at the neck. The pianist noticed and quickly ended the current song.

More applause. Suddenly, the ballroom was silent.

"Folks, you paid to be here, so you ought to know the rules," Donnie said into a microphone. "You're here because you want a demon and JoJo's your man. The auction will start in a minute. JoJo, want to say anything?"

A few people clapped as Donnie handed JoJo the microphone. JoJo scanned the crowd of shapeless faces that might as well have been blank in the dim ballroom light. Only now did he see the hundreds of flickering candles lining the ballroom walls, making the undersides of the curtains glimmer.

The demons came alive in his mind, laughing like jackals again.

He stared across the crowd again, long enough to make everyone uncomfortable. Meanwhile, Donnie helped him out of his mink coat.

"They're laughing," JoJo said eventually.

Murmurs of confusion spread through the crowd.

"The demons inside me laugh at you," JoJo said. "They say, what fools would be willing to pay for such misery?"

JoJo laughed himself. "I told them no, demons, these people aren't signing up for misery. They're signing up for something they believe in. A problem you can help them solve. But then, the demons laugh even louder."

He sensed the demons in his mind salivating.

"So, I'm here to help you. I'm here to help you make things happen, Jack. The demons in my mind are laughing at you because you don't have what it takes. But, if you want one, you do have to do something. You have to pay me. And what you pay is your dreams. Your soul. Your life. The life you live right now."

"So, what's the deal?" someone said.

JoJo grinned.

"A pimp once gave me some advice," he said. "He said, 'You can do anything you want out there, JoJo, but you have to know how to deal with people first.' Make your pitch. Make it good. Make it quick."

JoJo pointed. "What do you want a demon for, sir?"

The man cleared his throat. "I want knowledge."

"Dig it," JoJo said. "A professor type. I think I could find one for you. How about you, ma'am?"

"Protection," a woman nearby said.

"A proper Chicagoan!" JoJo said. "That's how we do it!"

Donnie handed him a glass of wine. He took a sip and raised his glass, eyeing Dominica in particular, who gave him a sultry smile.

"How about you?" he asked.

"I want to experience a side of life that I've been missing," she said. "I want to live on the dark side."

"You all are after my heart," he said, keeping a lingering eye on Dominica before turning to the crowd and raising his glass as if he were punching the sky.

"To demons," he said, then downed the glass in one gulp. The crowd roared with applause and laughter.

"To fools," the elder demon said. The other demons cackled.

"To food!"

"To hell!"

JoJo wandered over to the piano, set the empty glass down on the lid, and clapped his hands.

"Let's get this party started."

The elder demon in his mind stopped laughing and said, "Just like last time. We'll show them some sizzle."

Simone hopped on top of the piano like a woman getting ready to sing a jazz number. But she didn't sing. She watched JoJo intently before giving another sidelong glance at Dominica.

"Here goes," JoJo said to her.

JoJo felt pressure in his eyes, like a migraine was coming on. Then, blades of light erupted from them and his body rose into the air as if being crucified.

A black ball of shadow oozed from his eyes. The ball rolled across the room, gradually gaining speed as it went, until it disappeared under a table in the far corner of the room.

JoJo touched down gently, bending his knees. He yelled like a maniac. "Whoo! That always feels good!"

A woman screamed, then there was silence again. JoJo waited a beat then stalked over to the table where the ball had disappeared. He bent down and peered under it. Then he threw one of the chairs violently aside with a loud grunt.

"Come out, come out, wherever you are," he said in a sing-song voice.

On cue, the ball drifted out and landed on the floor in the middle of the room. A malformed cattle skull appeared first, then angular arms and legs. A beefy, triangular body materialized out of thin air, filling the space between the legs and skull. Chains rustled on the demon's body as if it were a long-lost Greek titan. The demon's back was to the crowd. It did not turn around.

The crowd gasped collectively as the demon swirled on the checkered ballroom floor. Meanwhile, JoJo crept back to Simone at the grand piano. He hopped on the piano and kissed her on the cheek.

"Hit it, baby," JoJo said.

"Rule 101 about demons," Simone said loudly in a disinterested tone, studying her nails, "is to never look at a demon directly. It is a sign of disrespect."

"Simone, what's this fine demon's name?" JoJo asked.

Simone's eyes flashed red and she spoke like a woman possessed. A demon had taken hold of her—a historian type who knew everything there was to know about demons and their whereabouts. One of the best reasons he kept Simone around. That old historian was too much for JoJo, but somehow his girl tolerated him just fine. She was never sexier than when the demon took hold of her.

"Before you stands Traxus, Lord of Agony, resident of the

fifth circle of hell, and trapped inside JoJo's body for seven years," Simone said.

"Good number," JoJo said. "Holy, even. Holy hell!"

A few people laughed.

"Lord Traxus, tell us about your last host," JoJo said.

"I clawed him from the inside out just to hear him scream," the demon said. "He tried to exorcise me."

"For the record, you all know what will happen to you if you do not obey his will," Simone said to the crowd. "What do you have to offer, Lord Traxus?"

"A thirst for blood," the demon said. "I can interpret someone's emotions in real time and detect their true intentions."

"In exchange for what?" Simone asked.

"The ability to cause random, unfocused agony everywhere we go," Lord Traxus said. "You will worship me by causing others to scream and cry for mercy."

"That's kinda boring, ain't it, Lord Traxus?" JoJo asked. "You can get all that in a night."

"It never gets old," the demon said.

JoJo shrugged. "Whatever makes you happy, man."

The red beams in Simone's eyes flashed away, leaving her human eyes. She blinked a few times, a little dazed from the possession. But she recomposed herself quickly.

"You heard him!" Simone cried. "You know what you want. If this demon can help you achieve your darkest dreams, we invite you to bid."

A slow hand rose. A woman in a red dress. "Ten thousand."

"Plus the fifty at the door?" JoJo asked. He pretended offense. Had to get them going. "Come on, now. You gotta do better than that."

"Fifty," a man said.

"That's my kinda guy," JoJo said. "Now it's a six-figure, wild moon kinda night. Care to bite back, ma'am?"

The woman in the red dress stared at the man who outbid her with the hardness of a woman who wanted to kill. "Seventy-five."

"Yes," JoJo said quietly.

Atop the grand piano, Simone continued studying her nails as if the exchange were the most trivial thing in the world. How many initiations had she been to? JoJo lost count. But there was something sexy about a woman unfazed by the hell that was about to unfold.

"Take over the bidding, baby," JoJo said. "It's sexier when you do it."

Speaking of sexy, Dominica remained by the piano. Her eyes locked on JoJo. He hopped off the piano as Simone picked up the bidding.

"One hundred and sixty," she said. "Going once…"

"Two hundred!"

"That's the spirit," he said, sauntering closer to Dominica. All the frantic cries of money and demons laughing in his skull fell away as he homed in on her.

"Not getting cold feet, are you?" he asked.

Slowly, she shook her head. She ran a hand through her dark hair. A ringed finger caught the light, dazzling him for a moment in rainbow light. A necklace of a skull with green eyes sat on the woman's neck. JoJo lifted it with a finger, stared at it curiously, then into her brown eyes.

"You're not one of those people who think they know what they want and then cowers at the first side of crazy, are you?"

"How about you find out?" she asked.

JoJo brushed a knuckle against her cheek. He traced a rune on her cheek with the pad of his finger. Then, with her ring, he made a small cut on her cheek with the ring's sharp prong. She winced.

On his palm, JoJo made a quick slice. The sliver of broken skin was as deep as a paper cut. He placed his palm on her cheek.

A blood exchange. Blood for blood. The first step.

"You strike me as a forever gal," JoJo said, slipping her bloodied ring back on. He embraced the woman's warm hands. "The kind of gal who doesn't want a demon. You need it. You need it like grass needs chlorophyll. You need it like a man needs mink. You need it…"

He leaned in and lowered his voice to a low whisper. "Because you ain't been livin' until now. You been dead, ain't that right?"

The scent of bed sheets and sweat drifted into JoJo's nose out of nowhere, a memory of last night. Skin on skin. Moaning and whispers.

Dominica said, "I need it. I need you."

Simone puffed.

"Three hundred!" a woman cried.

"We got a few rules," he said to Dominica, ignoring the bidding. "First things first, Simone is my main squeeze. I don't do cattiness. Second thing second, I'm a child of a far-gone time, you dig? You want to run with me, you got to wear my marks. You don't mind a wardrobe change or two, do you?"

"Just shut up and give it to me already," Dominica said.

JoJo smiled like a man who had just eaten the last morsel of the best meal of his life. His whole body was warm and a fire sparked in his loins.

"Then do it," JoJo said.

"Four hundred," Dominica said loudly.

"Four hundred!" Simone belted. "Going once…"

Silence.

"Going twice!" Simone cried.

"Sold!" JoJo said. "Lord Traxus is bonded to the beautiful woman in black!"

Four hundred large and the demon was hers. Four hundred thousand invisible, non-existent dollars that would never be collected. He'd cut her a deal—all she had to do was pledge loyalty to him and he'd pay the fee. By pay, what was really meant was that there would be no payment. He'd rigged this night like a good boxing match.

Quiet applause resounded through the room as several people congratulated Dominica.

"Demon rule 102," Simone said. "Lord Traxus will soon turn around to behold his new host—I never got your name—"

"Dominica," the woman said.

"Dominica," Simone said with disdain.

"*Dominica*," JoJo said, tasting every syllable as if he'd never heard her name before. "Everyone, while Dominica takes her prize, I suggest that you turn your backs."

The crowd turned away quickly, but one woman couldn't bear it. She stood, facing the demon resolutely.

"Turn around, ma'am," JoJo said sharply.

"I've come all this way," the woman said. "I must see its face!"

JoJo shook his head as he turned away. Why was there always one idiot in the crowd who had to look upon the demon's face as if it were the Messiah? Didn't make a difference to him. The mess was going to get cleaned up just the same at the end of the night.

The floor shook as the demon stomped his feet.

A bone-crushing female scream tore through the ballroom, followed by splattering blood.

JoJo's peripheral vision inked with red splotches. Nearby, a man in a tuxedo was covered in blood that wasn't his own.

Next to him, a headless stump in a dress thudded on the ballroom floor.

At first, confused screams grated JoJo's ears. Then, the timbres grew terrified when they realized that JoJo wasn't kidding about looking at demons being a sign of disrespect.

JoJo sighed and predicted pandemonium half a second before it started. A stampede erupted toward the door.

"Donnie, the doors!" he said.

"Already ahead of you," Donnie said. The pianist in muttonchops stared at JoJo through the window on the other side of the door and gave him a thumbs-up.

"It's locked! Oh my God, it's locked!" someone cried.

All at once, the sounds of jackal demons, the tortured screams, the buckling door, and the demon in the middle of the ballroom demanding obedience surrounded JoJo.

He took a look around and decided now was the time to do something about it. He turned and tilted his head so that he could see the shadowed demon, but only from the corner of his eye.

Despite the horror, Dominica stood fast next to the piano, her back turned to her impending demon host.

"Tell me, woman," Lord Traxus said. "Is my desire all *you* require?"

"I want to live," she said. "After that, I don't care. Have me as long as you want me."

"Talking dirty again," JoJo said. "She's yours, Lord Traxus."

The demon roared and JoJo looked away, keeping only the corners of the demon in his peripheral vision. Its shadowy body streamed into a long wand of dark light.

Dominica held out her hands and said, "Yes. Yes. Yes!" as the demon streamed into the cut on her cheek.

The elder demon came alive in JoJo's mind. "A splendid pair!"

"It's always splendid," JoJo said.

The demon filled the woman's body so fully that shadows leaked out of her eyes, ears, and mouth. She laughed like a super villain, then dropped to her knees as if her body had powered down. She wheezed in heavy, ragged gasps.

"Take it easy," JoJo said. "I'll be with you in a minute."

The door stopped buckling. The rest of the potential clients watched in horror as he strode toward them.

"You thought you knew what you were signing up for, but

you had no idea," he said. "Who here still wants a personal demon?"

No hands went up.

"Help me understand something," he said. He stopped at the corpse of the woman slaughtered by the demon. The blood stopped just short of his bluchers. "You're telling me that all of you pulled strings, lined up, and were willing to pay me hundreds of thousands of dollars *for a demon*, and at the first sign of blood, you're running like wimps?" He held out a hand and closed it into a fist. His voice went cold. "What did you think was going to happen?"

Someone spoke up. A man in the back of the crowd. "Just let us out of here and we won't say a word."

"See, that's the problem," JoJo said. "See, I let you all out of here and you *are* going to start talking. I'm going to have reporters knocking on my door asking me about why there's a woman dead on the ballroom floor."

He pointed down to the woman, wagging a finger at her. "And that's not good for business. I'd almost go so far as to say that you people wasted my time."

He took more steps toward the crowd. They flattened against the door.

"Before you entered, I asked for a deposit. Fifty thousand just to get in the door. You get your money back if you don't win the auction. But I got bad news for you: there isn't any auction, and there are no more demons for sale."

A gasp spread across the room.

"What I do need, however, are some good human minnows."

"You bastard!" someone cried. A man tore from the throng and ran at JoJo, fist raised.

JoJo stepped aside and hit the man hard in the back of the head with a sucker punch. He hit the floor cold.

"I'm done wasting time," he said, holding out his hands.

The demons in his head started laughing again. Slowly, he

lifted several inches into the air. He held out his hands long and wide and gave his best full-throated laugh.

One by one, shadows slipped out of JoJo and surrounded him in a voracious twister. A fierce wind blew through the room, snuffing out the candles. The ballroom curtains flapped like flags in a storm.

Electric eyes flashed in the shadowed twister as JoJo lifted higher into the air.

"It's all right," he said, as everyone screamed and cried. "This won't hurt none."

The twister engulfed the room. Demons broke off, flying through the air as shadowed, horned wraiths with sharp teeth. A demon swirled around each person.

JoJo's head nearly hit the ceiling, but he didn't care—he kept laughing and laughing and laughing as his demons swarmed their marks, engulfing them in shadow and blood.

Agonizing screams and the cracking of bones erupted throughout the ballroom as the demons feasted on their meal.

In a few minutes, there would be nothing left. No blood, no bones, not even any clothing. And for a while, these ravenous jackals would slake their thirst with these people's blood and be content. For a while, they'd finally shut the hell up and let him think with his own brain for a change. Plus, he'd have a new member of the gang. At least his new squeeze wasn't going to be demon food.

Just the thought of newfound peace made JoJo laugh even harder as his demons swirled at a dizzying pace below him.

CHAPTER TWENTY

Becca jolted awake from a deep, dreamless sleep.

She shot straight up. Her heart raced and she took quick, shallow breaths.

Fear gripped her insides and squeezed hard like a monstrous claw. She became aware of uncomfortable wetness. Warm, sticky sweat covered her face, drenched her clothes. Her bed sheet and comforter looked like someone had thrown a giant bucket of water on them.

She put a hand on her head. A slant of moonlight sliced across the bed. Dazzles of snow danced against her bedroom window.

Garamanthus spoke to her quietly but confidently.

"Do you sense that energy?"

"What energy?" she whispered.

"My brothers and sisters ride again!" Garamanthus cried.

"Screw them," Becca said.

Becca wanted a glass of water. Hell, she would've gladly drunk a pitcher of ice-cold water.

A quick glance at the green neon clock on her bedstand told her it was two-thirty in the morning. Nothing good ever happened after two o'clock. Her mother had taught her that.

The longer she lived with this demon, the more she believed it. At this rate, if she ever exorcised Garamanthus out of her, she'd convert to Puritanism.

She pushed her bed sheets aside and was about to step out of bed when the demon seized control. That familiar twinge spread across her body—the maddening, soul-crushing loss of control that made her feel disabled.

"No," was what she wanted to say, but Garamanthus took over. All she could do was watch as the demon stood in her body, stretched, and tiptoed silently into the living room.

Cyrus lay in a sleeping bag on the hardwood floor. He slept soundlessly with his back to Becca. Her mother was tangled in a bed sheet on the couch. She must've fallen asleep reading because her digital e-reader lay on her stomach.

Leave them alone, Becca thought. *If you hurt them, I'll—*

The demon stopped at the hallway mirror, put a hand to her mouth and said, "Ssssh."

Garamanthus moved in her body with the swiftness of a ninja into the kitchen, where she grabbed a small stainless steel saucepan.

I swear on everything. If you hurt them, I'll kill you.

She crept to the door. She slipped on her boots and her winter coat. The security chain on the door didn't make a sound as she placed it aside.

The apartment door shut behind her and she waited for a moment, her ear to the cold door, listening for any signs of stirring in the living room. There were none.

She pushed out into brutal winter night and snow as wet as rain. She stood under a streetlight and watched the Wicked Cat, which was dark now aside from the mason jar can lights she left on at night for security.

The surrounding street was a winter wonderland. Not a single footstep marked the pristine layer of snow that gathered on everything. The powdery wetness came up past her heels. She felt the frigid sting, but Garamanthus didn't seem to mind.

Where are we going? she asked as she trudged through the snow.

"To make a proposition," he said. Her voice came out from her mouth, flatter and lined with undertones of evil.

Thoughts of Desmond and the plans he made hours before flashed through her mind. Garamanthus sensed her thoughts too.

"Don't worry about your pretty little plans," he said. "Those men won't find us."

If they do, I sure hope they don't bring guns to the fight, Becca thought.

"We can both hope," Garamanthus said.

She became aware of the saucepan in her hand.

Why did you take one of my saucepans? she thought.

"Your question is perfectly timed," Garamanthus said.

A shadow flickered over them. Above, a raven perched on a nearby streetlight, watching them intently.

Rocco. Or Luna. In the snow, she couldn't tell which one it was.

Becca bent down and grabbed the nearest rock. She chucked it at the raven, and it cawed as it flapped away.

She waited for the bird to land on a nearby car and she launched the saucepan. It flipped through the air several times before it smacked into the bird and knocked it onto the sidewalk.

The bird let out a pained grunt, taken by surprise.

She tracked through snow, where the saucepan had landed on top of the raven. Then she ran into the alley, grabbed one of the shovels belonging to the Wicked Cat, and threw a heap of snow on top of the pan until it was a pyramid of snow.

Becca resisted and tried to take back control, but the demon's hold was too strong.

You're going to kill it! Don't do this!

Becca threw the shovel aside and wiped snow off her hands.

"Some things can't be avoided," Garamanthus said. "I'll make you a deal. If we finish our business early, I'll dig the bird's dead carcass out of the snow with your bare hands."

She took off in a run down the nearest alley, then emerged onto another street, slipping her scarf over her nose and mouth.

Bright lights blinded her as she stopped in the middle of a street. A car horn honked madly as tires screeched in the snow.

Becca shielded her face. The car missed her by inches and skidded to a stop in the middle of the street. A tinted window rolled down and an angry man yelled at her.

"Hey, watch where you're going!"

Seconds later, Becca had the man by the collar and stuffed him face-first in a mound of snow. Then she was sitting on the heated leather seat of a BMW, peeling away. The blood-red lights on the dashboard lit up the inside of the car in a demonic glow.

Oh my God, Becca thought. *I just committed grand theft auto.*

"Don't be a pest," Garamanthus said. "He never saw your face. There weren't any witnesses."

You don't know that. I'm going to jail.

Panic set in and sirens might as well have been ringing in Becca's head.

"I'm wearing gloves," the demon said. "No fingerprints. Live on the wild side, Becca. Besides, why would I commit myself to jail time? I can't wreak havoc there."

But all Becca could think about was that poor man in the snow. She hadn't even seen his face. Had he seen hers? What if the police caught her? She'd never see Cyrus or her mom again.

"Sit back and enjoy the ride," the demon said. "It's not every day you get to ride in a car like this."

Becca screamed inside her mind as the snowy city streets rushed by in a blur.

CHAPTER TWENTY-ONE

Cyrus dreamed he was riding his electric skateboard through the snow under a starry sky. His motor whined as he cut a path in the middle of the street that looked like miniature train tracks. He was in Logan Square with cars all around him. He skated through a light and hit a thick layer of snow, slowing down.

His earbuds were snug in his ears and he hugged himself as a katana-sharp breeze blew through him.

"Do you think this is really a good idea?" his mom said in his earbuds.

"Perfectly fine," he said as a car honked behind him.

He cradled the remote in his hand and pushed harder on the throttle. The wheels threw up snow as the engine chugged and burped.

"Come on," he said.

He suddenly remembered he had to return Fontanelli's equipment. The backpack sprayer was light on his back.

"I gotta get this equipment back to Font," he said.

"I told you it was a bad idea," his mom said. "Pull over and call a rideshare."

A car passed him aggressively, spraying up snow in his face. He yelled and cursed at the driver.

He pushed harder on the throttle.

"Just a few more blocks and then you can rest," he said to his board.

But the board cut off. He was trapped in the snow.

"Damn it!" he cried as another car passed him.

He stood in the middle of the street and picked up his board, inspecting it as cars streamed past him.

The motor was oven-hot. Ice caked on the axles. His board wasn't going to make it.

"You should call a rideshare," his mom said, this time more motherly.

"Fine," he said. "I'll listen."

"For a change," she said. "Because you and Becca never listen to me."

"We listen all the time."

Cyrus ran to the side of the road. He surveyed the damage on his board again.

"I have an idea," he said. "Just let me try this and if it doesn't work, I will call a rideshare."

"I don't think that's a good idea, honey."

"It'll just take a second," he said, throwing his board down into the snow.

If his board was overheated, maybe the snow could cool it down. Steam rose from the board. Cyrus jumped back to avoid an explosion of sparks.

"Aw, man!"

"Told you," his mom said.

"You win," Cyrus said.

Suddenly, headlights lit up his vision, turning everything white.

A menacing horn blared and swelled toward him. He froze like a deer.

Tires squealed, followed by a man screaming. He jumped out of the way.

Two hands grabbed him by his coat collar. A man hollered something in the distance.

Fear spread through him. Something told him to fight.

"Leave me alone!" he cried, swatting.

"Cyrus," his mom said.

"Mom, I can't talk right now!"

The hands shook him.

"Cyrus!"

He resisted, and his face landed in the snow, and he howled in pain.

"Cyrus, wake up!"

He sprang awake.

The nylon trappings of his sleeping bag replaced the snow and he was back on Becca's hardwood floor. His mom knelt in front of him. He startled and crawled back, yawning.

"Did you hear that?" Aurora asked.

"What?" Cyrus asked.

"Sounded like an accident," Aurora said. "Or an assault. A man was yelling."

She rose and looked out the living room window, hooking a blind down with a finger. "It sounded really bad."

"Just another night in Chicago," Cyrus said. "Trust me, I've heard worse."

Cyrus rolled over and repositioned his pillow. "I don't want to scare you, Mom, but Becca and I have heard much worse this time of night around here. You get used to it. I don't know what it says about me that I don't wake up anymore."

Hell, Bec was probably rolling over in bed right now too.

"I wish I could see better," Aurora said. "The snow is coming down pretty hard."

"Yeah, yeah," Cyrus said, settling into his sleeping bag.

"Maybe I can see something from Becca's room," Aurora said.

Cyrus closed his eyes and welcomed sweet, sweet sleep as his mom's footsteps walked into Becca's room. He wiggled and yawned again as the pace of the footsteps quickened, followed by a light switch clicking on.

"Cyrus," Aurora said nervously.

"Bad accident?" he asked, not opening his eyes.

"Becca's gone!"

"She's probably in the bathroom," he said. Warm, warm sleep invited him. The darkness in his eyelids began to coalesce into another dream, the shapes of another street taking form.

"She's not in the bathroom," Aurora said.

"Luna's on the roof," he said. "She probably went to chat. She doesn't sleep too well sometimes. Anyhoo, I've got a skateboard to fix…"

Something hit him hard on the shoulder.

He sprang up and tripped over the sleeping bag. One of his sister's sandals lay next to him. It took him a yawn and a few seconds of blurred thinking to discover that his mom had thrown it.

"Wake up!" Aurora cried. "Your sister is *gone*!"

Cyrus stood for a moment, staring as Aurora threw on her coat.

"Help me look outside!" Aurora said, motioning him to hurry up.

Becca was missing? She couldn't be.

He wobbled to the door, put on his boots, and grabbed his coat. He didn't zip it up; he followed his mom down the apartment corridor, into the dark foyer, and out into the night.

The cold sure woke him up. Suddenly, he was awake in the middle of the street, eyes burning.

The lights of the Wicked Cat were turned down low.

"She's not at the Cat," Aurora said.

He glanced into the sky. "Luna? You up there?"

He waited.

"Luna?" he asked again, a little louder.

A distant, muffled *gronk* replied.

Cyrus looked around but didn't see the raven he expected.

"It's coming from over there," Aurora said.

A few feet away, a two-foot mound of snow lay in the middle of the sidewalk. A shovel was staked on the summit.

"The hell?" Cyrus asked.

He grabbed the shovel and dug into the base of the mound. The shovel clinked against something metallic.

A few snow throws later, he spotted the handle of one of Becca's saucepans. He dug it out and a flutter of wings made him jump back.

A raven with blue-tinged wings leaped into the sky, wheeled over Cyrus, and then slammed onto the ground. Slowly, it morphed into Luna, who lay shivering face-down in the snow. She wasn't wearing a winter coat—just a leather jacket, flannel shirt, and jeans.

"She's hurt," Aurora said.

Cyrus turned Luna around. She blinked and smiled at him. "I…thought I was…a goner."

"Don't talk," Cyrus said, closing both of his hands around hers. "It's going to be okay."

"Becca," Luna said. "No…not Becca."

"Where did she go?" Aurora asked.

"No idea," Luna said. "It's…cold."

He cursed, looking around the street. Then he spotted a trail of footsteps leading into an alley.

Boots. Looked like Becca's size.

"Call Gilberto and call Desmond," Cyrus said to his mom. "Get Luna inside where she can warm up."

Zipping up his coat, he pulled himself into a run, following the footsteps into the darkness.

"Where are you going?" Aurora asked.

"After Becca," he said, rubbing the sleep out of his eyes.

The footsteps broadcast an obvious path through the alley next to the Wicked Cat, and then onto another street.

A man in a thick pea coat and a trapper hat blew into his hands on the corner. Red and blue lights washed out his face as he spoke with a police officer writing something down on a notepad.

"I think it was a woman," the man said. "I couldn't see her."

"What kind of car do you have, sir?" the officer asked.

"BMW."

"I'll give you a ride down to the station and we'll do the paperwork there," the officer said. "I hope we can get your car back."

Cyrus watched them, trying to understand what was going on. Then he picked up on the footsteps, which stopped abruptly in the middle of the street. A long skid of tire tracks tore up the road.

"Holy crap," Cyrus said.

If he didn't know any better, his sister had just stolen a car.

CHAPTER TWENTY-TWO

Kirk swore that, from now on, he would relish the finer moments in life. The last day had taught him not to take anything for granted.

No, he was going to be a new man, and he would savor experiences that mattered. Like getting onto the last flight to Chicago on standby because Catalina was extra nice to the front desk worker. Like the darkened airplane cabin, which meant that he didn't have to talk to Catalina for two hours. Or, like the captain coming on the intercom and saying that they would in fact be making a textbook landing at O'Hare Airport because of a break in the snow. Or, even better, the robotic buzz of the landing gears extending out, or the plane touching down on an icy runway, or the labyrinth of silver lights of the airport concourse in the distance like a contorted crown.

He even felt nice enough to hand Catalina her bag from the overhead bin.

He was back in Chicago, back in the game. Now he might have a chance of rescuing his dad and brother.

After a short wait at the baggage claim carousels, he and Catalina were sliding into winter coats as they exited into the horrid winter night. They waited next to a pillar with an airline logo on it.

"What now?" Kirk asked as he and Catalina stood on the curb.

Catalina thumbed something into her phone and slipped it into her coat.

"We wait," she said.

"Rideshare?"

Catalina looked around. "Something like that."

Kirk stared up at the belly of the sky. Snow began to fall again. He wondered if it was a miracle that he had gotten on that plane from Atlanta, a divine act that the plane made it to O'Hare Airport—of all places—and a greater miracle that the plane had landed in a break in the storm, a break that seemed to be rapidly ending.

"Why don't we continue our game while we wait," he said.

Catalina gave him a sly smile. For a moment, he wondered if they'd be stuck together forever, traveling and revealing information about their entire lives on a slow drip. "You first."

"Two things again," he said. "Ask away."

Catalina thumped a finger against her lips as she thought about the game. "Okay, I'll deal. What's the one thing in your entire life that you are most proud of?"

"What kind of a ridiculous question is that?" Kirk asked.

"You wanted to play," she said.

"Proudest moment? My dad telling me he was proud of me for the first time in a long time."

"That's deep," she said. "I didn't expect you to bare your heart so soon."

He wondered what she meant by "soon."

"What was he proud of you for?" she asked.

Kirk slipped a pair of sunglasses out of his breast pocket. He slipped them on. "Casting my first dark spell that didn't backfire for a change. My brother and I had just taken down a couple of real bad guys. It was a hundred-thousand-dollar contract, and these guys were into some pretty sick stuff. Animal sacrifice, human trafficking, you name it. They made even a necromancer like me blush. Anyway, the last guy was powerful. My brother and I had to run. I remembered a spell my father taught me years ago. I could never quite get it right."

"Death curse?" Catalina asked, suddenly interested.

"Not quite. It was a spell to get me from point A to point B. We're not talking halfway around the world or anything. More like sixty feet. Enough for me and my brother to double back and attack with the element of surprise."

He tipped his sunglasses down at her. "But that's not why Dad told me he was proud of me."

"Then why?" she asked.

"Because I beat the literal shit out of the guy that was chasing me. He just so happened to be a guy my father hated very much. He was proud that I made the guy suffer."

"Your proudest moment was a moment of evil," Catalina said. "Even a necromancer can't find any joy in the world, can he? Okay, I'll tell you another detail about me. I'm kind of a big deal."

A taxi passed just as the wind blew. Kirk wished he was inside a warm car right about now.

"A lot of people depend on me," she said, "and they look to me for guidance."

"I wish I had a better follow-up," Kirk said. "Care to tell me anything else?"

"I got this position ten years ago," she said. "My first order of business is vengeance."

"You've been doing this for ten years and this is your *first* order of business?"

"Vengeance takes a while when you do it right," she said. "Second question. Do *you* believe in vengeance?" she asked.

He rubbed his hands together to stay warm. He wondered

why the hell they were standing outside. It had seemed like a badass thing to do, but he was quickly regretting it.

"I've been on the vigilante side. It's not so bad. The money is good."

"I'm not talking about vigilantism," Catalina said, her face turning hard. "Anyone can be a vigilante as long as they can fight. I'm talking about fighting for something you believe in."

"Hypothetically," he said. "If something happened to my brother and father, and you were responsible—yeah, I believe in vengeance. Real bad. Otherwise, I'm ambivalent."

"Look at you and your big words," she said. "You and I, despite our differences, might not be so different after all."

A horn honked, and an unmarked black commercial van pulled up to the curb. Two men dressed in black winter coats and black medical masks hopped out.

"Here's the deal, Kirk McLeod," Catalina said, handing her leopard print suitcase to one of the men. "This is the part where we would normally point a gun at your face and tell you to get in the car. Or, if there weren't cameras or people watching, we would be more cavalier, hit you in the back of the head, render you unconscious, and drag you into the van. Since we can't do either of those things, just trust that my men are fully loaded and that we will subdue you if we have to."

She smiled. "I'm hoping that you'll just get in the van. It'll make all of our lives easier."

One of the men in black took Kirk's suitcases. Then, the man patted Kirk down.

Kirk told himself to think, think, think. Reluctantly, he climbed into the dark van and sat in a bucket seat. Catalina climbed in after him. The men slid the door shut.

The inside of the van was dark. Too dark.

"Thank you for your cooperation," Catalina said, sitting in the seat next to him.

As the van pulled off, the last thing Kirk saw was a passing car as he felt a giant *thwack* on the back of his head.

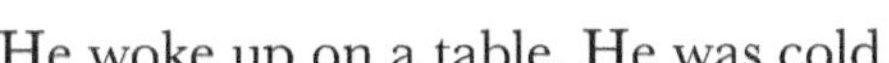

He woke up on a table. He was cold.

He was naked. His clothes were folded neatly on a cheap chair next to the table.

His eyes focused. A long fluorescent light buzzed in the ceiling. His arms and ankles were fastened to the table with metal clamps, and he couldn't move.

He struggled, trying to get his bearings. The back of his head felt raw, and he felt something dripping—had to be blood.

He was in some sort of green-walled room. There were cracks in the walls. A giant brown spider was nestled in one corner where the ceiling met the wall. On one end was a long window that he couldn't see out of. Whoever was on the other side could have definitely seen in. He didn't know why, but he felt like someone was watching.

A steel door opened and Catalina strolled in. Instead of the red sundress and denim jacket, she wore a leather jump-suit. Her hair was pulled back into a tight ponytail, and the skull necklace jingled against her leather zipper as she walked. An entourage of men in black coats followed her. They must've been the same men from the van, but their masks were removed, revealing faces covered in scars.

"Sorry about the hit," Catalina said. "But we couldn't risk giving away our location."

Kirk tried to wiggle himself out of the clamps. "What the hell is this?"

"My name is Catalina Parva," she said. "I am the leader of the Sacred Heart. We are dedicated to the eradication of evil wherever it may reside. And we are not afraid to resort to the darkness to do it."

"Sacred Heart?" Kirk asked quietly. "What is that, some kind of church?"

"We are secular, despite our name," Catalina said. "A

sacred heart means a heart that is free to pursue good, whatever that may be. But sure, we are people of faith, when you think about it. It's just so unfortunate that you had to get caught up in this, Kirk. I'm sorry for what we must do to you."

Kirk struggled again. "You listen—I came back to the States with you. I told you I would cooperate."

"And you are. Beautifully. But I suppose I wasn't entirely truthful. We at the Sacred Heart believe in vengeance. But we also believe in purity."

Kirk repeated her words. He didn't understand.

Catalina snapped her fingers and the men gathered around Kirk. One of them produced a knife and made a quick laceration on Kirk's arm.

Catalina unzipped the sleeve on one of her arms. The man tossed the knife to her and she made an incision in the same part of her arm.

"We have several specialties, Kirk," she said. "We can be vigilantes. That has been good money for the last few years. But there's another specialty that we've been longing to get back into, and the time is now."

She held up the knife and grinned. "Our best specialty is demon hunting."

CHAPTER TWENTY-THREE

If Becca ever took a driving test while possessed by Garamanthus, the student driver police officer would take her directly to jail.

She drove the BMW like she stole it—literally. Stoplights were just a suggestion and all the snow in the world wouldn't have stopped her from driving at fifty miles per hour, swerving through the gathering snow.

She fishtailed out of Logan Square toward downtown, a straight shot down North Milwaukee Avenue. She kept the same speed and cruised through all the lights on late yellow.

Becca waited for the police sirens. It was just a matter of time before someone called the cops. They'd run the plates, which would match the description of the vehicle, which was probably already being reported as stolen, and the police would stop Garamanthus. If she didn't kill the police, they'd take her to jail, and Garamanthus would conveniently cede control of her body back, just in time for an intense interrogation session. Becca had seen enough television shows to know that she was absolutely, positively screwed the moment the police showed up.

They crossed a bridge over the Chicago River where snow

gathered on the cracks between the barge-sized ice floes. Past the river, the buildings grew taller as they entered the River North district.

"Where are we going?" Becca asked.

"To the source of the energy," Garamanthus said. "Call it a family reunion of sorts."

Becca's heart pounded at the thought of encountering more demons tonight. She focused all her energy and tried to take back control, trying to move her arms and legs.

"Don't bother," Garamanthus said. "With all the demon energy in the air tonight, you're mine to control until I say so."

Demon energy. She didn't know such a thing existed. It explained a lot. She kept straining, trying to regain control, but the demon laughed.

She took a hard left, drifting across a big snowbank as she turned into a dark alley between a hotel and a parking garage. She cut the car off and hopped out, but left the keys in the ignition.

"Done worrying about going to jail?" he asked, slamming the door. "There won't be any tracks in about twenty minutes with the snow falling the way it is. Congratulations—you just lived on the wild side."

Despite the pure fear gripping her, she also felt pure adrenaline, every blood vessel in her body pumping like mad. Seconds later, she was at the end of the alley and crossing an empty street. All around, late-night Chicago was deadly silent. The gunmetal sky kept dumping snow-globe levels of snow. She tipped up her collar to give her a little more warmth.

Why do you want to reunite with your brothers and sisters? Becca asked, trapped in her mind.

"Unfinished business," Garamanthus said as she jaywalked across another street, "and familial courtesy."

Dangerous business? Becca asked.

"You'll find out soon, won't you?"

Becca wanted to curse.

"We had a rude awakening today," Garamanthus said. "I thought I had more time." The wind blew and she dipped into an alley. She walked halfway down and spotted the base of a fire escape that wrapped around an apartment building.

Time? Becca asked.

"To enjoy my newfound freedom," Garamanthus said. She broke into a run and hopped on a dumpster and then onto the base of the fire escape, which clanged under her boots.

Thank God the lights in all the apartments were off and that Garamanthus was a quiet creeper. If she were sleeping in her apartment and heard someone on the fire escape, she would have freaked the hell out.

"I thought I had at least a few years to wreak havoc with your body," Garamanthus said. "You could call it demonic freeplay."

I'm just an object to you, aren't I?

"You're far more than an object," he whispered. "Even we demons value human life. You could say that I value your life more than *you* do at the current moment."

She crept up a few flights of the fire escape, staying low to the steps.

"Then the strange men showed up and ruined our night," he said. "I had a chance to think on our little encounter long and hard. I've decided that I need to come out of hiding."

Wait—you're in hiding?

"I'm hiding for other reasons," he said. "A bitter feud with a vampire clan."

Wonderful.

"Lucky for you, we aren't fighting vampires," Garamanthus said.

A blaze of bright lights nearly blinded her. Garamanthus stayed crouched on the fire escape, staring across the street at a massive skyscraper that stretched at least sixty stories.

Various floors were lit up in yellow bands on the skyscraper, an assortment of offices, high-end lofts, and a hotel. A sign on the front of the building said *Montclair.*

"My brothers and sisters are there," Garamanthus said. "It's just a matter of getting in."

It's a skyscraper. Can't you just walk in? Becca asked.

Garamanthus laughed quietly. "Good idea. Actually, I like that a lot. Here I was thinking I'd have to sneak in… You have no idea what we are up against. We're sure to find some resistance in the lobby. This place is oozing with demon energy. But there are no wards, so your suggestion may work after all."

Hearing the demon speak with her own voice, dripped in sarcasm, made her wish she hadn't said anything.

Something tells me this isn't your average place, Becca said.

"You're learning quickly," Garamanthus said, sliding back down the fire escape. She landed in the snow with a puff. Becca held her breath as she jogged across the street, under the long red canopy, and into the revolving door that led into the Montclair Building lobby.

The lobby was like any other Chicago building in River North—opulent and immaculate. Giant ferns lined the walls, and the floor was a shining marble with some kind of Greek-inspired design. Somewhere, a waterfall gushed and provided ambient noise.

Garamanthus stopped in the middle of the lobby and looked around. Seeing the security desk, she grinned.

A black woman in a security uniform made eye contact. Her face hardened instantly.

"Ma'am, can we help you?" she asked.

"I'm here for the demons," Garamanthus said as loud as he could.

What the hell are you doing? Becca asked.

The security guard frowned as if Becca were some crazy person off the street that wandered into the lobby for warmth and attention. She wondered how many people stumbled into this lobby to make the security guard barely blink at such a ridiculous statement.

"We need to ask you to leave," the guard said.

"Why leave?" Garamanthus asked. "I could sense the energy from halfway across the city. Didn't you too relish it, sister?"

The guard's eyes widened for a split second. She pressed a button on the desk without looking down.

"I'll wait as long as it takes," Garamanthus said.

Suddenly, there were footsteps behind Becca—she turned just as a stun gun struck her. Her body crashed down onto the marble.

Every muscle in her body locked up. Her jaw seized and the skin on her face stretched downward. Her arms and legs pulled inward as if to protect her. A guttural moan escaped from her lips against her will.

A heavy man landed on top of her.

"Don't move," another guard said. Becca convulsed as the woman and another male guard handcuffed her.

Then, the voltage was gone and she had control of her body again. She could wiggle her hands. It would have been a relief if she weren't in handcuffs.

"What the hell have you done?" she asked with her own voice. This time, she didn't care that she seemed to be talking to herself.

Garamanthus laughed inside her skull as the security guards ripped the stun gun's copper wires from the back of her duffel coat and dragged her up.

"Please," she begged. "Let me go. I don't know what got into me."

"Quiet," the female security guard said, taking her by the arm.

"Just let me outside and I won't be any trouble—"

"We're not going to ask you again to shut up," the male guard said harshly.

Becca resisted all the way across the lobby to an elevator and said nothing as the car rocketed toward the upper floors of the Montclair Building.

CHAPTER TWENTY-FOUR

THE SNOW MADE Cyrus's boots and jeans soggy as he dashed through the three inches of snow on the ground.

Columns of snow blew in his face and he had to keep wiping sweat and frosty tears from his eyes. It was so cold, the tears on his cheek froze.

Freaking lake effect snow. During a regular spring, summer, or autumn day, he could have run a block in a minute. Now, it was taking him five.

The darkened streets of Logan Square seemed to ignore Cyrus, like all the buildings were turning their backs to him, offering nothing with their blackened windows and shadowed facades.

He was cold. Wet. Scared.

It dawned on him that he might never see his sister again. The last time he'd ever see her was her sitting on the couch, yawning and talking to his mom.

He wouldn't let this be the end. He wouldn't let Becca get hurt.

If he were his sister right now and he were infested with a demon, where would it take him?

He had no idea. There were no places he could think of

where Becca might be. That frightened him and forced him to keep pushing.

The wind sliced through him again and he yelled, leaned forward, and kept going.

In the distance, the lights of the Logan Square Blue Line station lit up the night. A long blue and purple mural stretched behind the glass entrance where escalators fed down into the station.

He kept Becca in his mind as he ran. He wasn't going to let her down. He just hoped she knew it.

He shook off snow from his boots as he rode the escalator down into the cool underground tunnel with tracks on both sides. There was no one on the platform.

He reached into his pocket and wrapped his fingers around warm metal. The pewter whistle Bart and Wendy had given him. He pulled it out and stared at it for a moment.

He couldn't believe what he was going to do. But he didn't have any other hope.

He stuck the whistle in his mouth and blew as hard as he could. It let out a pathetic shrill tone that reminded him of a failed birthday kazoo.

He blew again.

And again.

He waited.

Pacing across the platform, he wondered if it was just a dream. Maybe the gnomes wouldn't come for him after all.

He was just about to reconsider his options when the ground rumbled and a distant white-hot lamp appeared deep in the tunnel. Wheels whined on the tracks, making Cyrus want to put his hands over his ears.

The gnomes' L train burst into the station, filling it with the smell of fresh earth. Smoke rose from the lead car's giant drill. The blades on the drill were still revolving slowly.

The dirt-covered train slid past and slowed to a stop. The

lights in the cars flickered and then the doors opened with a hiss.

A window on the lead car opened and Bart stuck his head out, still grimy as ever. He wore his goggles now, giving him a steampunk vibe.

"Sorry it took me so long," Bart said. "We didn't seriously think you'd call so soon, Mr. Grant."

"My sister is missing," Cyrus said. "It's a life or death situation."

Bart's face shifted from silly to serious. "Say no more. Hop on."

Cyrus ran into the car, and as soon as the doors shut, he grabbed the nearest rail as the train rocketed into the tunnel.

CHAPTER TWENTY-FIVE

THE ELEVATOR STOPPED on the thirty-fifth floor. The bell dinged, the door slid open, and the guards kept their ironfisted holds on Becca's arms as they dragged her out.

"I told you to let me go!" she cried.

She bent her knees and her boots squeaked across the marble floor as they pulled her.

"Let me go!" she cried, hoping someone would hear her.

She was in some sort of hotel. One of those older, historic hotels that you often found downtown. The walls were plastered with candy-striped pink and white wallpaper, and the air was musty. Brass-plated sconces cast a glow that reminded her of candlelight. A subtle buzz from a nearby ice machine blanketed the hallway.

Every door they passed had brass numbers. She tracked the door numbers as she passed, keeping a mental note in case she got an opportunity to call for help.

If these guards dragged her into a room and killed her, no one would ever know. The rooms were quiet as tombs. She couldn't tell if they were occupied or if the occupants were sleeping.

"Just settle down and relax," Garamanthus said. "This will be over shortly."

"Next time we're in a difficult situation that I cause, I'll tell you to settle down and see how you feel," she said out loud.

"Ma'am, we really would prefer not to shoot you," the guard said. "For your sake, I recommend that you remain quiet."

That shut Becca up.

Further down the hallway, the single doors turned into double doors. They must've been penthouses or expensive suites.

The guards stopped at a pair of double doors at the end of the hallway. The woman unlocked one of the doors with an antiquated brass key. Becca hadn't seen keys like this at a hotel since she was a little girl. It reminded her of a motel she and her dad stayed at in the middle of God-knows-where Illinois. The innkeeper kept the keys on a pegboard behind the front desk. She didn't think any hotels used real keys anymore.

They carried her into a lavish suite. The living room alone was as big as the Wicked Cat, with a full kitchen, bar, and more chaise lounges, ottomans, and couches than she'd ever seen in her life. The suite had a snowy, panorama view of the Chicago River painted in the gold, blue, and pink lights of nearby high-rises.

The guards threw her on a green paisley-patterned chase. Her face hit the fabric hard.

"What's your name?" the female guard asked.

"Like hell I'm telling you," Becca said.

The woman searched Becca's pockets. They tore off her coat and inspected all the pockets. Thank God she had left her purse at home. She hadn't even brought her keys with her.

Garamanthus laughed inside her mind. "What a goose chase," he said. "No one's going to get hurt here as long as you repeat after me."

"Why are you here?" the male guard asked.

Becca listened closely to Garamanthus and repeated after him.

"I sensed the demon energy. Didn't you?" she asked.

"How did you know that?" the guards asked simultaneously.

"Everyone knows it," Becca said. "At least, everyone who's someone knows the secret initiation. You can smell the demon energy from the suburbs."

Becca couldn't stand the cryptic talk anymore. She lowered her voice. "If this is so important to you, why don't you take control and tell them yourself?"

"Theatrics, my dear Becca," Garamanthus said. "If there's one thing I've learned about you, it's that you have no flair for the dramatic…"

Becca was so focused on the demon's words that she didn't see the guards' faces shift. She couldn't tell why, but something on their faces was more malicious. Almost wicked.

The woman spoke, but this time, her voice was two octaves lower. "So, you are one of us."

Becca's eyes widened. "No, I'm not—"

"Not you, girl," the woman said harshly. The way she said "girl" made Becca's spine tingle. "We refer to the one you are carrying."

Becca swallowed hard.

"Announce yourself," the female guard said.

"I am Garamanthus, the Prince of Blood," Becca repeated.

The man and woman glanced at each other with concerned faces.

"Garamanthus the Coward?" the male guard asked. "You came here so that your enemies could finish you, then."

"I came here because we are all in great danger," Becca said. "I have news that the leader among you will desperately want to know."

A bedroom door nearby opened. A short man in a tuxedo

with a red tie walked out. He had sharp facial features and a mustache, and he walked with his hands behind his back. He reminded Becca of an evil butler.

"And what would that be?" the man asked.

"Donnie, she's all ready for you," the female guard said.

"Finally, a leader," Garamanthus said. Becca seized up as the demon took control. Her voice dropped in tone and took on the usual wicked sheen.

"There are demon hunters in the city," Garamanthus said. "I was accosted by several earlier this evening."

The leader smiled. "Befitting of a coward, isn't it?"

Garamanthus scowled. "You don't know the story."

"What else is there to tell?" the leader asked. "You chose to leave our collective. We refuse to hear you."

"These hunters are sophisticated," Garamanthus said. "I fought them off easily, but they are smarter than they look. You all know as well as I do that there haven't been demon hunters in the city for over a decade."

The man strode over to the bar and poured himself a glass of rum.

"So what if there are hunters?" he asked. "Our collective is strong."

He topped off his glass and screwed the cap back on the bottle of rum. "Is that all, coward?"

Garamanthus gritted his teeth. "You fools are making a mistake. You're risking our lives!"

"You risked your life by coming here," the leader said.

The man made a time-out motion. A forceful hand pressed on the back of Becca's head. Pain exploded across her skull.

She pushed back and resisted as the male security guard pressed harder, just behind her ear.

Her ears rang like a defective television.

The last thing she saw before she passed out was the leader sipping his rum and dialing a number on his phone.

CHAPTER TWENTY-SIX

"WE ARE STUCK, SIR," the chauffeur said.

The limo's engine revved and the tires squealed in the snow, stirring JoJo from his current thoughts.

"Goodie."

JoJo snuffed a cigarette in an ashtray in a console in the seat next to him. He exhaled a column of smoke out of one nostril and tasted bitter ashes as he strained to get a better look at the current predicament. He couldn't see a thing in the storm, and the tinted windows of the limousine didn't help.

Simone stirred on the leather seat next to him. "Terrible night to be driving, baby," she said. "I told you we should have hid in one of the hotel rooms. Why do we always have to run at the first sign of danger?"

"Old habit," JoJo said.

On his other side, Dominica Parva peered out the window. "Can't one of your demons do something about this?" she asked.

JoJo opened the limo door and stepped out into the snow. The damned limo was stuck in the middle of the skyscraper-studded street. There wasn't a single soul anywhere. They might as well have been the only car around for miles, and they were stuck in the *middle* of the street. A bystander would have thought they were parked. They had just been driving along, and the next thing JoJo knew, the wheels started spinning.

"You took a wrong turn back there," JoJo said as the chauffeur pulled a shovel out of the trunk.

The driver lowered his head. "I'm sorry, sir. I had orders to get you out of the hotel as soon as possible, and I misread the sign at the intersection. I thought this was Dearborn Street."

JoJo let the apology slide. He would have made a wrong turn in this storm too. A few minutes prior, he had received a call from Donnie telling him that they had an emergency in the lobby. For precaution's sake, Donnie told JoJo to leave immediately. JoJo grabbed Simone and Dominica, and they high-tailed it down to the parking garage where the chauffeur was waiting impatiently.

The timing, though terrible, wasn't as bad as it could have been. JoJo's demons had just finished their smorgasbord. The ballroom didn't have a single speck of blood or bone on the floor or walls. The place was cleaner than a penny run through a washing machine, just how he liked his crime scenes.

His staff had taken a robust guest list. The only thing they didn't gather about the clients were their dates of birth and names of their first-born children, though JoJo could have easily gotten that information. He had instructed his staff to scour the guest list, identify the vehicles by their license plates, and drive them to random places in the city. His men were instructed to leave the keys in the ignition and to wipe the cars down of any fingerprints. With the snow falling the way it was, any footprints and tire tracks would be erased by morning. Not even a whiz cop would know where to start. There would be no immediate connections for any of the guests tonight directly to the Montclair Building. And if prior demon auctions were any guide, guests didn't exactly advertise to their families that they were going to bid for some badass demons. JoJo counted on the fact that these guests would have been discreet. If there were any abnormalities, he would see to it himself that they were crushed.

And then Donnie came along telling them to get the hell out, fast. Here he was, stuck a few blocks away from the Montclair Building when he needed to be long gone.

He rolled up the sleeves on his mink coat and spoke to the demons in his head.

"Fellas, I know you're still digesting, but I got myself a little problem here."

The lead demon came alive in his mind. His elderly voice was agitated. "Ever heard of a tow?"

"You obviously never heard of a tow ban. What's your fee?"

"Always the pragmatist," the demon said. "That's what I always admired about you. I'll defer your fee."

"I don't play that game," JoJo said. "Give me some sort of tasks to do in the next week, and I'll make sure they get done. In exchange, I need this car unstuck from the ice and you need to ensure me a safe passage to my nightclub."

"You'll return the favor within the next few days?"

"You got it."

"Very well," the demon said. "A few hours ago—in the elevator. I told you that you could have had a second host tonight."

"Yeah," JoJo said. "I remember. Confused the hell out of me. What did you mean by it?"

"Sometimes when you suppress us, it is to your detriment," the demon said. "When you smoke, you lose your perception, JoJo."

"Give me one reason I should go into rehab and I'll reconsider, but I've kinda got a situation right now."

"Someone was snooping around your nightclub," the demon said. "Any other paranormal would've seen it."

"Who?"

"You still can't make the connection, can you? JoJo, you've got a rat in your midst."

JoJo paused. "Barry? He was going through my things when I got there.''

"Not figuratively, you dolt. Literally. The rat that bit you. That wasn't any normal rat."

The bite marks on JoJo's ankle pulsed again. In an instant, he felt the rat's sharp incisors piercing his skin again, followed by the white-hot pinprick of pain.

"You're kidding me," JoJo said. "You're telling me that rat was a spy?"

"I don't know what it was," the demon said. "I'm not omniscient. But I know when things aren't as they seem."

"So, what do you want?" JoJo asked.

"You can settle my fee by seeing what the rat wanted. It sounds like your man Barry just might have the answers."

"Done. Now get me out of here."

The demon took control of JoJo's body. It forced him to hold out his hand. Lead-colored wisps streamed from JoJo's fingertips, lifting the limo into the air. Inside the car, Dominica watched with awe.

The lead-colored wisps surrounded the tires, making them look as if they were drawn in living chiaroscuro as the limo landed on the snow.

"This will give you one hour," the demon said, relinquishing control. "Don't waste it, and don't forget my fee."

"You could have asked him to teleport us," Simone said sarcastically as JoJo climbed back into the limo.

"No matter," JoJo said. "We'll be on our way in a minute."

He turned to Dominica as the limo pulled off. "I hope you learned a thing or two from that transaction."

Dominica massaged her chin. "You made a deal. What do you normally have to give up?"

"Often, you give up a few days, weeks, or months of your

life," JoJo said. "Other times, you've got to do them a favor some point in the future whenever they want you to. That's why if you're smart like me, you time limit the reciprocation. Otherwise, you might be doing payments when you're eighty years old, and that's no good. Assuming you live that long."

"Genius," Dominica said. "I get it. Teach me more."

"There'll be plenty of time for that," he said, putting an arm around her, and pulling her close. He caught a whiff of sunflower perfume on the nape of her neck and studied the clasp of her necklace chain. "How's Lord Traxus treating you?"

"I don't feel a thing."

"That's because his belly is full of blood and bones," JoJo said. "Just you wait—he's gonna come alive in your mind and he won't shut the hell up."

"What do I do then?" Dominica asked.

"Do what we all do," Simone said, annoyed. "Deal with it."

JoJo wanted to say something to Simone, but he understood where she was coming from. It wasn't exactly good form to have both his squeezes in the limo at the same time. Donnie was supposed to bring Dominica back to the bar. He needed to separate these two, stat. But security was security.

Rinnnnng! Rinnnnnng!

The car phone on the wall rang loudly.

"It's probably Donnie," Simone said, scooting toward the phone. "Maybe it was just a false alarm."

She held the big, thick-antenna'd phone to her ear and dangled the kinky cord with her pointer finger. "Hey, Donnie. Any news? Why so tight-lipped? Yeah, he's here. He had to make a deal with a demon because we got stuck in the snow. Mmm, is that right? Here he is."

Simone jammed the phone into JoJo's hand. "Apparently, it's not a false alarm."

JoJo put the phone to his ear. "What's up, Donnie?"

His henchman's voice was quiet on the phone, like he was trying to stay out of earshot.

"We got you out of there for good reason. It's not safe to come back, boss. A woman wandered into the lobby asking about demons."

"How would some random woman know about what happened?" JoJo asked. "No chump off the street would have any idea what went down." He stopped, thinking. "Unless—"

"She was carrying a demon," Donnie said. "Garamanthus the Coward, to be exact."

"Doesn't ring a bell," JoJo said. "I traffic a lot of these buggers, you know."

He cupped his hand over the microphone and asked Simone, "Do a channel quick and tell me about Garamanthus the Coward."

Simone closed her eyes and took a deep breath. Her body tensed up, and JoJo knew that the historian demon in her was in control. Her voice was low and slow.

"Garamanthus, born in France in 1603. Relatively young. During the French Revolution, he is rumored to have inhabited Robespierre during the height of the revolution. He is responsible for at least 79 deaths in central Europe, 10 in South America, and 5 in the United States. His contributions to the macrocosm of demonic energy are small—no, minuscule at best. It is said that he abandoned his collective five years ago in favor of personal freedom. Ironically, this abandonment was on the same day that demon hunters launched an attack on his brethren. It has never been proven that he deserted them because they are all dead and cannot offer their sides of the story, but his title was earned by reasonable inference."

JoJo put the phone back on his ear. "Okay, so the guy is a hell of a coward. Or, he could be the most misnamed guy in history with a comeback story. I dig it."

"Don't dig it," Donnie said. "He came with a warning. He said that demon hunters are back in the city."

"Bullshit," JoJo said. "We ran those bastards out over a decade ago. They wouldn't be back unless they had death wishes."

"Not according to our fellow coward—or comeback artist."

"Huh. Did you capture him?"

"We're keeping her in the executive suite."

"Her?"

"The host, boss."

"Crap. Is she initiated, or did Garamanthus just pop into her?"

"She wandered around the lobby like a lost dog," Donnie said. "From what I can tell, she's real fresh."

"Let's say this demon is pulling our chains," JoJo said. "I'm not getting caught with my mink coat undone, if you know what I'm saying. But if he's right, he might have just done us a favor. A big one."

"What do you want to do, boss?" Donnie asked.

"Extract Garamanthus," JoJo said. "It'll be a bloody affair for the lady, but she'll thank me in the end. Absorb him and come quickly to the bar. I'll transfer him into me and feel him out."

"Got it."

"See ya."

"Wait—boss."

"Yeah."

"What about the woman?" Donnie asked. "She's unconscious right now. Should we drop her somewhere after the extraction?"

JoJo watched the snow fall outside. The limo took a left and Dominica brushed into him. If he didn't know any better, she was listening and learning. He loved her drive.

He thought about the random woman. If he let that

woman live, she might owe him a favor and probably be grateful as hell, especially if she was as fresh as Donnie said. She might also be a liability.

There was no telling who she was or where she came from. He'd already dealt with enough crap tonight.

"Kill her," he said.

CHAPTER TWENTY-SEVEN

"Hang on, gnomes!"

Cyrus held on to a metal rail as the train lurched to the side. Darkened shadows passed by as the train bulleted down a tunnel.

He was sitting in the lead car with Bart and Wendy, hanging on for his life.

The lead car was a contraption full of buttons and switches. Cyrus had no idea what any of them meant, but Bart maneuvered the control panel with the finesse of a rail engineer.

"Hit the power button on that box over there, will you, Cyrus?" Bart asked.

Cyrus stared at a steel box on the wall. It was the size of a bread box, covered in rainbow buttons, and had a glass screen. One of the buttons had the letters "I/O" and Cyrus pressed it.

The box vibrated. On the glass screen, a radar map of Chicago appeared along with a blinking green dot on the east side of the city. A red dot appeared downtown, just north of the river.

"Atta boy," Bart said. "I didn't even have to tell you which one. You're an engineering natural!"

Cyrus couldn't believe he was here. It had all happened so fast. When he stood at the Logan Square station and blew the pewter whistle, he wasn't sure if Bart and Wendy would fulfill their promise.

They arrived like they said they would. A quick ride to the underground lair later, Cyrus told Bart and Wendy everything. The King and Queen listened and, without hesitation, they ordered the gnomes into service.

They carried Cyrus back to the train, and the gnomes spilled into the passenger cars carrying picks, shovels, and spades. Now they were barreling through the earth.

"We're certain that your sister was overridden," Wendy said. "The demon probably took control. It explains why she snuck out."

"But she was managing the demon so well," Cyrus said. "We had a plan."

"Plan, eh?" Bart asked. "There ain't no such thing as plans with those pesky demons. They have a way of subverting anything you come up with."

"Where are we going?" Cyrus asked.

"That box is an energy sensor," Bart said. "A few hours ago, there was a concentration of demon energy like you wouldn't believe. It almost blew my beard off! Can't believe you didn't sense the demon energy yourself, Mr. Grant."

"Demon energy?" Cyrus asked.

Bart tended to the engine and steered the train to a sharp turn.

"I don't expect you to have sensed it, dear," Wendy said, "though if you were a rat, you might have felt it. The energy rocked the city."

"What happened?" Cyrus asked.

"A bunch of demons get together from time to time and wreak havoc," Bart said. "They're too dangerous to bother, so we paranormals just let them be. But now that the demon has control of your dear sister, we gnomes are going to get involved. No one messes with our friends!"

Bart grabbed the microphone and yelled into it. "A cheer for Cyrus and a cheer for Becca!"

On a television screen that switched rapidly between views of the passenger cars, the gnome passengers pumped their fists and cheered, shaking the train.

"I can't tell you how much I appreciate this," Cyrus said.

"Don't mention it, dear," Wendy said. "You would do it for us too. But, Bart, we really should pick up the pace."

Bart stuck a dirty finger on the screen of the energy sensor box.

"See, we're on the Northwest side," he said. "I built this box myself, and it measures paranormal energy. The closer we get, the bigger the red dot on the screen will grow."

The train picked up speed and Cyrus held on tight. Bart took control of a giant joystick. Cyrus's feet lifted off the ground as the train tunneled upward.

"I estimate we are about five minutes away at our current rate," Bart said. "So, what's the plan, Cyrus?"

Cyrus shrugged. "I was hoping you could help. I don't even know where we are *going*."

"Neither do we, hun," Wendy said. "That's why we brought our weapons."

Cyrus thought of Becca. He hoped she was safe. That she wasn't in any pain. If Garamanthus did anything to her, he would kill the demon himself.

He shouldn't have gone to sleep. Desmond's orders were clear: either he or Gilberto was to be with Becca at all times. He could have never known that Garamanthus would do this.

But then again, Garamanthus had been inside Becca's mind when the Regulators had their meeting, and he had been listening to everything.

Cyrus cursed at the realization.

Desmond had made a mistake. A giant mistake. Why didn't he plan for this?

Cyrus slipped out his phone. He needed to call Desmond, but there was no signal down here.

"Need to make a call, dear?" Wendy asked.

"I have a hunch," Cyrus said.

"Your hunch will have to wait," Bart said. "We're in for one hell of a ride, Mr. Grant!"

The red dot on the energy sensor grew into a dancing dot whose edges bounced outward like radar.

"Huh," Bart said. "If I didn't know any better, I'd betcha the concentration is downtown."

"I don't care where it is," Cyrus said. "As long as you take me to my sister, I'll figure out the rest."

Wendy gave him a warm smile. Her smile could have slowed down time even though the train was rattling violently. "You're so concerned for Becca. It's so sweet, dear. Just hang on."

Cyrus stared at the dot for an eternity as Bart steered down underground tunnels that only the gnomes knew about.

The train flew upward, dove down, jostled to the left and right, and did sick inversion loops. He almost lost his grip on the metal rail. He pushed the buttons Bart told him to push and he made small talk with the Gnome King and Queen, but Cyrus didn't take his eyes off the screen. He breathed in time with the dot's dancing, and he found stillness and quiet even though the train shook like the inside of a space shuttle during launch.

"We're definitely heading downtown," Bart said finally. "Under the river, we go!"

The train's green dot appeared directly on top of the Chicago River.

Cyrus couldn't believe his eyes. "How the—"

"The river isn't as deep as you think," Bart said. "It's a gnome tunneling trick. We have to repair this stretch of tunnel a lot because of leaks and such, but it's a fast way to get around."

The screen on the energy sensor refreshed, and a more detailed map of downtown Chicago appeared. The red dot bounced in the corner of a plot next to an intersection.

"Looks like River North," Cyrus said. "Bart, what's waiting for us in that red dot?"

"Beats the heck out of me," Bart said. "But whatever it is, they're about to get a mouthful of dirt and fistful of gnomes!"

Bart pulled the joystick down and shouted into the microphone.

"Gnomes, prepare for surfacing. Time to pound some dirt!"

The blades on the drill came alive and spun like something out of a hypnotic optical illusion. It let out a high-pitched whine that made Cyrus want to cover his ears.

"I told you to fix the interior insulation, Bart," Wendy said in a fussy tone. "It sounds terrible in here."

"Won't be long," Bart said. He started to whistle the same carefree tune that he whistled when Cyrus had met him for the first time. He pulled hard to the right on the joystick and the train snaked to the side.

The drill crashed into earth and a shockwave passed through the lead car. The impact threw Cyrus to the wall.

On the security camera screen, the shockwave passed through passenger cars and the gnomes held on as they weathered the impact.

The train lost speed and stopped shaking. Lights on the side of the train lit up the new tunnel the train was boring under the city. Outside, the ground rumbled as the drill tore through the soil and angled upward. Meanwhile, Bart kept whistling. On the energy sensor screen, they were only a few inches away from the red dot now.

The train stalled. Bart flipped a switch and the drill reversed for a moment, sending the train back down the tunnel. Then he flipped the switch again and the train charged forward through a stubborn patch of dirt and rock.

"Time to tango!" Bart cried. "For Cyrus and Becca!"

The gnomes repeated the chant.

"Dear, this is going to be over soon," Wendy said. She reached over and grabbed his hand. He looked into her frosty blue eyes, which showed motherly concern. "Whatever happens, I suggest you think fast. I don't want to explain to your mother how we got you hurt."

Cyrus nodded.

"Thanks, Wendy."

The drill slammed into something hard. Cyrus screwed up his face in confusion as the drill busted through a somber wall of gray and brown.

An eardrum-busting explosion rippled forward and the car turned into a fireball with a drill in front. A wave of heat passed in the car, soaking him in an instant sweat.

The train left the fire behind and the darkness in the tunnel blinked away like someone flicked a light switch.

The train shot upward through a parking garage. The drill obliterated several service trucks with a hotel logo on them.

Boom!

The train continued its upward trajectory through another level of the parking garage. The floor broke like a wooden block, and the next thing he knew, the train ripped into a marble-covered lobby. Dirt and concrete flew everywhere, and someone jumped out of the way.

"Bart, what the heck?" Cyrus cried as the train pushed through the ceiling of another floor, pulling down carpet and dirt and chairs and concrete into the void it left behind.

Then, the train hissed to a sudden stop.

The lead car stood straight up in the middle of what looked like a conference room, in the middle of a sea of chairs. An elevated stage had caved in from the impact. The drill had struck a chandelier, and it fell off and crashed to the floor in a flurry of glass shards. Steam rose around the car, and Cyrus tasted metal and dirt.

"Here we are," Bart said. Humming, he pressed a button and the doors slid open. He pushed another button and a bright yellow evacuation slide extended from all the doors to the ground followed by a noise that sounded suspiciously like a whoopee cushion.

Cyrus couldn't help but laugh. "I have no idea what you two just did or how you did it, but man, am I glad to be here. Let's just hope your energy sensor is right."

He glanced around the room. "Looks like some kind of convention center."

"Glad there wasn't anyone here," Bart said, waving from the car. "Or they would have really got a show."

The Gnome King's carefree face turned into a quick frown. "Uh oh. Looks like we're in the right place, all right!"

Wendy pointed to the doors. Uniformed security guards with guns ran into the conference room. Bullets ricocheted off the train.

Cyrus gulped.

Wendy pushed him forward toward the car door. "Time to think fast, Mr. Grant."

CHAPTER TWENTY-EIGHT

BECCA WOKE UP SLOWLY, and in a fuzzy grog. She felt as if she had been drugged. Her eyes tracked across the hotel room, but it took her brain half a second to catch up. The back of her head throbbed like someone had punched her. She wanted to rub the wound, but her hands were tied behind a chair.

Slowly, she remembered how she got here. Garamanthus taking control of her body after waking up from a dreamless sleep. Running through the snow. Stealing a car and driving downtown. Busting into a hotel with a death wish.

God.

The guards had detained her. They must have knocked her out. How long had she been asleep?

The hotel room sharpened around her. She was in the same lavish suite. A glass of half-drunk rum sat on the counter. It was the same glass the leader had been drinking before his henchmen knocked her out.

The room was empty except for her, but the doors to the bedroom and adjoining bathrooms were closed.

She listened, trying to discern any sound that would help

her figure out what was going on. But this damned hotel was so quiet. She couldn't hear a thing.

Her attention focused on her hands and feet, which were bound with thick knots. Whoever tied her up knew what they were doing. There was no amount of wiggling in the world that could have gotten her free.

She was truly trapped.

Garamanthus made his presence known and spoke in a berating tone.

"This is your fault," he said.

"My fault?" Becca asked. She kept her voice to a whisper. "You're the one who barged into the hotel and then left me to fend for myself, remember?"

"Not *that*," the demon said. "Your body. You were asleep for too long. I can't operate when you are asleep."

"I think you have a memory problem," Becca said. "Since I'm awake now, what do you propose, since you have all the answers tonight?"

"I had hoped you would come to as the goons were binding you," he said. "I could have worked with that. But now these ropes are too tight, even for me."

"In plain English, we're screwed," Becca said.

"That appears to be the case, Rebecca Grant."

Becca balled her fists. She wanted to scream, turn into She-Hulk and tear off these ropes. She wanted to rip this demon out of her head and rip him apart limb from limb. She wanted him *out*.

She missed her brother and mother again. She missed her mother's advice about life and her brother's cheesy jokes. She missed everyone at the Cat. The smell of roasted blends and alcohol being mixed at the bar. She closed her eyes and tried not to think about what could happen to her.

"We can use dark thoughts, girl," Garamanthus said, "but there's no time for tears."

"Shut up," Becca said. "I don't care what happens. They

could come in and kill me. But so help you God, if you open your fucking mouth one more time, I swear I will destroy you."

Garamanthus went quiet and left her with her thoughts. She stared at a painting on the wall behind the bar. A still life watercolor with a bowl of pears and grapes. It was surprisingly serene. She found herself staring at it blankly. She didn't want to think anymore.

Whatever was coming, she was ready.

The key turned in the door. The leader entered, followed by the two guards.

"How was your nap?" the man asked.

Becca kept staring at the painting.

"Don't want to chat, eh?" the man asked. "No matter. We weren't going to spend much time making small talk anyway."

As if on cue, the two guards stood on each side of Becca. The leader produced a serrated knife.

"Good news and bad news," he said with a devilish grin. "The good news is we are going to get that demon out of your head. You're going to feel like a new woman. If my suspicions are correct, you will immediately want to go out and do cartwheels in the snow. Normally, my boss would charge for an extraction like this. It takes a great deal of effort. But he decided to have mercy on you tonight, and you are getting this procedure done free of charge. We are very happy for you."

He pulled a self-defense knife from his tuxedo. It revolved several times in the air before he caught it by the hilt. He grabbed Becca's arm and made a quick, ragged cut.

She screamed as the blade drew blood. The wound was immediately warm and tender.

Becca balled her fist to manage the pain. It hurt, but it wouldn't be fatal.

"The bad news," he said, "is that after the extraction, we unfortunately cannot let you leave here alive. Sorry about that."

The leader took off his tuxedo jacket, undid a silver cuff-link, and rolled up his sleeve. He then made an identical cut on his arm, drawing a thread of blood.

"I'm not sure if you know this, but there is a ritual for this kind of thing. It's not the…cleanest procedure in the world. But there are messier ones."

He produced a sandwich bag from his trouser pocket and slipped the knife inside. He tossed it to one of the guards. "Be sure to get rid of that, will you?" he asked.

He turned back to Becca. "I have no idea how you became a host, and frankly, I don't care. But I see it as a moral respon-sibility to educate you on just how much trouble you got your-self in before you die. There *are* such things as ghosts, and you will soon become one before the night is over. I don't want you coming back and haunting me and telling me that you had no idea what was going on. First, I don't have time for that. Second, it would be far better if your eternal sleep was as restful as I could make it. I'm not a good guy, but I'm not a terrible one either."

Becca gritted her teeth. "You hold yourself in such high esteem. It's a miracle your head doesn't explode."

"You're feisty," the man said. "Anyway, I've said my piece."

He clamped his hand down on Becca's arm. She felt his warm blood on hers, followed by fiery pain that spread across her body like napalm. She cried out in agony. The pain was so severe, it made her close her eyes. Tears streamed down her cheeks.

"That's it," he said. "Go ahead and let him out. You don't need him in your body anymore. We'll take very good care of him—not that you're going to care anyway."

Becca bucked in the chair. Then, Garamanthus screamed.

"This is farewell," he said. "It's been a good ride, Becca. Have a nice death."

She pushed him out of her head. Donnie's face was inches

from hers, now wild with enjoyment. He looked like he got off on this kind of thing.

"We are almost done."

"Screw you!" Becca said.

"That is anger that comes from your pain," he said. "I won't take it personally."

Becca closed her eyes. If the strange man and Garamanthus were right, she would soon have the answer to her prayers that she had been waiting for, for six months. She would soon be free. Dead, but free.

Suddenly, she couldn't hear herself screaming anymore. She gave in to it. She found her peace among all the pain and burning and malevolence oozing around her from the man and his two goons.

She stopped screaming and took a breath.

"Mom, Cyrus," she said softly. "I'm sorry. I wasn't strong enough. Please forgive me because—"

The pain surged in her arm again and rattled every bone in her body. She screamed again.

The man let go of her hand. Footsteps strutted across the carpet. The man yelled an order Becca didn't understand.

Then, quiet. She was no longer screaming. She opened her eyes.

The man stood on the carpet, huffing and puffing. His hands were covered in blood, and this time, instead of excitement, his eyes were wide with fear.

"What did you do?" he asked.

Becca said nothing.

The man wrapped his bloody hands around her throat. "What the hell did you *do*?"

Becca couldn't answer. The man squeezed. His fingers dug into her flesh. She lost air and struggled to inhale. She closed her eyes again. She decided that if she was going to go out, she was going to go out like a boss.

She pulled up all the saliva she could muster and spat in

the man's face. Then, she banged her forehead against his. He stumbled back.

"You stupid—"

"Boss!" one of the guards cried. "We've got a serious problem!"

The man wiped Becca's spit off his face, gave her a lingering malevolent snarl, and ran to the door of the suite. Becca could hardly keep her head up. The suite spun around her vision and she wondered if this was it, if this was what it was like to die.

Hands suddenly unbound the ropes around her. She was lifted into the air. Someone was carrying her. She watched as the two guards carried her down the candy-striped hotel hallway.

"Get the damn elevator," the leader said. "If we can't do it here, we'll do it by the river."

Becca closed her eyes and drifted off.

CHAPTER TWENTY-NINE

Cyrus slid down the evacuation slide and ran for cover amid an explosion of bullets.

The conference room was crawling with armed security guards.

He crashed into the carpet, covering his head as bullets flew over him.

Who the hell were these guys and how did they get here so fast?

A staticky voice cut through the gunfire.

"Whoever youse are, you picked the wrong fight tonight. Gnomes, unite!"

A loud, unified cry erupted from the train. A swarm of gnomes poured out, their picks and shovels and axes and spades raised. A pick flipped through the air over Cyrus and struck one of the guards in the chest. The man dropped his gun, hollered, and fell back, clutching at the pick's handle.

From the lead car, Wendy closed her eyes and her hands glowed with golden energy. She opened them and slung an earthen blast, blowing up a table and sending two guards diving.

Wendy's voice echoed in his mind. He had to think fast.

He pulled himself into another run, this time grabbing a nearby chair.

A guard stood between him and the door. Cyrus threw the chair before the guard saw him.

The chair cracked against the man's nose and exploded in an array of splinters before the man dropped.

Cyrus grabbed the guard's pistol as he passed. "Thanks."

He turned to run, but an iron grip seized his ankle.

The guard stared up at him with a hardened face. The man spoke in a deep, otherworldly voice. "You aren't going anywhere."

A demon.

Cyrus pointed the gun at the man and pulled.

The muzzle flashed and the gun jumped in his hand. His ears rang.

The bullet had hit the man in the shoulder.

Cyrus stared for a moment in horror at what he'd done, then he ran.

He was definitely in a convention center. Broad aisles. Fancy carpet. Giant rooms on either side of him.

He hesitated. He didn't even know where the hell he was. How was he going to find Becca?

He ran as fast as his feet carried him, hoping that he would find her somehow. He passed a sign hanging from the ceiling that said "Elevators."

He crossed into a carpeted lobby with a building directory on a nearby wall. The words said "Montclair Building."

He scanned the directory. Convention center. Apartments. Luxury lofts. Law offices.

If he were a group of demons, and he was going to set off an explosion of energy that would ripple across the city and alert paranormals, where would he do it?

His mind blanked. He had no idea. Maybe he could find one of these guards and use his gun to get them talking.

A voice called after him.

"You! Stop!"

Cyrus dashed toward the elevator bay.

One of the elevator doors opened and more guards ran out. Cyrus cursed.

The guards aimed at him and fired, and he jumped behind a wall. He waited for a lull in the gunfire, and then he peeked around the corner and unloaded.

He pulled the trigger until it clicked.

He didn't hit a single guard…

"Crap!" he said.

It was suspiciously quiet around the corner.

He guessed that the guards were formulating a plan. They had probably counted his bullets. They would know he didn't have any left.

Panic set in as he glanced around the hallway. He spotted a rectangular grate in the wall. He ran to it, and warm air flowed onto his hands. A duct. It was fastened with thick bolts.

The grill—it was just the right size…

He concentrated and willed himself into a rat just as the footsteps of thick boots ran toward his position. His tail sprouted from his back. His claws bloomed from his hands.

He touched down on the floor and squeezed through the hole in the grate just before the guards jumped around the corner.

"Where did he go?" one of the guards asked.

"He probably ran down the hallway," another said. "Let's go."

Cyrus charged into the dark duct as the guards ran past.

His claws didn't make a sound on the aluminum sheeting. It was warm in here—uncomfortably warm.

He could still hear the gnomes with their battle cries in the conference room down the hall.

He couldn't rely on his eyes. Combined with the darkness of the duct and his rat's poor eyesight, he was completely blind. Instead, he let his whiskers do the work, sweeping the duct ahead of him and feeding his brain with a steady stream of information. The acrid tang of gun smoke drifted into the ducts. He could almost taste the bullet casings, and also fragments of dirt and construction concrete from the train crashing through the floor.

But there was something else in the air, something he'd never smelled before. Something rotten, like decaying flesh, bowels, and blood. The smell was electric in the air, sparking against his whiskers and setting off little explosions across his brain.

His mind filled with faint screams as if he were living a memory that wasn't his. A man laughing like a supervillain. Violent, whipping wind. People screaming.

Cyrus closed his eyes and turned his head away. The emotions faded, but the smell was still there.

He opened his eyes reluctantly. This had to be demon energy.

He sniffed and ventured forward, deeper into the duct. A whining sound stopped him in his tracks.

He stood on his hind legs and sniffed. The air smelled different, colder and fresher. A loud whine rattled the duct around him and made him wonder if an earthquake was imminent. Then it stopped, followed by a metallic ding and a rush of metal gears rubbing and grinding.

His feet carried him cautiously through the duct. His whiskers worked even faster.

He ran, stopped, sniffed. Ran. Stopped. Sniffed.

A pinpoint of light appeared at the end of the duct, and he scampered cautiously toward it. His whiskers detected a drop-off, and he stopped just as light washed over him.

Even his terrible rat eyes knew an elevator shaft when they saw it. A giant metal car cruised past on its way downward, inches away from his whiskers, and he scurried back.

He glanced down the shaft. The car stopped on the floor below.

His whiskers directed his nose upward. The demon energy was stronger in the shaft. His instinct told him that the energy was stronger higher up.

If the car was below him, that meant that it could only go up from here. A distant ding in the elevator told him that his window was closing. Soon, it began to rise.

I can't believe I'm doing this, he thought as the car swept up the shaft. He leaped and landed on top of the car. He was unsteady for a moment as his rat body adjusted to the shift in equilibrium.

The crossbars on the roof were covered in a permanent layer of dust. The warm air rushed around him as he ducked.

His rat brain didn't like what he was doing. The shaft was big. Really big when you were a rat. Something told him it was safe to change, and he morphed back into his human form.

He stared up the shaft. It was impossibly tall. Then he glanced over the edge of the car and peered down at the lengthening chasm below him. He was going to be sick. This was the kind of crap heroes did in thriller movies, not in real life.

The car passed numbers etched into the wall.

Four.

Five….

The elevator stopped and the doors opened.

Cyrus crawled over to a grate where he could see into the car. There were two guards.

"Command only wants one elevator working," the guard said. "We stopped the others in the bay. I want you to stay in this car and make sure the boss is protected."

Boss, Cyrus thought. That sounded awfully paranormal.

"Are they done already up there?" the other guard asked. "I mean, we installed extra insulation in all those rooms, but somebody is going to hear her screaming at some point."

"Doesn't matter. Even if they call hotel security, they're among us. They'll just pretend to call 911."

Cyrus scowled. He didn't know if they were talking about Becca. Even if they weren't, no one had any right to be treated the way these men were described.

"No one comes in or out of this elevator without your permission," the first guard said, running out.

"No one, huh?" Cyrus asked. He inspected the elevator car around him as it climbed up the shaft. To his surprise, he found a work light. He switched it on, lighting up the shaft and an inspection box nearby.

The inspection box was a great rectangle of metal with a few buttons: stop, run, up, and down. He also spotted the outlines of the escape hatch in the roof of the car. The hatch had a simple switch on one side and another connected to a wire that ran into the inspection box.

The car passed the tenth floor.

He could have shifted back to a rat, found the nearest duct on any floor once the car stopped, and jumped off. That would have been safer, but if this elevator was the only way in and out, he decided to wait.

The elevator rose higher. Cyrus transformed back into a rat and sniffed the air.

Good God. The demon energy was more concentrated. It overwhelmed his rat brain. That was all he needed to know to confirm he was on the right path.

He transformed back into a human again. The car cruised past the twenty-fifth floor.

How high was this building? He wondered what it looked like on the outside.

Thirty-fourth floor. The car began to slow down…

Cyrus held his breath as the car screeched to a halt on the thirty-sixth floor and tried to remember the directory he had seen earlier. He thought there might have been a hotel on the higher floors. From what the guards were saying, the woman they were referring to was almost certainly in a hotel room.

Through the grate, the guard held the doors open.

"Hurry up, hurry up!" the guard cried.

"What the hell happened down there?" someone asked.

"You're not going to believe this," the guard said. "But an L train busted through the floor."

"Get out of here."

"I have orders to escort you guys down to the parking garage."

Two guards entered the car, carrying someone.

Becca. She was covered in blood. She looked delirious.

Cyrus wanted to fly into a rage.

A man in a white dress shirt splattered with blood entered after the two guards.

"I hope they catch whoever did this," the man said. "This ruined our night. The extraction failed."

Cyrus studied the inspection box. There was no way in hell he was going to let these guys escape with Becca.

The car shot downward. Cyrus waited until the car was between floors, and he punched the stop button. The elevator jolted to a stop.

"What the hell?" one of the guards asked.

Cyrus cut off the fan to the car too.

"Now the fan's off."

Then Cyrus cut the lights in the cabin.

"Did someone cut the power? To the building?"

"You're about to find out, assholes," Cyrus said, opening the escape hatch. The hatch opened easily and with a metallic groan.

"Someone's coming in from the top!" a guard cried.

Cyrus threw the hatch door aside and gave a loud war cry but didn't jump in.

Gunfire exploded from the car. Cyrus turned away and

shielded his head as the men unloaded their guns. He counted bullets.

Cyrus let out another scream, and the men fired again. One of the guns clicked.

"What was that?" one of the men asked.

Cyrus shrank down into a rat. With his claws, he cut the lights on. Then, he arched his back, launched himself into the car, and pointed downward. He landed on the leader's face and bit into an eyeball. The eyeball collapsed like jelly and the man cried and brought his hands to his face as blood poured down his nose.

"Jesus!" the man cried.

Cyrus used the element of surprise and bounced off the man's body onto another man, digging his claws into the man's eye too. Now two men were screaming.

Cyrus jumped off the second man's head and transformed into a human. He smashed the butt of his pistol in the man's face, making him stagger back into the elevator doors.

He drew his empty gun and aimed it at the three men.

"You're going to let me and my sister out of this elevator or I'm going to blow you away," he said.

The third man put a hand on his face and said, "You're making a big mistake, buddy."

"How about you look at your friends," Cyrus said. "You made the mistake."

Becca lay on the floor, eyes open and breathing, but not moving.

"Press the button for the third floor," Cyrus said.

The guard pressed it, but the elevator didn't move. The guard laughed.

"You idiot. When you opened the escape hatch, it stopped the elevator."

Cyrus gulped.

"So go ahead and shoot us," the guard said. "We're stuck on this elevator until reinforcements arrive."

Cyrus thought hard. He had to act, but he didn't know what to do.

The guard sensed his hesitation and took a step toward him.

"Back!" Cyrus cried.

"Gun's empty, ain't it, kid?" the guard asked.

"I said back!" Cyrus said.

The guard pounded a fist into an empty palm. His face sharpened and he spoke again, but this time, his voice was deeper. Demonic.

"Why don't we show you what a real fight looks like," the guard said.

The leader's voice changed in an instant. He was no longer clutching his face. He laughed as the blood ran down his cheek. So did the other guard.

Their voices were deeper now too.

"Crap," Cyrus said.

He was stuck in the elevator car with three demons.

CHAPTER THIRTY

The first guard ran at Cyrus, eyes wild with murder.

Cyrus's heart skipped a beat. If he was going to die, he was going to die fighting his hardest.

He reared back with the gun.

Wham!

The elevator car spun and Cyrus found himself on the ground. His cheekbone swelled with pain. His gun clacked to the floor.

He jumped up and ran at the guard. The man grabbed him by the shoulders and slammed him against the wall.

Cyrus fell to the ground and yelled in pain. He landed next to his sister but rolled out of the way as the guard tried to stomp on his head.

The leader grabbed him and put him in a half Nelson.

"Let's see what it feels like for *you* to lose an eye."

The first guard ran at Cyrus. Cyrus jumped up and kicked the man on the bottom of the chin. The hit knocked him out cold.

The second guard with a bleeding eyeball raised his fists and said, "Pure dumb luck."

Someone stirred below Cyrus. There was a dazzle of red. A foot sweeping out across the floor.

The guard fell flat on his face. Becca landed a fist on the man's face. She pulled him up and put him in a headlock.

Cyrus's eyes widened. Becca panted. She didn't have much energy. But when she spoke, the voice Cyrus expected didn't come out.

"Funny how circumstances change," Garamanthus said. "What an admirable feat you've pulled off, little brother."

Cyrus shook his head.

The leader pulled hard on Cyrus's arms. "I'll kill the little brother and you can kill the guard. Then we'll have a fair fight, won't we, Garamanthus?"

"I don't think that's going to happen," Garamanthus said, grabbing the guard's gun and chucking it directly at Cyrus's head.

Cyrus yelled, but the gun barely missed him. It struck the leader in the face. He let go of Cyrus.

Becca snapped the guard's neck and the man toppled to the floor like dead weight. She dashed across the elevator, pinned the leader to the wall, put him in a chokehold, and banged his head against the wall. Again and again and again until he was a bloodied mess on the floor.

"Becca, stop!" Cyrus said. He grabbed his sister, but she pushed him into the wall. She smashed the man's head several more times until he went unresponsive. She threw him to the ground. She was covered in even more blood, breathing hard.

"You always were a little shit," the demon said, "but you made yourself useful tonight. For that, I promise not to murder you."

"Shut up and give my sister control back!" Cyrus cried.

"Your sister needs me more than she needs control right now," Garamanthus said. "If you know what's good for you, you'll stop complaining so we can work together. If we do, we just might survive."

Cyrus growled. As much as he hated it, the demon was right.

"That was some quick thinking," Garamanthus said, "but you disabled the elevator. We need to get up top. You first."

Becca crouched down and motioned for Cyrus to put his foot in her palms. He did, and the demon launched him onto the lip of the hatch. He pulled himself up and extended a hand, pulling his sister into the shaft.

Becca bent down and inspected the control box. She replaced the hatch, reengaged the circuit that Cyrus had tripped, and pushed the run button. The elevator hummed downward.

"Third floor," Cyrus said. "I've got an escape route waiting."

"Look at you," Garamanthus said. "Never in a million years would I have imagined that you were capable of this."

"Screw you."

The ride down felt like an eternity. Cyrus noticed every floor. Becca stopped the car just below the third floor so they could access the doors. Becca wedged her fingers into the doors and pulled them open.

"Go," she said. Cyrus squeezed through the doors first and held them open so that Becca could follow.

Together, they ran through the carpeted lobby, back toward the conference room where the gnomes were.

"You're sure about this?" Garamanthus asked.

"Very sure," Cyrus said.

Several guards took cover outside of the conference room. They didn't see Cyrus and Becca coming.

Becca landed a sharp punch to the back of one guard's head, then flew around the hallway like an anime character, landing roundhouse kicks, gut punches, and uppercuts until all the guards lay on the floor dead or groaning.

Bart and Wendy were taking cover in the lead car when Cyrus and Becca entered.

Wendy saw them first.

"There he is!" Wendy cried. Bart immediately fired up the engine. The drill whirred loudly.

"Let's go!" Bart cried to the loudspeaker. The army of gnomes were huddled in the train, axes and spades raised. They cheered as Cyrus and Becca jumped onto the train. The pneumatic doors hissed shut.

"Hold on to one of those metal rails," Cyrus said. "And whatever you do, don't let go."

Garamanthus obliged.

"We were getting worried," Bart said.

"I'm still worried," Cyrus said.

"Good thinking, Mr. Grant," Wendy said, patting Cyrus on the back. "Did your rat sense come in handy?"

Cyrus nodded.

"It's so good to see your dear sister." Wendy extended a hand to Becca, but when Becca snarled at her, the gnome queen jumped back in fright.

"Dear, did you know that your sister is—"

"I know, I know," Cyrus said. "I'm trying to figure it out."

"Figure it out later, Mr. Grant," Bart said, "because we're out of here!"

More guards entered and fired at the train as it reversed into the hole. Cyrus's stomach dropped as the train entered freefall.

Metal groaned and the drill whirred and time seemed to slow down…

A fierce impact jostled the cars. Then Bart flipped a switch, pulled back up on his joystick, and the train surged forward. Subterranean darkness spread across the windows as the drill made a new hole.

They rode in silence for several minutes until Bart let out a sigh of relief.

"That's the most excitement we gnomes have had in over a

century!" Bart cried. He turned to Cyrus. "Hey, is your sister all right?"

Becca lay on the floor, covered in blood.

CHAPTER THIRTY-ONE

BUZZSAW-SHARP PAIN GROUND down Kirk's arms. He screamed.

The pain was so intense that it temporarily blinded him. All he could see was a sea of white.

His arms might as well have been sawed off. Rivulets of blood ran down his arms, his legs.

Harsh voices around him spoke French. He had no idea what they were saying. It didn't sound like they were wishing him well.

Then, the pain changed. The searing hot needles gave way to an intense pulling. Like someone was pulling on all his limbs from every direction.

"What do you want from me?" he asked. "Whatever it is, you've got the wrong guy."

He could hardly stand listening to himself talk like this.

He'd tortured men before. Every man had his pain threshold. Ratchet up the pain, and eventually, they would talk and give you their secrets.

He wasn't at his pain threshold yet, but maybe he could make them think he was. Maybe then they would relent.

The voices kept on droning in French. The pulling intensified.

Just when he thought his arms and legs would pop out of their sockets, the pain stopped.

Suddenly, he felt…lighter.

A rash of stillness spread across him. For the first time in what seemed like an eternity since they began this torture session, he breathed again. Long and slow.

The whiteness in his vision warmed to shades of green with florescent slants. Catalina was standing on the other side of the room. He could only make out her shape clad with leather, but not her face. She spoke, this time in English. The language transition confused him, and he didn't understand her at first.

She wasn't speaking to him.

Next to his table, a hulking gray mass of shadows swirled in place.

The demon was on his knees, severely weakened and dejected. It was one of the many demons that resided within Kirk, one of the quieter ones. His back was turned to Catalina,

For the first time ever, Kirk saw this demon's face. The skull smoldered with maggots and lead-colored magic. Its golden teeth were covered in splatters of blood here and there. Its broken horn leaked out wisps of magic like a chimney. Normally, Kirk would have expected a demon's face to be confident, smug even. But the demon shared the face of so many human faces he'd seen in his life—the face of someone who knew he was going to die.

"This doesn't have to be so bad," Catalina said. "You can redeem yourself by telling us any secrets we need to know about."

The floor shook as the beast staggered onto one knee.

"I will never betray my brethren," he said.

"That's a shame, because your brethren would very easily abandon you," Catalina said.

The demon exploded with rage, shaking Kirk's table.

"Just do it already!" he cried.

In an instant, Catalina leaped across the room. The next thing Kirk knew, a blade entered the demon's neck and emerged on the other side. Catalina said a small prayer in French before pulling out the blade, turning around, and in one sweeping motion, lopping off the demon's head.

The beast's body tumbled to the ground. Its body decayed into a spectacle of maggots in light. Soon, it was gone and the only remnant of his existence was scratch marks on the floor where its claws had dug into the concrete.

Catalina lowered her sword.

"How does it feel, Kirk?" she asked. "Do you feel better, or are you still ravaged by the pain?"

He mustered the strength to curse her out.

She shrugged. "Someday, you'll come to thank me." She snapped her fingers at the men in black who surrounded Kirk again. The needling pain came back and he roared in agony as his vision went white again.

"Time to extract the next demon," Catalina said.

CHAPTER THIRTY-TWO

JoJo PUSHED through the wooden door into his bar. A sickly wall of dull cigarette smoke hit him, followed by the hard stench of sweat and human warmth. Loud dance music thumped from the speakers in the wall, rattling his bones. The lights, turned down low, were shot through with purple and pink spotlights isolating from the ceiling. He wove through a maze of bodies, clad in nightwear, corduroy, and velour. Simone and Dominica followed behind him, trying to keep up.

Someone saw him. "Hey, JoJo!"

JoJo ignored them, making his way to the bar.

Barry was mixing a black and tan. JoJo slid into a stool at the bar and stared daggers at Barry. Simone and Dominica stood on either side of him.

That blockhead Barry didn't know when someone was staring at him. He navigated the bar blithely, joking with the patrons and pouring his drinks with the finesse of a toddler. He was wasting product the way he poured, eating JoJo out of the little profit margin this bar was supposed to make.

Finally, after the fourth drink—a blue Hawaiian with too much blue Curaçao—his eyes met JoJo's.

"What's happenin', boss?" he asked, slinking toward JoJo, Simone, and Dominica. "Want the usual, Simone?"

"Always," Simone said, lighting up a cigarette. She inhaled and blew out a puff of smoke as if the cigarette were a release valve.

Barry pointed at Dominica. "And you are…"

"How about you ask her what she wants to drink, Barry-O?" JoJo asked in a low, growly tone.

The remark caught Barry off-guard.

"Sure thing, boss. What'll it be, miss?"

"Screwdriver," Dominica said loudly to cut through the banter and the music. She tucked a strand of hair behind one ear as Barry walked away. "Some place you got here, JoJo."

JoJo grunted. He didn't take his eyes off Barry. "Welcome to the home base."

"You don't have any problems with the city with all this cigarette smoke?" Dominica asked.

"We bought the city officials," Simone said. "It's Chicago. It's not that hard."

Dominica didn't take the insult personally.

"You're going to burn a hole in the back of that guy's head," Dominica said, changing subjects.

"That's the least of what I'm going to do," JoJo said quiet enough for Dominica and Simone to hear.

Barry returned with a rum and coke and a screwdriver.

"Come with me," JoJo said, slipping off his stool.

Barry gulped. He wiped his hands on a rag and followed JoJo across the floor, up the spiral metal staircase, past the VIP section where a couple was French kissing in the shadows, and into JoJo's stuffy office. JoJo let Barry in first. Then he entered and locked the door behind him.

Barry sat on the corner of JoJo's desk. "Everything all right, boss?"

"You tell me, Barry."

JoJo didn't sit down.

"I get the feeling that you're not happy about something," Barry said.

"Detective Barry Evans!" JoJo said. He gave the bartender a slow clap. "You're the employee of the month."

Barry's face hardened. "I'm sick of this shit," he said. "When I pledged loyalty to you, I didn't sign up to be verbally abused every day."

"You signed up to do whatever I say," JoJo said, stepping toward Barry. "And if I say you're my bitch, you say what do I wear, JoJo?"

Barry slid off the desk and took several steps backward as JoJo stalked toward him.

"When I say protect the bar and keep a watchful eye, you're supposed to say 'got it, boss.' When I ask you for a report, you're supposed to tell me the truth."

JoJo was now inches away from the bartender's face.

"I don't know what you're talking about," Barry said.

JoJo pointed at the door. "That pest control kid! He was a spy!"

Barry stammered.

"You were so busy trying to save me a buck that you couldn't even see it!" JoJo said.

"Come on, man," Barry said. JoJo punched Barry in the face, knocking him to the floor.

"I'm beginning to think you asked that kid to come," JoJo said.

Barry cried like a little girl. "JoJo, stop—"

"I need one reason to restore my faith in you, Barry."

"I told you, I don't know what you're talking about!" Barry cried. He whimpered, nursing his cheek. "The kid came in here and said that he got a call from management to inspect the place for roaches and rats."

"That's the oldest trick in the book," JoJo said. He felt his anger rising like a mercury thermometer. "And?"

"I told him he had the wrong address. He looked around

and that was it," Barry said. "He offered to put down a few traps for free and that was that. I swear, JoJo! I told him to come back in a couple of days and we would talk. I had no idea the guy was a spy. Who's he spying for?"

"Wouldn't you like to know?"

"You're accusing me of something I didn't do," Barry said, trying to stand.

JoJo landed a swift kick on Barry's chest. His head hit the wall. He coughed and his voice went up an octave. "JoJo, you have to believe me."

JoJo crouched face-to-face with Barry. "See, that's the problem, Barry. I do believe you. What I didn't believe is that you could be so stupid."

"It won't happen again," he said.

"No, it won't."

JoJo rose and walked back to the door. "I gave you a mighty fine demon," JoJo said. "You were a disappointment to him."

JoJo slipped a hand into his mink coat. He pulled out a pistol with a suppressor.

"I'll have to recycle that demon, and that's going to take considerable effort."

JoJo whipped around. Barry saw the gun and screamed.

"Please, no! Don't—"

Bang. Bang. Bang.

JoJo shot a triangle into Barry's body. A bullet in the forehead. One to the shoulder. One to the neck. Barry bled out on the floor.

JoJo slipped the gun back into his mink coat and waited.

A lead-colored twister streamed from the bullet holes. JoJo turned his back quickly. A demon stood over Barry's corpse.

"This is a setback I did not expect," the beast said in a low female voice. "You owe me for this, JoJo. I had plans for this body."

"You know the rules," JoJo said. "You didn't see anything

off when you saw that kid walk through the door? It didn't raise any suspicions for you either?"

"That is not my responsibility," the demon said.

"Clean up this mess," JoJo said. "Make this office spotless and I'll forgive you."

"We should first discuss my fee—"

"You don't get a fee for a mistake like this!" he cried. "Test my patience and I'll charge *you* a fee, got it? I'm going to count to ten, and this office better be spotless when I turn around. One, two, ten."

JoJo turned around and a column of lead-colored magic poured into him, making him stagger backward. The demon's voice echoed in his head. "Be glad I'm feeling charitable tonight."

"I'm the one who's charitable," JoJo said.

He looked around the office. Barry's body was gone, and there wasn't a drop of blood on the floor or wall.

JoJo grinned.

Dominica was sitting outside the office holding two drinks. He ignored her as he walked to the metal railing on the balcony.

He lit a cigarette and watched the bodies bumping and grinding on the dance floor below. Everyone in this goddamned bar had a demon and he'd use every one of them to kill those demon hunters if he had to.

Dominica brushed up next to him and handed him a glass of bourbon.

"Where'd the bartender go?" she asked.

"He's been let go," he said. And he said no more.

All he could think of was that damned rat. When that kid came back, he was going to give him a grand welcome.

CHAPTER THIRTY-THREE

Two Days Later.

"My, it sounds like you had a harrowing last few days, Becca."

Becca closed her eyes as she sunk into Carolyn Davidson's couch. She imagined herself floating as she told Carolyn the events of the past days. How Garamanthus had wrested back control of her body. How he made her do unspeakable things. How her brother had miraculously rescued her…with the help of gnomes, which she still couldn't believe.

It had all unfolded like a dream. She awakened on a dirt mound in an underground lair with dozens of faces of little gnomes staring at her. That made her faint. When she woke up again, Cyrus was there, telling her it would be okay. The gnomes took Cyrus and Becca to the Logan Square Station, where Desmond, Aurora, and Gilberto were waiting.

She spent the next twenty-four hours in bed in a delirious state. Her mom never left her side.

Today was the first day she felt semi-normal, thanks to Gilberto's healing spells. The first person she wanted to talk to was Carolyn. She asked for an emergency session, which

Carolyn obliged. Cyrus and Gilberto escorted her to Carolyn's new location, the same quaint greystone, but this time in another area of Logan Square. When Becca walked through the doors and saw Carolyn's warm smile, she knew this was the best place for her to be.

Carolyn's leather couch, book-lined office, and copper tin ceiling were the same as last time, and she felt like she had been coming here her whole life. Carolyn made tea, and a mug of hot peppermint herbal steamed next to the couch.

"How are your wounds?" Carolyn asked.

Becca patted her arm, which was wrapped in bandages. She would have to change them when she got home. "Better."

"I don't understand something, Becca," Carolyn said.

Becca took a deep breath. "Fire away."

"The exercises we discussed seemed to work," Carolyn said. "It sounds like you practiced them to great effect. I just don't understand how the demon was able to steal control from you."

"My brother says it was something about demon energy," Becca said. "Somebody—we don't know who—unleashed the paranormal equivalent of an atomic bomb. Apparently, it got Garamanthus excited. All the training I had wouldn't have made a difference."

She opened her eyes and turned to Carolyn, who was sitting back in her leather chair, listening intently. "I remembered what you said."

Carolyn raised both eyebrows.

"About none of this being my fault. Everything has been a blur. I feel...like I've completely lost control. Like I'm watching everything unfold. I've never felt so lost and so dark as I felt the other night. But I am trying to be kind to myself."

She stared up at the copper tin ceiling. "There's a man who had to suffer a blizzard without his car because I stole it. At least a dozen security guards at that hotel are dead, and I killed them with my bare hands."

"And you don't blame yourself?" Carolyn asked.

Becca paused. Now would have been the time when Garamanthus came on in her mind. But the demon had made a truce with her. He too had been grateful for Cyrus's intervention.

"I don't," Becca said. "I really don't. I have forgiven myself for the other night."

She took a deep breath.

"Carolyn, what did you mean when we met and you told me that the old me was dead?"

"Well," Carolyn said, taking the bag out of her teacup, "The joyous, innocent Rebecca Grant is no more. It's kind of like paranormal puberty, hon. There's a day when all of us in this life are never the same. Some of us choose this life. Some of us are dragged into it, like you and your brother. But some are robbed of their innocence. There is a sharp line in their lives: before the moment and after the moment. It's not an easy thing to process, and some of us never truly develop the tools to address it. It's like any other trauma, but it's unique in so many ways."

"I think I understand," Becca said. "That night, when those guys were extracting Garamanthus from me, I thought I was going to die. Maybe I did die. I gave up fighting. Suddenly, nothing mattered anymore. I just wanted the demon out so I could rest."

"But the bad guys failed, didn't they?" Carolyn said.

"Yeah, big time," Becca said. "I was minutes away from being free forever. And I wanted it. You have no idea."

"I have a minuscule idea," Carolyn said.

"And yet this damned demon is still inside me," Becca said. "It has to be fate. There's no explanation for any of this other than that this happened to me for reason. I don't know what it is, but I have decided to stop fighting it."

She sat up. "I just kept running away and trying to resist, but I've come to terms with my own death."

She gave a sarcastic laugh and looked away from Carolyn. "I don't know what any of this means. I don't even know what I'm rambling about. I just…"

"Needed to talk?"

Becca nodded. Carolyn set aside her notebook and pen. "I, for one, am glad that you are alive. I am also glad that you called me. You have no idea how much it means that I was the first person you thought of, Becca. I think you're going to be just fine. As far as fate and the lesson in all of this—I am just as curious as you are. When you find out, I hope you will call me."

When Becca exited the front door of the Davidson Therapy House, Cyrus and Gilberto were waiting for her. They rose upon seeing her.

"How did it go?" Gilberto asked.

"God, that felt amazing," Becca said. She wrapped her good arm around Cyrus and said, "But I don't want to talk about it, okay?"

"Got it," Cyrus said. "Heard that, Gilberto?"

"Amen," Gilberto said.

As they closed the wrought-iron fence in the front yard, a raven wheeled overhead. It let out a loud gronk to let them know it was there. It was Rocco. They walked in silence for a little while.

"How's Luna?" Becca asked.

"Shaken, but okay," Gilberto said. "I've got her on an accelerated healing plan. She'll be fine."

"It's a good thing I found her when I did," Cyrus said.

The blizzard had been the worst weather event of the year. It took the city plows forever to clear the snow, and even then, it was still piled up in big mounds on the sides of the streets. Though the snow had relented and the day was filled with warm sunshine, the bitter cold hadn't stopped. The air still cut through Becca just the same as she walked with Cyrus and Gilberto.

"Desmond still hasn't found out who was behind the concentration of demon energy," Cyrus said. "Did Garamanthus say anything?"

Becca shook her head. "He's been quiet."

Cyrus shrugged. "Funny how a demon can be true to his word for a change." He checked his watch. "I've gotta run. I promised Fontanelli I'd give his equipment back. He may want me to do an odd job or two for him."

"I'm sure Font isn't missing his equipment right now," Becca said. "We're kind of in the aftermath of a snowstorm."

"You'd be surprised," Cyrus said.

"Just remember your priorities," Gilberto said jokingly. "If Desmond catches you missing your duties, he might not like it."

"My errand is Desmond-approved," Cyrus said, saluting as he walked. "See you guys soon."

"You're sure you're okay walking home?" Gilberto asked. "I would understand if you were apprehensive. Given what happened last time."

"It's like I told the therapist," Becca said. "I got dragged into this kicking and screaming. I don't blame myself anymore. I told the therapist that there is a lesson in all of this. The way I see it, every step I take puts me closer to finding out."

"Man, that's the spirit," Gilberto said. "You're the toughest woman I've ever met."

Becca blushed. They walked for another moment in silence.

"Seriously," Gilberto said. "I don't know anyone who has taken being infected by a demon as gracefully as you."

"You think I'm taking this gracefully?" Becca asked. "If this is graceful, I don't want to know what the alternative is."

They came to a stop light and waited as a chain of cars passed.

"It's beyond graceful," Gilberto said. "I know it sounds weird, but I'm proud of you. We all are." They crossed the street.

"Thanks," Becca said. "I'll be proud when this is all over."

"That makes two of—uhh…"

The Wicked Cat was half a block away. Becca stared at Gilberto, confused by his trailing off.

Then Becca saw him.

A black man in a black puffy coat and sunglasses. Kirk MacLeod stood on the sidewalk outside the coffee shop, looking around nervously. He had cuts on his face and a bruise on one cheek.

Sitting next to him was an olive-skinned woman in a black parka and snow boots with fur trim, sipping a to-go cup from the Wicked Cat and laughing mirthfully. She sat close to Kirk, so close her hip touched his. She said something and rested her head on his shoulder.

"It's him," Becca said.

"And…his significant other?" Gilberto asked, incredulous.

Garamanthus came alive in her mind. "It's about time you got some answers," the demon said.

CHAPTER THIRTY-FOUR

Cyrus stood in front of JoJo's Dive. Snow gathered on the second-floor windowsills and the sidewalk hadn't been shoveled free of snow and ice.

He took a deep breath. He had lied to his sister. Sort of.

He did tell Desmond that he had to run an errand, and he did take the sprayer back to Fontanelli's. His boss had wanted him to do an odd job or two. ("Hey, champ, if you got a minute, I wouldn't mind you doing a few things for me…")

Cyrus had refused, saying that his sister was unwell today and he needed to be with her. He told Fontanelli that she had an autoimmune disorder, and ol' Font didn't ask any further questions. Then, he took the L, then the bus, and a few blocks later, he was standing here at JoJo's.

It was time to get the demonsharp's attention. If Rocco was right, and if JoJo respected crazy, he was going to talk his way into an audience with the enigmatic man. Cyrus just hoped he was there.

He skated across the sidewalk, careful not to slip. His shoes scratched across the surface, and for a moment, he thought he was going to crash, but he reached out and grabbed the door just in time. Swinging it open, he threw himself inside.

All the lights in the bar were on, but it was still darker in here than it was outside. The blackened gradient of light hurt Cyrus's eyes and he squinted as his eyes adjusted.

The air smelled of even stronger cigarette smoke than it did before—this time laced with weed and stale beer. Chairs were flipped on top of the tables.

A sole purple spotlight lit up the wooden dance floor. A grim-faced employee with muttonchops and a bushy mustache mopped the dance floor. A nightclub Igor.

The man spotted Cyrus, studied him, and resumed his mopping as if he were the saddest man in the world. His facial expression didn't change a single inch. Cyrus felt bad for the guy, though he didn't know why.

He walked toward the bar, passing a bulletin board of posters advertising strip clubs, full of women with glitzy cherries over their breasts and men wearing only shirt cuffs, ties, and tight-fitting underwear. The posters had tear-off addresses with models' faces on them, which creeped Cyrus out.

A cloud of smoke caught his eye behind the bar.

A woman was reading a magazine and smoking behind the bar. Cyrus recognized her by her energy—and her shoulder-length hair. She had been the woman in the mink standing on the corner waiting for JoJo. Today, she wore a floral crop-top shirt tied off above the belly button and a little too open at the top.

She glanced up at him, then back at the magazine, as if he didn't exist. Then, as if her brain caught up with the fact that he was there, she lifted her head. Her eyes were red, as if she had been crying.

On the street, she had seemed attractive and pretty. Here, up close and personal, she was haggard and mean, like the universe had performed a bait-and-switch. Every muscle in her face was tight, like she was going to snap.

"Yeah?" she asked, annoyed. "We're closed."

"I was looking for the…bartender," Cyrus said nervously. "Is he around?"

"Who? Barry?" the woman asked.

"I never got his name."

"Had to be Barry," she said. "He doesn't work here anymore. He got fired for being shitty at his job."

The woman spoke as if her throat were lined with knives. "What do you want?"

Cyrus rubbed the back of his head. "I was here a few days ago about pest control," he said. "Your guy—I think it might have been Barry—told me to come back and chat with him in a few days. I set some traps and sprayed for free."

Her face brightened a little. "Oh, you."

Her tone turned familiar. "Why didn't you say so, honey?"

The woman curled her finger, beckoning him closer. He leaned on the bar.

"Since Barry is gone, JoJo made it clear that any requests have to go to him now," she whispered. "Are you sure you want our business?"

She studied him up and down. He felt as if her eyes were x-rays and her look was sizing him up not only physically, but sexually. It made him uncomfortable. That day when he saw her on the street, she was pretty in a seductive way. But up close, she disturbed him. He didn't know why.

"We're not good clients," she said, shaking her head. "There's no loyalty in this goddamned place. JoJo will love you, and next thing you know, he'll be using another…service behind your back."

Cyrus shrugged. "So long as I get paid, I don't care what he does with the rest of his money," he said.

The woman sighed and smacked her head, closing her eyes for a long moment. She opened them again.

"How old are you anyway, baby?" she asked.

Cyrus stiffened and tried to stand taller. "I'm old enough to do this job, and I'm not your baby."

"Just go home," she said. "We have roaches and rats just like everyone else. You don't want our business…baby," she said. She hesitated before she said the word "baby," as if she were tempting him and mocking him at the same time.

Cyrus leaned in closer. "I'm not going anywhere. I want to talk to JoJo." He stared her in the eyes for what seemed like a minute until she smirked, threw out her hands, and said, "Fine, just fine. Don't say I didn't warn you."

She held up her fingers and snapped. The man in muttonchops mopping the dance floor rested the mop against a nearby table and shuffled up the stairs to the VIP section.

"He'll let JoJo know you're here. You can go on up now. By the way, I don't think I ever got your name—"

"Doesn't matter," Cyrus said.

Desmond had warned him about never giving his name to paranormals he didn't know. Sometimes one could do dangerous things with your name. This woman was a five-alarm fire. Whatever kind of paranormal she was, she didn't need to know his name, let alone the fact that he existed. He walked away with the intense wish that he had never met her.

She called after him. "Talk fast and be sure to make JoJo your best offer. He doesn't like to screw around. I don't want to clean your guts off the wall. I had planned on relaxing today."

Cyrus ignored her and walked up the spiral staircase. The man in muttonchops stood next to the door.

He grunted. "The boss will see you now." He opened the door and Cyrus entered.

Another woman was sitting at the desk. She wore a red dress with a silver skeleton necklace and dark hair pulled into a ponytail. She had a smirk on her face.

"So you're the pest control kid," she said.

Cyrus screwed his face up at her. "You're not JoJo."

The door slammed behind him. The hammer on a gun cocked into position.

Cyrus turned to face the barrel of a pistol. Behind it was JoJo's face, his blood-veined eyes crazy and his grin wide and malevolent.

"Hey now, rat."

way here to talk to me about because you're right: I do respect crazy."

JoJo circled in closer, so close that Cyrus could smell the weed on his breath. It was pungent and sticky.

"But if I'm left, this is your one and only chance to get the hell out of my sight," he said. "Because you have no idea what I am capable of, despite what you've heard. You don't want to die, and I don't have time to be bothered by a kid like you, so it would be in our mutual interest if you stepped on out the door. What do you say, Jack?"

"My name's not Jack," Cyrus said.

"It's an expression, man," JoJo said. "But okay. We'll play."

JoJo stared Cyrus up and down. His voice deepened and he spoke as if in a trance as he circled Cyrus. The hairs on Cyrus's arms stood at attention.

"You're the kind of cat who has never experienced any kind of hardship in your life. You grew up in a suburb. Your mommy and daddy weren't rich, but they weren't poor. Anything you wanted, you got. Even today, any time you need something, Mommy and Daddy are just a phone call away. You've never done drugs and the thought of being drunk on alcohol scares you senseless. You like your girls plain, and there's been many a night where you lie awake wondering whether there truly are enough fish in the sea for a freak like you."

JoJo paused to test Cyrus. Cyrus kept his face stoic.

"Which brings me to the rat inside you," JoJo continued. "You didn't come into this paranormal world wanting to be a rat. Maybe you lost a bet or someone played a sick joke on you. Nobody—and I mean nobody—wakes up in the morning and says they want to be a rodent, you dig?"

JoJo snapped out of his trance and lowered his gun. His voice returned to its normal timbre. "Remember the rules," he said in a singsongy tone. "Right...or left."

Cyrus stared the madman in the eyes. JoJo was right. Too right. How someone could have sized him up after only having met him once sent a shiver through his entire body. But he hadn't come all this way just to walk away. He didn't know what type of balls he had, but he was about to find out.

"Right."

"Right on!" JoJo cried, letting out a victorious whoop. "My instincts are still hot even after all these years. Okay, I'll buy it: you got crazy balls, kid. What the hell do you want?"

JoJo tucked his gun into his jeans, folded his arms, and gestured for Cyrus to speak.

"I need you to take care of a demon for me," Cyrus said.

JoJo laughed. "What kind of a demon could possibly be causing you trouble in *your* pretty little sheltered life?" he asked.

"Not mine," Cyrus said, shaking his head. "My sister. She was infected against her will. I'm trying to cure her."

JoJo's lips arched downward and the lines in his forehead sagged. Cyrus had caught him off-guard.

"What did your sister do?"

"In the wrong place at the wrong time," Cyrus said. "That's all you need to know."

JoJo sauntered over to the desk and ran a fingernail along the faded wood. "Who is the demon?"

"He goes by the name Garamanthus."

JoJo stopped. He regarded the name, betrayed a quick glance to Dominica, then shook his head. "I've dealt with hundreds of demons. Maybe I know him, maybe I don't. But his name isn't ringing a bell. What did nasty old Garamanthus do to your little sister?"

Cyrus resisted the urge to correct JoJo.

"He's making her life difficult. She's ambitious. A lot of people depend on her. She needs the demon gone."

"So you are performing an act of sibling sacrifice?" JoJo

asked. "Admirable, but I don't think you understand what you are risking."

"I came here to do a deal," Cyrus said. "Do you want to do one or not?"

JoJo studied Cyrus. His eyes scanned him like a jackal ready for murder.

"Say I do want to do a deal. What do you suggest?" the demonsharp asked.

"You wouldn't be talking to me if I didn't have skills as a rat," Cyrus said. "I'm here to offer my services to you. If you need someone spied on, or followed, I can do it and I can do it without being seen. I'll get you whatever knowledge you want. I'll do it on a one-time basis. In exchange, I need you to extract the demon from my sister permanently. No bullshit. I do a favor for you and you do a favor for me, and if we're lucky, we'll never see each other again."

"Now, now," JoJo said. "There are those crazy balls." He sat on his desk and Dominica shuffled closer to him.

"You are thinking too transactionally," JoJo said. "That's how businessmen do deals. No—that's how commoners do deals. I'm not a scratch your back kind of guy. If I do something for you, you pay it back—with interest."

Cyrus dug his hands into his wool coat. "I don't hear you negotiating."

JoJo slapped his knee. "My God, you are something else!" His face hardened. "I'll let you get away with that one because you're ignorant and you don't know any better. But if you talk to me like that again, I'll blow your face off."

Cyrus said nothing, but he didn't avert his gaze.

"Here's my counter. I will use you and your rodent services as you described. Ironically, I have an immediate need for someone like you. I will extract the demon from your sister, no problem. It's as easy as snorting a line in a pew at ten o'clock on a Sunday. But here is what you are also going to do: you are going to carry your sister's demon."

"No," Cyrus said.

JoJo shrugged. "I didn't stutter, and you didn't seem to misunderstand me, so we must be at an impasse."

"What makes you get off shuffling demons around?" Cyrus asked. "You've got a stable of demons. What's another one?"

"Because I need to make sure you want what you're asking for," JoJo said. "And I may need your services again."

Cyrus backed toward the door. He didn't like where this was going.

"Scared?" JoJo asked. "All those predictions I made were true, and you're ready to piss your pants."

Cyrus deepened his voice just a little. "I told you I wasn't here for any bullshit."

JoJo held up a hand. "I don't normally bid against myself, but I *am* intrigued. You will carry your sister's demon for one year. Then I will eradicate it and you can return to your sister and live your merry little life."

JoJo grinned wickedly. "Just imagine how happy she'll be when she can return to her old life. Isn't that worth it? You're telling me you don't want her to be happy?"

"You can't guilt me," Cyrus said. "Six months."

Cyrus held out a hand.

"Six months?" Dominica asked. "Is that really long enough? It takes six months just to get acquainted with the demon, JoJo, doesn't it?"

Cyrus gave the woman a mean glance. What did *she* care about how long it took?

"I don't know," JoJo said, thinking about her comment. "Any other fool that would've come in here would have been on their knees begging me for at least a year. You don't know how good you've got it, kid. But okay—I never got your name—"

"Doesn't matter," Cyrus said.

"Okay, Mr. Doesn't Matter, you've got a deal."

JoJo strode across the office and grabbed Cyrus's hand so hard, it almost cut off his circulation.

JoJo pulled him in close. "But let's be clear. If you fail or cross me, I will kill you and your sister."

Cyrus gulped.

CHAPTER THIRTY-SIX

"Why didn't you kill him like you said you were going to?" Simone asked. She took a drag from a cigarette and leaned against the doorframe to JoJo's office.

JoJo paced around his office.

"I got a hunch," he said.

"If I had a shot every time you had one of your hunches, I'd be in the hospital with alcohol poisoning," Simone said.

JoJo ignored her.

He couldn't get that kid out of his mind. As much as he didn't want to admit it, Mr. Doesn't Matter had rattled him.

"You've got that historian demon in you, and you still can't see the signs," JoJo said. "It's as plain as sunlight, baby. That kid isn't just any typical requester."

Simone pulled the cigarette out of her mouth in a ragged arc. "You said the night of the feeding that your sign was a latticework," she said. "I didn't see any lattices."

Dominica rose from the desk and put her hand on JoJo's shoulder. "Are you sure about this? He doesn't exactly seem like the type you would send on a mission."

"We are going to stop those demon hunters," JoJo said. "If it's the last thing I do. I ran those fools out of town ten years ago, and they didn't learn their lesson. Don't they know this is my city?"

JoJo punched the wall. The wall didn't budge, and he brought his fist into a roundhouse punch toward the desk, sending a stack of papers fluttering to the ground.

Simone stared at him, her lips twitching. "I still don't know why you didn't do it," she said, turning to walk away.

Anger rose in JoJo. Who was she to question his intentions?

"If it weren't for me, none of you would have anything," he said. "This lifestyle wouldn't exist and you would be back wherever you came from."

Simone paused. He could sense anger rising in her too.

"What exactly do I have?" she asked.

"You know what you have."

"The monsters within me are negative space," she said. "This bar ain't nothing anyway. In an alternate universe, I could get all the herb I want. And I'm not your main squeeze anymore, so what exactly *do* I have, JoJo?"

She still hadn't turned around.

JoJo bristled. "The fact that you even have to ask—"

Simone whipped around. "Call me ungrateful!" she shouted, pointing a finger at him. "You wouldn't have any of this without me!"

JoJo thought about her words. "You're right. This was a team effort. But if this is going to stay a team effort, then we've got to nip this in the bud, baby."

Dominica ran a hand down JoJo's arm. "Maybe we all ought to cool off," she said.

"I wasn't talking to you," Simone said. "Why don't you butt out of this conversation for a change?"

"Maybe JoJo ought to step out of the room for a minute, so we can talk," Dominica said softly.

"There was never anything to talk about with you," Simone said.

"Baby, go home and get some rest," JoJo said. "I'll deal with you later."

"I'm not going home," Simone said.

"If you want to make yourself useful, then why don't you prove that the kid is up to no good?" JoJo asked. "Since you have such a bad hunch about him, why don't you go with him tonight?"

Simone put a hand on her hip. "And?"

"I'll make you a deal," JoJo said. "If my gut is wrong, you can kill him."

A devilish smile spread across Simone's face, wicked and toothy. "And if I'm right, I want all the credit," she said.

JoJo brought her in for a kiss on the cheek.

"If you're right, I'll never trust my hunches again."

Simone snuffed out her cigarette and an ashtray on the desk. She snapped her fingers and barked for Vince to go get the limo.

"I'm going to show you why you shouldn't trust rats," she said.

CHAPTER THIRTY-SEVEN

BECCA FROZE as Kirk MacLeod waved at her. She stood in the snow, staring at him and unable to move as a ragged wind blew around her.

She wanted to punch him in the face. She also needed his help.

"I love your confusion," Garamanthus said.

"Shut up," Becca said.

"I can help you," Garamanthus said.

"I said shut the hell up," Becca said.

The demon said no more.

"I can handle him for you," Gilberto said. "I'll tell him to take a hike."

"No. I need to talk to him."

Becca took a deep breath and started toward the Wicked Cat. Gilberto trailed behind her.

The woman sitting with Kirk whispered something to him, eyeing Becca with a friendly smile.

Kirk stood.

"I don't know where to start or what to say," he said, holding out his hands so that his palms showed.

Wham!

Becca punched him in the face, sending him spiraling into the snow. Her fist stung from the blow.

"Oh my God!" the woman cried.

Kirk waved her off and staggered up, knees in the snow. "It's all right. I deserved it."

"That's not a fraction of what you deserve," Becca said.

Gilberto pulled Becca back. "Hey. I get it. But this isn't a good idea."

Garamanthus came alive again. "To hell with that! Hit him again!"

Becca shook the demon's voice away.

"Quiet!" she cried.

"Please," the woman said. "We don't mean you any harm, Miss Grant. We just want to talk."

"What she said," Kirk said, rubbing his cheek. "You've got a hell of a right hook, by the way."

Kirk stood and the woman doted on him, inspecting the cheek where Becca punched him.

"Honey, that's going to leave a bruise," she said.

"Honey?" Becca asked.

"Can we talk?" Kirk asked. "It's important."

Becca stared at Kirk and his—girlfriend? Wife? She walked quickly past, motioning them to come in.

The Wicked Cat was mostly empty save for the morning seniors, who drank coffee, ate croissants, and read newspapers. The morning light reflecting off the snow lit up the restaurant in a golden magic hour glow even though it was almost noon.

Becca found a corner booth away from the customers that gave them privacy and quiet. She and Gilberto slid into one side and Kirk and the woman slid into the other.

Becca tried to suppress her rage at the man who had given her this demon. It took all of her strength to listen to Gilberto's advice and not give in to Garamanthus.

"I know it seems weird that I'm here," Kirk said. "But I've changed, Becca."

The woman hooked an arm around Kirk's and patted his arm. Becca spotted a thick gold ring with a giant diamond. Kirk wore a matching gold band.

"This is my wife, Catalina," he said.

"I'm so sorry for what happened to you," Catalina said.

"Are you paranormal?" Becca asked curtly.

"She's not part of the life," Kirk said. "I'm trying to put that behind me."

A waiter strolled to the table, but Becca gave him a "don't bother" look and pointed him away. She folded her arms and settled into the booth.

"Then you've told her about your necromancy, the demons you carry, and all the horrible things you, your brother, and dad have done?" Becca asked. She turned to Catalina. "Congratulations. You found yourself a real keeper."

"I know about his past life, and it scares me," Catalina said. Her eyes turned fearful for a moment. "But I believe that anyone can be redeemed. I'm willing to find out."

She hugged Kirk tighter. "But we aren't here because of me. We're here because of you."

"I came to warn you," Kirk said. He pointed to the bruise on his cheek. "A few days ago, I received a visit from some goons."

"What kind of goons?" Becca asked.

"They wore black, so I couldn't see their faces," Kirk said. "They wore silver crosses too. They ambushed me in the middle of the night. Said they were demon hunters."

"Ay, dios," Gilberto said. "This is bad."

Becca shushed him.

"I think they're going to come for you next," Kirk said. "They're after Garamanthus."

He snapped off his sunglasses and made eye contact. His dark eyes were troubled and sad. "After what I put you through, I just thought you should know."

"How about you take him back, then?" Becca asked. "You can deal with it."

"I told you, I've changed," Kirk said. "I promised Catalina I wouldn't take any more darkness. I'm sorry."

Becca's lips quivered. "Do you have *any* idea what you've put me through? While you confess your sins and try to move on, I'm stuck in a living hell. I will never forgive you. So while I appreciate that you came to warn me, it's not enough. It will *never* be enough."

Kirk started to reply, but Catalina stopped him.

"I hope one day you will find it in your heart to forgive Kirk," Catalina said, "and we *know* this isn't enough, but you need to leave town. Now. Somewhere secluded where the demon hunters can't find you."

"I can hold my own," Becca said.

"No, you can't," Kirk said. "The only reason I got away was black magic. You won't be so lucky."

"They already visited me too," Becca said. "And I was luckier than you, if you want to know."

"Glad you're okay," Kirk said.

"Anything else?" Becca asked.

Kirk shook his head. "Don't be stubborn about this. Hate my guts if you want, but I really am trying to look out for you."

Catalina smiled at Becca. "Thanks so much for hearing us out."

Kirk and Catalina slid out of the booth. Kirk stopped as he slid on his sunglasses. "You're not going to take my advice, are you?"

"Not for all the demons in the world," Becca said. "Now do me a favor and get out."

Kirk shook his head. He and Catalina left and stood on the corner speaking for a moment. Becca watched as they walked away, across the street into Logan Square Park, and away.

"What do you think?" Gilberto asked. "Did Kirk really find the light?"

Becca shrugged.

Gilberto put a hand on her shoulder. "You okay?"

"No," Becca said.

"Kirk's right," Aurora said, emerging from the kitchen. "Maybe you should leave for a few days while Desmond and Cyrus take care of the demon hunters."

Crap. Her mom had heard everything.

"Mom, not now," Becca said.

"Yes, now," Aurora said, blocking the door to the kitchen. "I don't know why you can't see it. We can go to your uncle's farm for a few days."

"Mom, no," Becca said. "I'm not leaving the Cat."

"You should reconsider," another voice said.

Desmond walked out of the kitchen. "Becca, some fresh air would do you good."

CHAPTER THIRTY-EIGHT

"You might just free your brother and dad at this rate," Catalina said as she and Kirk settled into the backseat of a black car. A driver in sunglasses and a black suit guided the car out of a skid as he pulled off from a parking spot.

Catalina slipped off her wedding band and forced Kirk's off. Kirk opened and closed a fist a few times, then massaged his ring finger.

That damn ring had itched. He might as well have been allergic to it. He didn't know how anyone could wear uncomfortable hunks of metal around their fingers all day.

"You play the matrimony card well," Catalina said, slipping the rings into a clutch purse.

"How about you play the release my family card now," Kirk said. "You wanted me to deliver Becca. Now she's yours."

"Is she?" Catalina asked, crossing her legs. She was reading a map on a tablet.

"You found Garamanthus," Kirk said. "With all the demons you extracted from me, that should keep your lot happy for a while, shouldn't it?"

Catalina had pulled every demon from Kirk's body and

killed each one before his eyes. He felt lighter, bruised, and empty. Any other person would have been thanking the good Lord. He was cursing fate. He hadn't known what it was like to live without darkness in his soul. He hated this new feeling…it took him back to his awkward high school days, the days before he'd known evil, when the most trouble that he and his brother got into was playing fighting video games well into the night.

"You know as well as we do that the Wicked Cat is a fortress," Catalina said, handing him the tablet. A blueprint of the Wicked Cat stared back at him.

Kirk studied the map. He quickly identified the booth they sat in and oriented himself. Before Becca arrived, Kirk and Catalina had cased the place while Catalina ordered a latte.

"The place is a fortress," he said.

"Who was the bird in the sky?" Catalina asked, reaching over him and tapping an area on the roof. A blue dot appeared.

"Shifter," Kirk said. "She's friends with a pair of them."

"That bird had its eyes on us from the moment we approached," Catalina said, speaking into her watch. "We'll need a tranquilizer gun and a man on a roof across the street."

"Got it, ma'am," a voice said.

Kirk shook his head. "High-tech demon hunters. I would have thought that was an oxymoron."

"A necromancer coming clean from evil and getting married is an oxymoron," Catalina said. "Who was the guy with Becca?"

"Healer. Useful guy to have around."

"I bet. What's in the kitchen?"

"A back office and…a kitchen. What do you expect? A BDSM dungeon?"

"We'll need at least two men to infiltrate the rear. That

kitchen is making me nervous. Too unpredictable. We'll need to make sure we secure it. What's on the second floor?"

"Apartments."

"Her apartment?"

Kirk shrugged. "I think so, but I don't know for sure."

Catalina spoke into her watch. "We'll need two men upstairs to secure the residential hallway. There's a separate side entrance that looks to have keycard access. The windows face the street. We'll need to break in the alleyway doors."

Soon, the map of the Wicked Cat was covered in a dozen blue dots.

"You're sure about this?" Kirk asked. "It's a sick plan, and I don't mean that as a compliment."

"I've never been more sure about anything in my life," Catalina said, packing away the tablet in her purse. "She's not going to listen to a word we told her. After tonight, she will reconsider. When she does, we'll follow her. We'll extract Garamanthus in relative seclusion, where the coward won't be able to call for help or hide in the city."

"And I thought my necromancer ways were bad," Kirk said.

"You know you like it," Catalina said.

She glanced out the window wistfully.

"When night falls, the Wicked Cat will be under siege."

CHAPTER THIRTY-NINE

CYRUS SNEEZED. The dramatic aroma of some godforsaken blend of chemicals invaded his nose and wouldn't leave.

He shifted in the back of a beat-up sedan as it parked on the side of the road somewhere in an industrial district. The car, driven by JoJo's chauffeur, had made so many twists and turns that Cyrus lost track of what neighborhood he was in. If he had to guess, he thought he was somewhere on the east side, south of the Chicago River. The area was all warehouses, shipping companies, and taxicab and freight company depots. The further the chauffeur drove, the more run down and dilapidated the buildings became, and the lower the sun sank in the sky, heightening Cyrus's paranoia. Twilight was in the air, casting slanted rays of orange and gold across the street and buildings.

It didn't help that sitting next to him in the backseat, smoking a cigarette and taking cheap shots at him...was Simone.

He had wished that he never met this woman. Now he was stuck in a car with her. He couldn't wait for the moment he could escape her. Malice and sarcasm slithered out of Simone's mouth in equal parts. Either she was attacking him, attacking JoJo covertly, or bitching about her miserable status in life.

Cyrus rubbed his nose and tried to ignore her as she spewed a cloud of smoke across the back seat.

"Got cold feet yet, boy?"

It took everything Cyrus had not to curse her out. That wouldn't have been a good idea, even though it would have felt amazing.

"I told you, I'm not a boy," he said. "I'm not a kid. I'm not your baby, honey, honeybun, ratty boy, or any other stupid thing you want to call me."

He glanced across the street at a boarded-up building that looked suspiciously like an old Burger King. "If you want to call me anything, call me Mr. Doesn't Matter. Or, don't call me anything at all. Better yet, how about you don't *talk* to me at all? It would make this mission a lot easier."

Simone puffed her cigarette. Something he said had irritated her. He didn't know what.

"A rat shifter like you shouldn't even exist," she said. "It would have done me a big favor if you didn't exist at all."

"Why don't you go find a time machine so you can make that happen?" Cyrus said, rolling his eyes.

"Sir, madam, we have arrived," the chauffeur said. The wan-faced man adjusted a Cardinals baseball cap and nodded across the street at the old Burger King. Cyrus wondered how any man could wear a Cardinals in the heart of Cubs territory. The first time he had seen this man, he was wearing a chauffeur's uniform and driving a seventies limo. Now he looked like any guy off the street. No one would have thought twice about a beat-up sedan driving in this part of the city.

"It's *there*?" Cyrus asked, pointing at the Burger King. "I think we have the wrong address."

"If our man says it's there, then it's *there*," Simone said. "Did anyone teach you how to follow instructions?"

The chauffeur hushed them. Across the street, two men in

black hoodies with their hoods up appeared out of nowhere and moved a large board away from the main door of the restaurant. A black commercial van rumbled out. Somehow, they'd managed to widen the door opening so it could fit a car. Cyrus's jaw hung open as the men replaced the board, then climbed into the van, looking around suspiciously.

The van rolled out into the street and passed the sedan. Cyrus, Simone, and the chauffeur ducked as the van passed. None of the men saw them.

"So maybe you're right," Cyrus said as the van rounded a corner. "This'll be easy."

He put his hand on the door handle, but Simone grabbed him by the coat and pulled him in close. He smelled alcohol, marijuana, and cigarette smoke on her breath. She stared at him with her reddened eyes.

"Let's get one thing straight, Mr. Doesn't Matter," Simone said sharply. "Your orders are to find a way inside that building and tell us what you find. I hope that little rodent brain of yours can reconstruct a map and tell us what is in every room so that we can infiltrate the place and obliterate these demon hunters. At least, that's what I hope, because if you can't, I am going to recommend to JoJo that we lop your little rat head off. You better not be playing a game, Mr. Doesn't Matter, because if you are, I am going to make sure that my man destroys you and your sister. And when he does, I will be there, laughing my head off every single second. I might even recommend to him that he resurrect both of your dead bodies and kill you again. JoJo's not beneath that, and it wouldn't be the first time we did it. Got it, Mr. Doesn't Matter?"

Cyrus swallowed.

"JoJo and I had a deal," he said, pulling away from her. "Let me do my job or I'll tell him that you interfered."

"Ooh, a tattletale," Simone said. "Exactly what I'd expect."

Cyrus paused and took a deep breath. He told himself to shut up and stop letting her push his buttons.

He started out of the car, opening the door. Then he stopped and glanced back at Simone. "Don't forget that JoJo doesn't know me any better than I know him. Something bad might happen if you were to hurt me. I have friends in high places and several people know where I am today."

Simone laughed in his face.

"Where did you pick that up?" she asked. "Let me guess: you heard that on television, didn't you?"

Cyrus pursed his lips and left Simone laughing in the car and the chauffeur staring ahead, as if the conversation never happened.

"What did I get myself into?" he muttered to himself as he dipped into an alley.

CHAPTER FORTY

"Becca, I really think you should reconsider."

Desmond leaned over the bar, nursing a scotch and soda. "I don't like Kirk any more than you do, but he has a point."

Becca wiped down the counter. The bar was in its late afternoon lull. It was starting to get dark outside. All the coffee shop patrons had left, but it was still too early for the bar patrons to arrive. The Wicked Cat was so empty that their conversation bounced off the wall.

"I made my decision," Becca said. "I am *not* leaving. How about you stop asking me and let me take care of my bar, please?"

Desmond drank the last of his drink and handed it to her. He shrugged. "Okay. You win."

Further down the bar, Luna drank a strawberry daiquiri.

"Want another one?" Becca asked. "Your drinks are on the house for a long time. Payback for injuring you."

Luna raised her glass but shook her head. "I'm good. I was just injured in the line of duty. You don't have to worry about me."

Becca wandered around the bar, glancing at all the tables to make sure they were clean.

Her mom was reading her e-reader in one of the booths near the kitchen. Becca slid into the booth.

"Desmond didn't change your mind, did he?" Aurora asked, closing the lid on the e-reader.

"I'll give you zero guesses, Mom."

Aurora sighed. Her sigh wasn't angry; just frustrated. "I know you can't be separated from this place for very long," she said, "but there's nothing wrong with your uncle's farm. You used to go there as a kid, remember?"

Becca did remember. Her uncle's farm in God-knows-where Illinois. Her dad's brother. She, her dad, and Cyrus would wake up at first light and clean out the horse stables. They shot clay pigeons during the day, rode ATVs around the expansive property, and spent so much time looking up at the stars at night. That was the only favorable thing she truly remembered about her Uncle Marty's farm. There were so many stars that she thought she was in an astronomy documentary. She and Cyrus lay there on a grassy hill, staring up at the infinite pinpoints in the dark blue sky.

But that was then. She wasn't sure if she would even be able to enjoy the farm's beauty now.

"I remember the farm well, Mom," Becca said. "But I am not going to run away. I have never run away from my problems. What would it say about me if I fled at the first sign of danger?"

"This isn't about your ego, honey," Aurora said. "It's about making sure that you live to see another day. This is all very scary."

Becca grabbed her mother's cup of coffee, which was dangerously low. "This is the absolute safest place I can be, Mom. Desmond said it himself. If you want, I won't leave the Wicked Cat for several days. I will stay holed up in my apartment and the Regulators can keep watch on me. But it will be a frigid day in hell before I leave this place. Let me get you a new coffee. The pot is fresh."

There was a coffee machine on the bar. Becca poured a steaming hot mug, added creamer, and swirled a flower petal into the top of the coffee. Then, a shadow outside caught her eye.

Becca saw the shadow first, followed by the grill of an engine. A wall of glass shards rained across the bar.

She instinctively dove to the floor with her hands over her bandanna.

Screams and the sound of a dying engine filled the bar, followed by a series of car doors slamming. Becca's ears clouded with a metallic *rat a tat tat.*

After a wave of silence, she glanced up to see a group of black-clad men standing with assault rifles on the floor of the bar. They wore all black, silver crosses around their necks, and their faces were covered in ski masks.

"Everybody down!" one of the men cried. "Shut up and nobody dies."

Holy shit... Becca was staring at a van on the floor of the Wicked Cat. It had driven through the wall. The entire structure of the building was at risk.

One of the men in black spotted Becca. He pointed at her and said something unintelligible to his friends. Boots clomped across the floor toward her.

A deafening growl cut across the air and something brown slammed into the man, sending him through the broken window and out into the street. The man bounced a few times, then stopped moving.

A giant werehyena stood in front of Becca, heaving. Desmond in his shifter form. In his leather trench, he looked like something out of a comic book. Saliva dripped from his jaws and he wrinkled his snout in fury.

Becca hid behind him. The men aimed their guns at Desmond.

"We can do this the easy way or we can do this the hard way," the leader said.

Desmond's vocal cords couldn't say intelligible words, so he growled and roared again, shaking the floor beneath her.

"I'll translate," Becca said. "Get the hell out of my bar."

The leader pointed his gun at Becca. "We have orders to bring you in with us. Surrender yourself or we will murder everyone in this place. You could have made this easier on yourself if you had just allowed us to extract the demon when we attacked you a few days ago."

"Not on your life," Becca said.

Aurora was hiding. Becca spotted her out of the corner of her eye.

"It sure would be nice if your brother was around during times like this," Aurora whispered.

"Maybe not," Becca said.

She cursed under her breath. Kirk had been right. They had come after her. She wasn't so tough now that the Wicked Cat was filled with crazy men.

Desmond sprang and grabbed the leader by the neck. He suplexed to man onto the floor, knocking him out instantly. The remaining man fired, but Desmond was too fast, leaping into the air and bringing the back side of his fist down against the man's face.

All went quiet as Desmond surveyed the area. All the men were down. Desmond transformed back into a human.

"Is everyone all right?" he asked.

"We're fine," Becca said. "Mom, you okay?"

Aurora nodded.

"Only one question remains," Desmond said, frowning. "Where is Rocco, and why didn't he—"

A thud stopped him. A raven landed on the ground at his feet. It was still breathing, but asleep. Someone had thrown it.

Outside, a man in a ski mask and black hoodie crouched on the bed of a pickup truck. He had a metal tube in his hand and a gunsight on his eye. He pulled the trigger.

A dart struck Desmond in the neck. Desmond furiously

ripped out the dart and cast it aside. He transformed into a werehyena and ran at the man. He barely made it outside the Wicked Cat before collapsing onto the sidewalk.

"A tranquilizer," Becca said.

The man on the truck shrugged. Another van pulled up to the curb and more men jumped out.

One of the men had a megaphone. "Becca Grant," the man said. "It's time to surrender."

CHAPTER FORTY-ONE

CYRUS EXPECTED the smell of old food and grease as he sniffed around the foundation of the old fast food restaurant, but the air was surprisingly sterile. He scampered over dust and debris, pausing here and there to listen for danger. His rat eyes used the last bits of twilight that they could, but he couldn't see well against the foundation.

He navigated along the wall of brick and vinyl, rubbing his whiskers against the surface as he went. He stopped, sniffed, stopped, sniffed until his whiskers led him to a rush of flat air.

He found a board in the back of the building. The doorway looked like a loading bay for a semi. Cyrus imagined this building in its heyday, with a semi rolling up every week full of hamburger patties, frozen french fries, and parfaits. He wondered how long the place had been abandoned.

He sniffed the board. An explosion of cedar and iron filled his nose. Whoever boarded up this building used new materials. The board smelled as if it came from the hardware store yesterday, and the nails were cold and fresh.

There was an opening between the board and the wall, big enough for him to fit his head in. He squeezed his head in first, then the rest of his body collapsed and slid through the gap with a pop.

He was inside. He waited a few seconds as his eyes adjusted to the darkness. Vacant buildings were always dark. They didn't have electricity and the boarded-up windows ensured permanent shadows.

But this building wasn't dark. A fluorescent light hummed in the ceiling. Cyrus would have never seen it from the outside. His hair stood on end.

The floors. They should have been dusty and cracked and neglected. The floor itself was old laminate, but it was clean as if it had been swept recently.

In the air, he detected the faint smell of rubber. The kind you found on shoes. Cyrus instinctively hugged the nearest wall and waited.

His heart beat like a hammer and he waited a few more seconds before it calmed down. He ventured forward through what seemed like a storeroom replete with wire shelves, a desk, and stainless steel doors that looked suspiciously like freezers. The doorway to the storeroom was open and he slipped through the frame into what he thought would be the kitchen.

He wasn't in a kitchen. He was in an open room. There was a table, a few chairs, and what looked like an interior window. Cyrus's whiskers detected the faint coppery odor of blood splotched on the floor. The energy in this room was intensely negative. It sent his hairs into a buzz saw. He didn't know why because there was no one in the room.

Something told him it was safe to shift.

He found a corner, waited a little, then shifted back into his human form.

His rat instinct was right. It was an interrogation room of some kind, like the ones he had seen in police shows. The interior window shone his reflection back on him.

His heart sank as he spotted a surveillance camera in the corner of the ceiling.

Crap. Now he would have to move fast. Faster than he expected.

He swept his gaze across the room and settled on the table, which had metal clamps mounted onto it. In the center of the table was a white envelope with something written in flowery handwriting. Cyrus inched closer and squinted his eyes at the envelope. Then, he couldn't believe his eyes.

The envelope was addressed to JoJo.

CHAPTER FORTY-TWO

Dear JoJo,

Congratulations on a terrific hunt. You did exactly what we expected you to do—used your demons to find us.

A decade ago, you banished us from the city. We never forgot that. We have been preparing for our return ever since.

Our informant told us everything we needed to know. Yes, that's right —you have a traitor in your midst. That is all we will say.

You have made your move. The next move is ours.

We would suggest you prepare for war.

Ever yours,
The Sacred Heart.

Simone read the paper. If it weren't addressed to JoJo, she would have ripped it apart.

She shouted at the top of her lungs and set upon Cyrus with mad eyes.

"You did this," she said.

Cyrus shrugged. "I'm not the informant, if that's what you're insinuating."

"You *have* to be!" she cried. "How would they have known we were coming?"

"Like I said, it's not my problem."

The chauffeur said nothing as he drove through the streets.

Simone panted. She read the letter again, then balled a fist. Her hands were shaking as she lit a cigarette and rolled down the window.

"I'm not convinced it *wasn't* you," she said. "But if it wasn't—"

"Why would I come to you if I was an informant?" Cyrus asked. "Use that half a brain cell in your head to think about that. Why would I volunteer myself for that kind of harm? I may be young, but I'm not stupid."

Simone exhaled a cloud of smoke and said nothing. Silence settled between them.

"If you're so smart, who do you think it is?" she asked.

"How should I know?" Cyrus asked. "That's your problem. As far as I'm concerned, I upheld my part of the deal. I just need JoJo to see that I did. After that, you can settle your feud with those demon hunters."

"It's your problem too, you know," Simone said. "You're going to serve JoJo for six months. Don't think you can get out of this."

Cyrus wanted to say that if these demon hunters were as smart as he thought they were, JoJo and Simone might not be alive much longer. But he held his tongue.

Soon, the chauffeur pulled up to the corner at JoJo's Dive. He hurried around to the back of the car and helped Simone out.

"We'll see if you're right," Simone said.

The chauffeur stood with his hands behind his back.

"How do you put up with her?" Cyrus asked.

The chauffeur said nothing.

"On second thought, maybe that's the answer to the question," he said, walking to the front door. "Just be quiet and say nothing."

JoJo was reading the letter calmly as Cyrus entered the office. Simone stood next to the desk with a hand on her hip. Dominica sat on JoJo's lap, eyeing the letter curiously.

"I'll be damned," he said, crumbling the paper. He met Cyrus's gaze. "You plan this?"

"For the second time," Cyrus said, "if I planned this, why would I be here now?"

"I don't believe him," Simone said. She strolled past Cyrus and slammed the door to the office. She latched the lock. The sound made Cyrus jump.

"He's a rat," Simone said. He felt her voice on his neck as she hovered behind him. He didn't like his back turned to her, but there was no way he was going to turn his back on JoJo.

"If you want to believe that I'm the informant, fine," Cyrus said. "But I guarantee you that you're wrong. And *if* you're wrong, then what?"

JoJo pushed Dominica off his lap and pulled into a pace in his office.

"I'll buy it," JoJo said.

"Then are we good?" Cyrus asked. "I upheld my part of the bargain."

JoJo stopped and grinned. "Yes, you did," he said. "I'm a man of my word, Mr. Doesn't Matter. Give me a few days. I'll send you an address to the place you and your sister can show up for the extraction."

Cyrus didn't like the sound of that.

JoJo held up a hand. "Don't worry, I'm not going to kill

you. Unless I find out that you were the informant. Then, you'll be on a one-way trip to heaven."

"Why should we let him leave?" Simone asked, her breath hot on Cyrus's neck. "We should keep him just in case I'm right."

"Keep me, and some very powerful paranormals are going to come looking for me," Cyrus said. "You don't want to do that."

Simone gave a harsh laugh. "What do you think for a change, Dominica?" Simone asked. "Or are you too busy in your honeymoon phase to have an opinion?"

Dominica's face hardened. "This is between you and JoJo."

"Just what I like to hear," Simone said. The lock on the door unlatched and the door creaked open. Simone stood in the doorway, gesturing for Cyrus to leave. "I'm done with you, rat. Come to think of it, I'm done with *you* too, Dominica."

Cyrus found himself standing on the balcony with Dominica as Simone slammed the door in his face.

"I can't stand her," Cyrus said.

"That makes two of us," Dominica said with a lingering glance at the door. She turned to Cyrus. "Some exploration job you did."

Cyrus waved in assent. "Just doing what I have to do."

Dominica started down the spiral staircase. "I need a drink. Want one?"

Cyrus glanced back at the office. He didn't hear anything. He wanted to know what Simone and JoJo were talking about.

"I don't drink from places I don't know," he said. He didn't see that Dominica had stopped. He banged into her back, sending her flying forward on the staircase. She cried out in pain.

"Watch it!" she cried, turning back to him angrily.

Cyrus caught her from falling down the stairs.

"So sorry," he said.

Dominica brushed him off. A flash of silver drew his eye.

He hadn't noticed it under her dress before. A skeleton necklace with emeralds for eyes. Dominica quickly tucked the necklace into the top of her dress.

"You've got a death wish, don't you?"

"I said I was sorry," Cyrus said.

Dominica hurried down the stairs and helped herself to the bar. She wouldn't look at Cyrus.

Cyrus took one last look at the sordid bar and walked out of JoJo's Dive, hoping he'd never have to come back to this place.

CHAPTER FORTY-THREE

"Let's see how well you absorb the darkness," Garamanthus said.

The demon laughed so hard, it was a miracle he didn't wind himself.

"I can help you," Garamanthus said. "But this time, I won't do it for free. If you want to survive, Becca, you've got to ask me for help."

The men in black approached. Becca stole a glance at Desmond on the floor. What a crappy time to make a decision.

"Even if these guys kill me?" she asked. "I thought you needed my body more than me."

The men took another step toward Becca and her heart raced.

A drunk patron told her one time that there comes a moment in every person's life when they are one decision away from death. Decide this and you live; decide that and you die. The patron, a chubby goth with a preference for Crown Royal straight, had stared into the depths of his glass and said that no one sees it coming, and no one could ever truly prepare.

A warm sweat broke out across Becca's body. She felt flush. This was that time her patron had warned her about.

"Okay," she said, "You win. I need your help. You knew I was going to say that, didn't you?"

Garamanthus laughed again. "You bet I did. I just wanted to hear you say it. I wanted to hear Becca Grant admit that she can't live without me, that the part of her that I occupy is essential to her life. Let's take care of these goons, shall we?"

The demon took over. Suddenly, she clenched her fists and assumed an attack stance with her fists in front of her face. Then, she was flying across the room at lightning speed. She tripped one man and brought her knee into his face. She grabbed his gun and shot the other two men. Her ears buzzed from the assault rifle noise.

Across the bar, a goon fired at her, but she dove under the bar at the last moment. The bullets struck the glass and alcohol bottles behind the bar, creating a waterfall of glass and alcohol.

She waited for a dip in the noise. She poked her head up and the man fired another round at her, spraying the bar with bullets.

She pulled herself into a crouching run, clearing the bar and hopping over one of the rails. The man didn't see her coming, and she punched him in the face. She took his gun and hit him in the temple with the butt.

She counted. Two left. They were standing by the door, backing away and trying to figure out what to do.

Becca slung the assault rifle around her shoulder and approached the two men.

"You've got all these people and you can't bring me down," Garamanthus said. "Which one of you wants to take a message to your leader?"

She floated the assault rifle's aim between the two men.

"Who's going to be the messenger and who's going to die?"

she asked. "Or do both of you want to be the messenger? Your choice."

"This isn't over," the man said.

"But it is," Garamanthus said. "Here's the message: you will *never* take me. I will come and find every one of you, and I will obliterate your kind. The best thing you can do is leave me and Becca Grant alone. If you don't, consider this your final warning."

Becca jerked her rifle to the right and fired, shattering another window. The men jumped.

"Get out!" Garamanthus shouted.

The men looked at each other, gave Becca a lingering glance, then turned around and ran.

Garamanthus relinquished control and Becca was in her body again, holding the giant assault rifle. Glancing down at it, she startled and threw it aside.

Two arms slid around her. Aurora. Becca hugged her mother.

"We've got to get out of here," Aurora said.

Becca's eyes scanned the floor where Desmond and Rocco lay.

"This is my fault," Becca said, backing away. She wanted to run.

"It's *not* your fault," Aurora said sternly. "But we have *got* to get ready to leave. Now. Where the hell is your brother?"

CHAPTER FORTY-FOUR

BECCA SWEPT a mound of broken glass into a dustpan. She was still trembling from the attack.

Desmond in werehyena form and Rocco in raven form lay sleeping on the floor of the Wicked Cat. Aurora and Luna watched over them. Luna sniffled as she ran a wet rag over Rocco's raven body. All was quiet across the bar.

Normally, the police would have been on site after an attack like this, but these were paranormal circumstances. No one was going to show up. Becca was on her own.

She fought back tears as she glanced around her ravaged shop. The shop she had spent years of her life building. Sure, there had been damage to the building before—a drunk patron punching a wall or a delivery truck backing into a bollard—but never anything like this. She didn't know how she was going to make repairs.

Nearby, one of the demon hunters stirred, woke up, and jumped to his feet.

"Crap," he said, eyeing her. He turned and ran.

Becca sighed. Hopefully, all of the hunters on the floor would have the same response. She didn't feel like fighting anymore.

She shoveled the dustbin into a trashcan, and the glass shards jingled as they tumbled to the bottom.

She wanted a drink. The hardest, stiffest drink she could muster, but she knew it wasn't a good idea. She needed her mind sharp. She just needed to calm down.

A horn honked, drawing her attention to the street. A white fifteen-passenger van with a church logo rolled up to the curb. Gilberto was in the driver's seat.

"Time to go," he said.

"There's only one problem," Luna said. She pointed to Desmond's body. "I have no idea how we're going to get him into the van."

"Teamwork," Becca said.

Becca, Luna, and Gilberto picked up Desmond and carried him to the back of the passenger van. They set him in the trunk. They all groaned as they carried him. Desmond had to weigh at least 300 pounds—it must've been all of that shifter muscle.

Becca's muscles burned and she leaned against the side of the van, huffing and puffing.

Footsteps crunched on glass, followed by a voice.

"Whoa, what the heck happened?"

Becca stared daggers at Cyrus as he stood in front of the Wicked Cat, surveying the damage.

"I disappear for a couple of hours, and this is what happens?" he asked.

"So nice of you to join us," she said.

"Is everyone okay?" he asked.

"Aside from Desmond and Rocco being shot with tranquilizer darts and my shop being completely ruined, everything is just peachy," Becca said.

Cyrus's eyes widened. "Was it the demon hunters?"

"Great detective work, genius."

"I had a run-in with them too," he said.

Aurora rushed out of the Wicked Cat with her purse. "Save your talk for later," she said. "We've got to go."

"Where are we going?" Cyrus asked.

Becca shushed him and dragged him toward the van. "Be quiet. I'll explain later."

Gilberto, Becca, Aurora, Luna, and Cyrus piled into the van.

"I made a call to some other Regulators," Gilberto said. "They'll work on repairing the place while we're gone."

As Gilberto pulled away, Becca stared at the remnants of the Wicked Cat and wondered if she would ever return.

CHAPTER FORTY-FIVE

"Where do you think they are headed?" Kirk asked.

The driver of Catalina's car hung back a few cars as the church van pulled away from the Wicked Cat.

"It doesn't matter," Catalina said. "What matters is that they're falling into our trap."

Catalina reached over and patted Kirk's hand. "Just one more step and I promise to give your brother and father back." She smiled at him. "How does it feel to be fighting for a noble cause for change?"

Kirk pushed her hand away. "I wouldn't call you noble. Not by a long shot."

She shrugged. "I suppose noble is in the eye of the beholder."

Kirk squinted and tracked the van as it made a left turn.

"I'll bet they're heading out of town," he said.

He stroked his chin. "If it were me, I'd be headed to Mexico right now. There would be no place in the city that was safe."

He puffed. "But with all those people in that van, there's no way they're leaving the country. I'll bet they're going to the country."

"We'll see if you're right," Catalina said.

Her phone rang. Her watch rang. She accepted the call. A voice echoed from her wrist. "We've got a problem," a female said.

"Relax, sister," Catalina said. "In a few hours, this is all going to be over."

"We don't have a few hours," the woman said. "JoJo got the letter."

"Who's JoJo?" Kirk asked.

Catalina hushed him.

"That was just a little game," Catalina said. "Besides, you warned us. We had to do it."

"He's stark raving mad," the woman said.

"All part of the plan," Catalina said. "Just do what we discussed to allay his suspicions, Dominica. I know he's a slimeball. But like I said, this will be over soon."

"Is that kid with them?" Dominica asked.

"Yeah, he's in the van we're following," Catalina said.

"He saw my necklace."

"So what?"

"He kept staring at it, like he thought it was important. Maybe he knows."

"How could he know?" Catalina asked. "You're just paranoid. That's what happens when you hang out with a man like JoJo."

Kirk folded his arms, listening carefully.

"JoJo's rooting his ranks for an informant," Dominica said. "They don't suspect me, but I don't trust his girlfriend. She's trouble."

"Trouble or not, who cares?" Catalina asked. "We'll send you coordinates. Just make it sound like the demon inside you gave them to you. Bring JoJo and his girl along, and we'll take care of them and Garamanthus at the same time. It's almost over, sis."

Dominica said something Kirk didn't understand and hung up.

Catalina sighed and stared out the window.

"Hang back," she said to the driver. "In a few blocks, tell the others to pick up the pursuit. I don't want them to suspect anything."

Kirk waited a little while before he spoke. "Got a sister, huh?"

"She's the wicked one," Catalina said.

The car took a right turn, cutting the van out of Kirk's line of sight.

If there was one thing Kirk knew, it was that these demon hunters didn't know who they were dealing with. The rat shifter and his sister were smarter than they looked.

But if there was another thing he knew, it was that the shifter and his sister had no idea who they were dealing with in Catalina.

All he cared about was his father and brother. He held their wispy forms in his mind's eye. He was so close to rescuing them that he could feel their presence around him.

He closed his eyes and went to sleep.

CHAPTER FORTY-SIX

"Where are we going?" Cyrus asked.

He munched on a bag of chips that Becca swiped from the Wicked Cat.

Gilberto drove quietly and hadn't said very much during the drive. They had left Chicago a long time ago. They were on an interstate, riding toward a vanishing point in the stars. Around them, the red flashing lights of windmills blinked on and sizzled out like sentinels watching them. It was so dark that Cyrus could barely see his hands in front of his face.

Aurora shifted in the front passenger seat. She turned on the radio. Crappy top 40 music began to play. Cyrus rolled his eyes.

"We're going to your Uncle Marty's," Aurora said. "I called ahead and he agreed to let us stay in his barndominium."

Cyrus sighed. "Uncle Marty," he whined. "Please don't tell me we're going to have to shovel after pigs this time, will we?"

"Only if you don't stop complaining," Aurora said.

"I don't like this any more than you do," Becca said, "but I was wrong and Mom was right."

"I think I'm going to record that," Aurora said. "It's not

every day your children tell you that you're right about
something."

Becca folded her arms and stared out into the night. "I
didn't trust Kirk. Why should I have? He doesn't exactly have
the best intentions. But I didn't listen to what he was saying.
All I cared about was punching him in the face. Because of
that, Desmond and Rocco were hurt."

"This isn't your fault, Bec," he said. "Not your fault at all."

Behind him, Rocco stirred. Luna, who had been riding in
the backseat, gave a startle. "Baby? Guys, he's waking up!"

Rocco groaned.

"Take it easy," Cyrus said. "And please don't throw up."

Becca elbowed him. "Such a nice thing to say to someone
who's just been shot with a tranquilizer dart, doofus."

Cyrus shrugged. "We've got a while yet until we get Uncle
Marty's. Fine. Rocco, if you want to vomit, aim it in Becca's
direction, okay?"

Becca elbowed him again and Aurora told them to be
quiet.

"This drive sure has gone by quick," Gilberto asked.

"That's because there is nothing outside the city," Becca
said.

Gilberto wiped his nose and craned to see the street
ahead. "I wouldn't say that. I lived on a farm for a while, you
know."

"You're a man of mystery," Cyrus said.

"I like the peace and quiet," Gilberto said. "There's
nothing like getting away for clearing your mind. That's what
I liked about living in the country."

"Maybe you're right," Becca said. "But I can't be out here
forever. I've got the Cat. And all of our friends."

Gilberto whistled. "Just you see, Becca. We'll be out here
for a couple of days, then hopefully will have this all put
behind us."

"What he said," Cyrus said, finishing his bag of chips. He

reclined in the seat, put his hands behind his head, and said, "I just hope that barndominium is nicer than I remembered it."

Uncle Marty lived on a corn farm an hour south of Chicago. The sky grew a deeper shade of navy and the stars just a little brighter as they neared the exit to the country road he lived on.

Aurora guided Gilberto down the long, winding gravel roads with no streetlights—just stars to illuminate the path. They turned onto a hilly road and then made a right onto a bumpy gravel road that wound through a cornfield, and toward a Victorian farmhouse in the distance.

The windows of the house were lit. Cyrus glanced at the clock. It was almost ten o'clock. He yawned.

Uncle Marty was sitting on a rocking chair on the porch. He was Cyrus and Becca's father's uncle. He had a mop of silver, thinning gray hair, and he wore a polo and jeans that emphasized his stick-like frame.

"Good to see you all," he said, rising from the rocking chair. "Though I wish it were under better circumstances."

Aurora didn't tell him everything, just that they needed a place to stay for the night.

"Marge and I prepared the barndominium for you," Uncle Marty said. "Hopefully, you will find it comfortable. Come on down to the house in the morning and we will make you breakfast. We laid out towels and toiletries for all of you."

Aurora kissed Uncle Marty on the cheek. Cyrus shook his hand and Becca hugged him.

"I can't believe how old you two are," he said. "I bet Dave would have gotten a kick out of this."

The barndominium was a white pole barn with a mosaic quilt painted on the front and a gabled rooftop that reminded Cyrus of a rooster. Gilberto parked on a gravel lot next to the pole barn.

"Pretty nice place," he said. "This will be a scenic place to hide out."

Becca turned to Luna and Rocco. Rocco was awake, but still blinking hard and groggy.

"You guys going to be okay walking?" Becca asked.

Luna nodded. "Desmond is the problem."

Desmond still lay sleeping like a stone in the back of the van.

Cyrus grimaced at the realization that they were all going to have to carry him into the pole barn.

The inside of the barndominium was like a loft apartment. It had an open floor plan with a living room, television, and kitchen with a range hood. There were plenty of couches and chairs for everyone to relax. A wooden staircase led up to the upper-story loft where two beds and several sleeping bags lay on the floor.

"Uncle Marty, always looking out for us," Cyrus said. "I got dibs on the sleeping bag by the AC."

"No, that's mine," Becca said, shoving him playfully.

They carried Desmond into one of the beds. Aurora stayed with him, keeping a cold rag on his forehead. Rocco sat on the other bed, trying to shake off the grog.

"Man, that dart was intense," Rocco said.

"That's because it hit your raven body," Luna said. "God, they could have killed you." Luna threw her arms around Rocco.

Cyrus looked away. The two of them had been through a lot in the last few days. If there was anyone who deserved a break, it was them.

Another staircase led up to the third floor of the barn,

where there was a balcony under the stars. Cyrus walked into the balmy night and sat on a wicker chair, staring up at Orion.

Becca joined him, and for a while, they stared up at the sky without saying anything.

Now was as good a time as ever to tell Becca the truth. She was either going to thank him or throw him off the balcony.

"Bec, I've got something to tell you," he said. "And I just want to say sorry in advance for not being honest with you."

She frowned at him, her face bright in the moonlight.

"Cy, is whatever you're going to tell me make me throw you off this balcony?"

"Fifty-fifty chance," Cyrus said. "But I'm prepared to die."

Becca glanced up at the stars. "I like the bravery."

"Remember a few days ago when you got attacked by those guys when you were walking home from your therapy session?"

"How could I forget?"

"Before all of that happened, I told you that I was going to Fontanelli's to do an odd job. That wasn't true. I did go to see Font, but I didn't work."

Becca narrowed her eyes at him. "So?"

"Rocco and Luna told me about someone in the paranormal world who could potentially help extract Garamanthus from you. I went to see him. Well, I *tried* to see him and failed miserably."

"Okay," Becca said, her tone leading him on.

"He's a loan shark, but for magic," Cyrus said. "They call him JoJo the Demonsharp."

"Like a cardsharp?"

"But for demons."

"Oh my God."

Cyrus rubbed the back of his head. "I did a deal with him. He needed my rat senses, so I lent those to him earlier this evening. In exchange, he's agreed to extract Garamanthus from you."

Becca was speechless. "Cy, I—"

"There's a small cost, but it was worth it, Bec. But if there's anyone who can do it, it's him. In the next couple of days, he's going to call me and we're going to get that demon out of you once and for all."

"Did you pay him?" Becca asked.

"I just have to work for him for six months," Cyrus said. "He can use my skillset."

Becca stared at Cyrus searchingly. "Why did you do this?"

"It kills me to see you like this," Cyrus said. "And I'd do anything to help you. But I couldn't tell you because I didn't want Garamanthus to know. Now, it doesn't matter."

"I don't know what to say," Becca said.

"Are you going to throw me off the balcony?" Cyrus asked.

"Haven't decided yet."

A tear jumped into Becca's eye. She wiped it away.

"It's been a hard six months," she said. "I want it to end like you do. Sometimes I think this demon is going to be inside me forever. I keep swearing to myself that I'll fight to the death, but I've come to terms with it."

"You don't have to anymore," Cyrus said. "This is all going to be over soon, Bec."

Becca pulled him into a hug, and they embraced for a while. Then Becca pulled away and punched him on the shoulder.

"Ow!"

"That's for lying to me," she said.

"I accept my punishment," he said, rubbing his sore arm.

~

Kirk and Catalina stood in the shade of a cluster of poplar trees, watching Cyrus and Becca hug through binoculars.

Kirk swept the binoculars across the perimeter of the pole barn, which was lit up like something from a quaint painting.

"Peaceful place," Kirk said.

"And quiet," Catalina said. "Just like we expected."

"I'll channel Nostradamus and tell him to give you an award," Kirk said flatly, setting his sights on Cyrus and Becca again. Becca punched Cyrus on the shoulder and he recoiled, rubbing his shoulder.

"Wonder what they're talking about," Kirk said.

"Looks like they got in a fight and are making up," Catalina said. "You don't read body language well, do you?"

"I have spirits to help me with that," Kirk said.

"Ah, right."

They waited for a while in the shadows until Cyrus and Becca walked off the balcony and back into the pole barn.

"The whole crew is in there," Catalina said. "Hopefully, Desmond's still asleep. That tranquilizer will wear off soon. We made a special formulation for him, but even we can't keep him down forever."

"Your problem, not mine," Kirk said. "I've been beaten up by that werehyena, and it's not in my plans tonight."

"They look like they're settling in," Catalina said, holding her watch to her mouth. "I'm beaming our coordinates to all units. Make your way here now."

She turned and motioned for Kirk to follow.

"Time to hunt us a demon," she said.

"You're sure about this?" JoJo asked.

JoJo watched Dominica intently as she closed her eyes and massaged her temples, listening to her inner demon. "Divination isn't the easiest thing in the world, you know."

Simone sat in JoJo's office blowing on a joint. She giggled. "If you had let me do it, baby, we would have found them by now."

JoJo snapped his fingers at Simone.

"That demon inside you doesn't sound right to me," he said. "Why would they hide out on a farm?"

Dominica opened her eyes and shook her head. "How should I know? But I did what you told me. I listened to him. Why would *he* lie? Unless there's something you're not telling *me*."

"What else did the demon see?" JoJo asked. "Divination isn't always accurate. Sometimes parts of it are right, others aren't."

"He just told me that a battle would take place on a farm," Dominica said. "He told me he could lead me there, but the cost is significant."

"How much?" JoJo asked.

"I don't want to say," Dominica said. "It's my cross to bear, JoJo."

JoJo nodded to her gently. He walked around his office, lost in his thoughts. That kid could have been pulling his leg. But why would he? He didn't look like the smartest kid in the world, but he didn't look like an imbecile either.

His mind kept going back to that steel lattice at the hotel. A latticework that held up the canopy.

He had thought then that that was a sign. It had to be. But he didn't see anything converging yet.

"You ought to give me a sign," he said to the demons inside him.

The jackals came alive and laughed.

"A sign? What are we, angels?" the leader said.

"Well, I've got a demon here that says that Garamanthus is on a farm. It doesn't make any sense to me."

The leader paused as the others laughed. "It doesn't make sense to me either, but it's the only lead you have. "

"What if it's a trap?" JoJo asked.

"A trap from Garamanthus?" the leader asked. "He's a coward. That is impossible."

JoJo grabbed his mink coat off the coat rack along with a pork pie hat. He set the hat on his head sideways.

"Tell Vince to get the limo," he said. "Looks like we're going to the country."

CHAPTER FORTY-SEVEN

A FEW HOURS PASSED.

Cyrus channel-surfed on the TV in the living room. Three hundred channels and there wasn't a damn thing on other than a bad action movie that was perfect for Gilberto.

"*Lethal Weapon*," Gilberto said, cooking eggs at the stove. "Not my favorite, but I can definitely relate. I'm getting too old for this sh—"

"Gilberto," Aurora said. She was reading her e-reader on a sofa next to the fireplace, beside which Rocco and Luna were tending to the fire, covered in blankets. Uncle Marty had an almost-expired bag of marshmallows in the pantry, and Rocco, in his grog, demanded s'mores. Luna was helping him toast the marshmallows. Becca sat on the couch with her arms folded, constantly attacking Cyrus's channel-surfing skills.

"It's almost the top of the hour," he said. He tossed the remote to Becca. "Maybe *you'll* have better luck. Gilberto, is there any coffee left?"

Gilberto scooped a skillet full of sunny-side-up eggs onto a plate. "No, Becca drank the last cup, but if you asked nicely, maybe she'll make you one."

"Not on your life," she said.

Cyrus screwed his face at her. "Technically, you still owe me a pot of coffee. Your turn to brew, remember?"

"If by owe, you mean that lousy roast you did the night I vanished with Garamanthus," she said, "then I don't owe you anything."

"Hey, I learned how to brew coffee from the best!"

"The spoon literally stood up in the cup," Becca said.

Cyrus glanced at Gilberto and made puppy-dog eyes. "Since you're over there, man…"

"What, are you scared of a foreign coffee pot?" Becca asked.

Cyrus recoiled. "If you don't want me to fall asleep again, then coffee would be a good idea. But whatever. I need to stay awake. I'm going to go make a snowman."

"What are you, seven years old?" Becca asked.

"What are you? Mean?"

Silence. Becca and Gilberto burst into laughter.

Gilberto slid into a chair at the tiny kitchen table. "You're the king of terrible comebacks, man."

"Bye," Cyrus said, swiping his coat off the hook. "I'm going to enjoy this winter wonderland all by myself. Plus, it'll help me stay awake."

"Stay in the front of the house where I can see you," Aurora said with a chuckle.

"Ha. Ha."

He pushed out into the merciless cold.

Now *this* was exactly the thing he needed to stay awake. Frigid air on his skin, pale moonlight, and glittering snow. But he wasn't going to go back in and be ridiculed.

Becca would have joked that he needed that little toboggan with the *Teenage Mutant Ninja Turtles* on it that he had when he was a kid. He clucked his tongue at the thought.

He trudged through the snow until he was out of the last slant of light from the living room in the pole barn. The only thing lighting him up now was the twinkling snow, starlight, and the bone-white moon.

"Here's a good a place as any to have some fun," he said.

He bent over and clumped a malformed snowball between his hands.

CHAPTER FORTY-EIGHT

CYRUS GOT A GOOD BASE GOING, although it was more rectangular than circular. Becca would have laughed at it. He himself laughed at it and tried to shape it to look more snowman.

His fingers were starting to tingle, even through his gloves.

"Gotta stay awake," he said, yawning. "Can't...let...Becca...down."

He tripped and fell knee-first into the snow. He decided to lie on his back and make an angel. The cold snapped him out of his current sleeping reverie. He moved his arms and legs up and down and his ears swelled with the swishing and swashing of snow. He stood up and examined his handiwork. The result was a giant crater in the snow that didn't even closely resemble a snow angel.

"Oh well," he said.

The twig snapped behind him.

An owl fluttered away over him, flapping its wings gracefully. Cyrus stood for a moment, watching the owl as it flew over the roof of the pole barn.

His mind wandered. What would it be like to be an owl shifter?

He sighed. He really needed sleep.

Behind him, a branch broke, followed by a soft tumble of snow.

Cyrus turned around just in time to see several men in black jumping from a nearby tree. They landed in the snow, grinning at him through their ski masks.

"Crap," he said, backing away.

"Making angels in the snow and then getting beat up," Kirk said, watching Cyrus getting ambushed through his binoculars. He and Catalina were deeper in the woods, out of sight. "That's pretty lousy, even for you guys."

"Do you want your family back or not?" Catalina said. She spoke to her watch. "All units, descend upon the pole barn."

She adjusted her knitted winter cap. "Just let us handle this, and it will be over soon," she said.

Becca hit the switch on the coffee pot and started a new batch of coffee. She had ribbed Cyrus enough, so she had to balance out the sarcasm; her brother was going to come in, covered with snow, and he would need something to warm him up. Plus, she needed another cup of coffee herself.

"Sure you don't want to go outside and make a snowman with your brother?" Aurora asked. "It would be like old times."

"Old times like twenty years ago," Becca said.

"It's not like there's anything else to do," Gilberto said. He finished his eggs and was raiding the pantry looking for something else to eat.

Someone groaned. Upstairs, Desmond shifted.

Upon hearing him, Becca and Aurora raced upstairs to the loft.

Desmond opened his eyes. He was wrapped in a quilted bed sheet with a cold rag on his forehead.

"Uncle Marty's?" he asked.

Desmond tried to reach in his pocket, but his hand missed.

"What do you need?" Aurora asked.

"Right pocket," Desmond said.

Becca dug into Desmond's jean pocket. His body was as warm as a volcano. Her finger seized on something warm—a wallet—and something cool—a whistle with a leather strap.

She ran her fingers along the whistle. "What is this?"

Along with the whistle was a metal cone the size of a walnut. A red beacon flashed on the tip.

"What is this?" Becca asked.

"Press the red button twice," Desmond said.

Becca pressed the red tip of the cone. It depressed like a cheap toy and made a sound like a kazoo.

"Now blow the whistle three times," Desmond said. "Blow with all your might. Just… Trust me."

Becca stared at the whistle, unable to believe her eyes. She slipped it into her mouth and blew. The whistle made a buzzy, ratcheting sound that reminded her of a cheap kazoo.

She blew again.

And again.

"Okay, that was weird," Becca said.

"Now help me," Desmond said.

Aurora helped Desmond out of bed.

"I could use something to eat," he said. "My head is swimming."

"You were hit with a tranquilizer," Aurora said. "Gilberto made some eggs, and Becca has a pot of coffee going."

"You're singing my song," Desmond said, grinning.

Becca and Aurora each took an arm and guided him down the stairs to the kitchen table. Becca placed the whistle and beacon into Desmond's jacket and shook her head. None of this made any sense.

The front door in the living room slid open. A cold gust blew into the room. She shivered.

"Cy, shut the door!" Becca cried. "In case you haven't noticed, it's freaking freezing outside!"

There was no one in the doorway.

Becca stared out into the night. "Cy, I know we were harassing you a little while ago, but this isn't funny," she said.

Silence. Then, a shadow arced through the air and landed on the coffee table in front of the television, crushing it.

Cyrus. He had a cut on his lip and he groaned.

Aurora screamed.

Ten men in black piled into the pole barn, gathering on the wall. They carried assault rifles and pointed them at Becca and the group.

Becca's heart raced.

Garamanthus came alive. "Look alive, Becca," he said. "It's a surprise attack."

The last two men parted from the doorway, making space. The woman Becca had seen—Kirk's wife—walked into the room.

"No," Becca said under her breath. "You—"

"Don't take it personally," Catalina said. "And don't get too mad at Kirk. I'm kind of extorting him right now. Isn't that right, honey?"

"I'm not your honey," Kirk said, entering. He took off his sunglasses and slid them into his coat. Then he cracked his knuckles. "And, Becca, it's nothing personal at all."

CHAPTER FORTY-NINE

JoJo TURNED his head sideways as the limo crested a hill and approached a barn.

"You've got to be kidding me," he said. "Vince, turn around. There's no way this—"

"Trust me," Dominica said. "Lord Traxus wouldn't lie. I'm doing what you told me." She grabbed his hand and looked into his eyes pleadingly.

Simone laughed derisively. She was a shadow puffing smoke against the window. "What's the worst that could happen? We'll encounter some pigs in a barn, and then you can see what a fraud that Lord Traxus is."

She made a circling motion with her wrist. "Vince, turn this limo around and I'll kill you myself."

She turned to JoJo. "Do you or don't you believe her?"

JoJo pursed his lips at Simone. "I told you what I believed."

Simone puffed again and said nothing, looking out the window.

JoJo made an open palm and struck it with a fist. "You did like I told you, Dominica. I'm just surprised, that's all. Doesn't seem right. But I'll hear you out. If Simone's right and we find that barn full of pork, I'm cutting that demon out of you so I can have a word."

He tapped Simone on the shoulder. "If Dominica's right, you owe us both an apology. Among other things."

He met Simone's eyes in the dark, starlit shadows. "A bunch of things, Simone."

Simone exhaled out of the corner of her mouth. "We'll see."

JoJo snapped his fingers. "Vince, don't go all the way up. Park on the side of the road over there. We'll walk the rest of the way. Hope you two can deal with a little bit of snow."

"I brought my boots," Dominica said.

"I've got my mink," Simone said, opening the limo door. "Among other things."

JoJo helped Dominica out after Simone and Dominica rolled her eyes.

JoJo told Vince to keep watch and come running at the first sign of trouble.

Dominica and Simone shivered. Dominica huddled next to JoJo. Simone flicked her cigarette and it smoldered for a few seconds in the snow.

"We're going to find pigs or we're going to find a demon," JoJo said, leading the way.

As he charged through the snow, he realized that the cold didn't bother him any.

No, the cold didn't bother him at all. He patted the pistol in his interior coat pocket and readied himself for whatever he was about to find.

Meanwhile, the demons in his head fell over themselves in laughter.

CHAPTER FIFTY

CYRUS PULLED himself up amid splinters and broken glass from the coffee table that he landed on. His head swam from where one of the men hit him in the head with the butt of their gun.

His cheek was raw from a fist with a ring on it. Who needed the snow to stay awake when a punch in the face could do the trick?

"You… assholes," Cyrus said. He staggered in front of Becca, pushing her aside. "Leave us alone."

"Aw, the little brother is standing up for the big sister," Catalina said. "That's really noble, sweetheart, but you have no idea what you're doing. Go sit down over there and I promise your big sis will be just fine."

Rage swelled in Cyrus's breast and he had no choice but to let it out. "What's with everybody calling me a kid! I'm not a damned kid!"

"You hit a nerve, Catalina," Kirk said, staring at Cyrus. He cracked a grin. "But he's right. He's not a kid. He's a rat."

Becca stepped next to Cyrus. Her voice was deeper, angrier. Garamanthus had taken over.

"What do you want?" he asked. "I've done nothing to you or your clan."

"Nothing?" Catalina asked. She strolled around the pole barn, admiring the wooden walls. "You don't remember a man by the name of Victor Girardieu, do you?"

Becca's eyes narrowed as the demon considered the name.

"Of course you don't remember him," Catalina said. "Why should you? You probably won't remember Becca Grant's name in a few years either, will you?"

Catalina's voice turned hard, cool. "Victor Girardieu was my father."

The comment took Kirk off-guard. His eyes widened, but then he turned his face stoic. It was a split second, but Cyrus caught it.

"My father was the founder of the Sacred Heart," Catalina said. "He was an ex-monk, and the Sacred Heart began as a peaceful organization, attending to exorcisms and demon possessions across the city."

"You call this peaceful?" Cyrus asked.

Becca hit Cyrus's chest with the back of her hand.

"Quiet," Garamanthus growled.

"You possessed a little girl fifteen years ago," Catalina said. "You didn't care that you were ruining her life. You didn't care about the nightmares she was going to have every night thinking about what you did to her."

"As it should be," Garamanthus said. "You seem to forget that I'm a demon."

"That little girl was my sister," Catalina said. "And you didn't just ruin her life. You ruined her mind too."

She advanced, her eyes wild with rage. "You fled from the body of the man my father was trying to cure, and you possessed my sister in front of his very eyes. And then you killed him with his own blade. She watched him die as you fled."

"Such a tearjerking origin," Garamanthus said. "So, the two sisters have come back for revenge, eh?"

Becca assumed an attack stance with her fists in front of her face. "We can settle the score. If I had known you missed your father so much, I would have helped you meet him sooner."

Catalina checked her watch. Cyrus noticed it for the first time; it was a high-tech smartwatch with a glass watch face. On it was a satellite map with two blinking dots. One inched closer to the other.

Catalina pointed at Becca. "Detain her," she said.

"Over my dead body!" Cyrus said.

Suddenly, Cyrus was on the floor. Becca had struck him on his back, winding him.

"Hey!"

The men in black approached with their rifles aimed at everyone.

Cyrus glanced around. Gilberto and Desmond had their hands up at the kitchen table. Aurora was standing on the stairs where she had left Desmond. And Rocco and Luna—they were gone.

Cyrus gasped. The muscles in his back blazed like fire from where Becca had hit him. The men aimed their guns at Cyrus, and he put his hands up.

"I know *you* don't care very much about the kid," Catalina said, "but you don't want your host to turn on you. That would be very bad for your situation."

"Her body is mine to do with as I please," Garamanthus said.

Catalina clucked her tongue. "I wouldn't be so sure about that." She snapped her fingers. One of the men pulled a syringe from his pocket. The sparkling green liquid inside glowed. He raised the needle toward Becca's neck. Cyrus's eyes widened. Garamanthus roared and knocked the needle out of the man's hand.

But the needle was a diversion. Another man behind Becca had also pulled out a syringe. He jammed it into Becca's shoulder. The demon screamed in his sister's voice.

Becca staggered sideward, ripped the syringe from her arm, and launched it at the wall.

"What did you do to her?" Cyrus cried.

One of the men nudged his rifle into Cyrus's Adam's apple. "Quiet, kid. You'll thank us when this is all over."

Garamanthus panted. "What did you… do to me?"

"Oh, you mean aside from faking you out in making you think that my men would be so stupid as to try to attack you so openly with the syringe?" Catalina asked.

The man with the first needle tossed it to Catalina. She held the needle up to the light. "Inside you, and inside this needle is a psychotropic chemical infused with magic. I could go on and on about how we had this developed, but I'm just going to wave my hands and hope you'll take my word for it. The compound separates the demon from the host. It allows the host to always remain in control no matter what. Even if the demon wanted, it wouldn't be able to take control."

"I…don't get it," Cyrus said. "You put us through all of this just so you could cure her?"

"It's a small thank you for the pain that we put you through," Catalina said. "But it's not actually for Garamanthus. Becca, this spell is a vaccine. Never again will you suffer the loss of your mind, body, or spirit because of the demon. The compound is forever."

Catalina checked her watch. The red dots were almost kissing. She switched over to a timer. "The compound should begin working any minute now."

"You ignorant son of a—" Garamanthus said.

"Watch your language," Catalina said. She smirked at Cyrus. "There are children present."

Her eyes went to the door. She snapped her fingers and motioned for her men to move away from the door.

The storm door creaked open. Suddenly, a brown tower with a tilted pork pie hat, mink coat, and brown and orange gradient sunglasses stood in the doorway.

JoJo took a look around the pole barn, slack-jawed. "Now I've seen everything."

"You're just in time," Catalina said.

JoJo settled on Cyrus, who was on his knees with guns pointed at him.

"At least I know you weren't the informant," JoJo said.

"Aren't you a certified genius," Cyrus said under his breath.

The storm door creaked open again and two female frames stood on both sides of JoJo. Simone and Dominica. Simone was just as slack-jawed as JoJo. Dominica had a stoic expression.

"Looks like we got us some pigs, girls," JoJo said, grinning.

CHAPTER FIFTY-ONE

GARAMANTHUS WAS in full control of Becca, but her vision wavered. The events of the day began to simmer across her field of vision as if her reality were soup.

"No," Garamanthus said. "No!"

The demon's voice banged around in her head as her body stumbled backward, onto a couch.

"What's happening?" she asked.

Who was the man at the door?

Someone called him by his name. JoJo?

The man Cyrus had made a deal with.

Catalina. The woman Kirk had made a deal with.

Her heart pounded and her vision rippled.

"You will pay for this!" Garamanthus cried.

"I am not a commodity," Becca said in her mind. "I'm not an object. I'm tired of people deciding my fate without my consent! I'm tired of it!"

She screamed. Her voice ping-ponged around her mind, but then she realized that she was screaming in her own voice.

She had control. Her arms and legs felt weak, as if she hadn't used them in forever.

"I'm sick of all of this!" she cried.

She screamed again, and the next thing she knew, she was using all of those moves Garamanthus had taught her. She flew around the room with the intensity of a hawk. Two men crumpled to the floor underneath the fist and a kick.

"Minor side effect," Catalina said, shrugging.

"Side effect!" Becca cried. "I'm a person, not a lab animal!"

Instantly, Becca's hands closed around Catalina's throat. The woman's skin was warm, and Becca brought her face into Catalina's. Catalina looked at her with no fear.

"This too will pass, Becca," Catalina said. Her voice went soft. "Just hang in there."

"I can't stand this anymore!" Becca shouted.

A flurry of shapes darted around the pole barn. Cyrus jumped on one of the men and was giving him a piggyback ride, punching him on the head.

Aurora threw a frying pan across the living room, hitting one of the men in the nose.

JoJo stood in the middle of the room, unbuttoning his mink coat, like a man preparing for a casual boxing match.

"I'm sorry I had to do this to you," Catalina said. "But this is bigger than you. It's bigger than me. Let me go and I'll show you the way."

"I'm not joining your stupid order," Becca said, throwing Catalina to the floor.

Wham! Something hard hit Becca. It might as well have been a tree trunk. She fell back onto the couch and rolled onto the floor.

The woman in the long black winter coat and dark hair in a bun stood where Becca had been, a fist still outstretched.

Becca ran at her.

Something hit Becca again and she wheeled to the floor. Her mind reeled.

The woman in the winter coat. She had drop-kicked her. She didn't look like the type that knew martial arts.

"If you come at my sister again, I'll hit to kill," the woman said.

Someone screamed.

The woman in mink in the doorway had her hands to her cheeks, a gob-smacked look on her face. JoJo glowered at the woman in the winter coat.

"Say it ain't so, Dominica," JoJo said. "Say it ain't so."

The woman in the winter coat threw off her coat, exposing a flowing red dress. Catalina jammed the needle into the woman's arm and depressed it.

"I am so sick of being your girlfriend," Dominica said.

Kirk waited in the corner in the kitchen, watching the battle.

Everything was going according to plan. The woman in the red dress being Catalina's sister sure threw him for a loop too, but he was able to put two and two together. Catalina had let it slip when Dominica had called her.

Two sisters fighting to avenge their father. Maybe Catalina was right. Maybe there wasn't that much different between him and her. Either way, it didn't matter. His job was to make sure that the man in mink didn't pull any bullshit. Apparently, the guy was full of it.

In full BS fashion, JoJo pulled a gun from his mink coat and aimed it at Dominica. "I'm going to make sure that Hollywood gets you an Oscar," he said.

Kirk pulled out a pistol from his jacket and aimed it at JoJo's head.

"You need an Oscar for costume of the year," he said. "What are you, a pimp?"

The woman in the door wearing the mink coat cried out.

She stood in the door frame with a glossed-over expression in her eyes, like she was channeling something.

"Necromancer," she said. "Free and clear of demons. Freshly clean. Empty. Vessel. A shell of his former self."

"Those are the nicest things anyone has said to me all night," Kirk said. "When I'm done with your crazy boyfriend over here, I'll say a few things about you."

"You won't be saying anything, necromancer," the woman said. Her mink coat rose around her body as if invisible hands were pinching it and pulling it upward.

"How about we continue this conversation, just you and me!" she cried.

Something knocked the gun out of Kirk's hand.

JoJo. His girlfriend had distracted him. Kirk blocked a fist to his face and landed a punch into JoJo's gut. The blow barely fazed the man.

"A fighter!" he cried. "I'm ready to dance, sweetheart!"

Kirk swept a kick across the floor. JoJo fell onto his ass. Kirk spotted the gun a few feet away and sprang toward it.

Something slammed into him again. Something soft and hot.

Not JoJo. The big man was still on the ground, grinning. At first, the only thing he saw was a wall of fur. Scratch that— a floating wall of fur.

He blinked several times. JoJo's girlfriend hovered a few inches in the air. Her eyes glowed crimson and her voice doubled upon itself.

"Why let him dance with just one partner, baby?" she asked, her voice infested with a demon's timbre. "I was hoping this would be a ménage à trois affair." The corners of the woman's fur coat glowed with plasma shaped like mink heads. The heads' eyes glowed crimson and snapped at the air as she hovered toward Kirk.

~

JoJo laughed as Kirk tangoed with Simone.

This was his kind of fight. Wild. Unpredictable. And in his favor.

He trusted Simone to handle whoever the hell the guy in the sunglasses was. He glanced across the frenzied pole barn and spotted Catalina and Dominica standing shoulder to shoulder, staring right at him.

"You broke my heart, Dominica," JoJo said.

"This is the part where you say that you trusted me and how dare I, right?" Dominica asked.

"You just saved me a few words," JoJo said. "I appreciate that."

The cackling demons came alive in his head and he knew it was time. He cackled along with them as he lifted into the air. A wind blew out of nowhere and he laughed his head off as a twister began to form in the barn. Black slip shadows poured from his eyes and into the twister.

Dominica's and Catalina's faces turned worried in an instant as electric eyes appeared in the gray mist.

The demons yipped inside his mind. He waved a hand, and horned liquid wraiths poured out of the twister. Their teeth were dripping stalactites of blood and their claws were hunched toward their bodies like a T-Rex. They laughed uncontrollably as they blasted around the room like bottle rockets.

One by one, the wraiths rounded up Catalina's men, grabbing them by the collars and ripping them into the air. The men's screams were drowned out by the demons' laughter. The men begged for mercy as the demons dragged them into the twister. The barn erupted with the sound of cracking bones. Then, the screams were cut violently short, as if all the men slammed into a rock face at the same time.

Then, there were no henchmen. The liquid wraiths poured back into the twister, and the voices crescendoed in JoJo's head. Their leathery voices begged for more.

"Just wait your turn, guys and gals," JoJo said. "I'll let you out to play one by one." He held out his hands, laughed at the top of his lungs, and pointed at the two sisters. Inside the twister, the demon eyes narrowed and laughter electrified the air.

"What the heck is going on?" Cyrus asked. He grabbed his mother's hand and led her to the second floor of the barn. "Marty's going to kill me," Aurora said.

"We got bigger problems, Mom," Cyrus said, pointing to the living room.

JoJo was laughing like a maniac. Simone attacked Kirk. Her fur coat was something out of a Ghostbusters movie.

He pulled his mother further and deeper into the second floor. He bumped into someone.

Catalina and Dominica. They had climbed onto the second floor from the other side.

Cyrus jumped back and balled his fists. "Stay back!" he cried.

Two emerald glints caught his eye again. The skeleton necklaces.

Catalina and Dominica wore a matching set. He couldn't shake it, but he got the feeling that it wasn't a coincidence.

"Your sister ought to be grateful," Catalina said.

"I'll remind her if we both survive," Cyrus said.

A black shape dive-bombed out of the air and struck Catalina in the face. She staggered backward and cried out in pain.

Another black shape hurtled down from the rafters, hitting Dominica in the face.

Rocco and Luna in raven form. Both sisters beat back the birds as they pecked at their faces.

Rocco and Luna let out mad gronks.

Dominica drew a gun from her coat and jumped back.

"Sorry to do this," she said. Her finger inched toward the trigger, but something yanked the gun out of her hand.

A slow growl shook the floor. Desmond grabbed Catalina and launched her down into the living room. She landed on a couch and bounced to the floor, just under JoJo.

Desmond grunted with pain and fell to one knee.

Becca crawled through the carnage. She didn't know if she could stand.

She sensed the demons all around her with their electric eyes.

Garamanthus spoke. His voice was frenzied. "You must escape or they'll kill us both!" he cried.

"Who, the demons?"

"I tried to warn them, but they didn't listen! Now those demon hunters have gone and made a mess of things. You listen carefully, Becca. We'll get through this. And if we do—"

Becca huddled in the corner next to the television. "They said I don't have to listen to you anymore," she said.

"You may not *want* to, but you're going to—"

"They said I don't have to *listen* to you anymore," Becca said. She discovered her words as she spoke, as if they were revelations sent to her from somewhere else. "If you wanted to take control, you would have done it," she said.

"Shut up and obey me, you—"

"Ah, the true colors," Becca said. "You know what? I don't feel like listening to you today."

"You're going to get us killed!"

Becca stood and stood tall. A strange calmness ran through her like a rising creek in a rainstorm.

"I don't know what those sisters did to me," Becca said. "But if I die, I'm taking you with me."

She waved her hand at JoJo. "Hey! I'm here!"

Garamanthus's voice was suddenly small. Like a child's.

"Becca, you wouldn't do this, would you? After all we've been through?"

"That's exactly why I'm doing it," she said, swiping up an assault rifle nearby. She aimed it at JoJo's girlfriend.

JoJo saw her immediately and pointed at her, yelling. The twister of electric eyes swirled around her. The demon voices had dropped to whispers. They whispered her name.

"Becca. Becca. Becca."

A forceful wind parted the rifle from her hand, melting it into liquid metal on the carpet.

Becca screamed as the twister engulfed her.

~

"Bec!" Cyrus cried.

He had watched JoJo devour Catalina's henchmen in that twister. Now it was devouring Becca. The gray vortex with a hundred electric eyes washed over her.

He ran to the edge of the wooden railing on the second floor.

"You asshole!" Cyrus yelled at JoJo. "We had a deal!"

JoJo, who was floating in the air, turned to Cyrus. "And the deal's still on, kid."

Cyrus leaned on the railing, measuring the distance.

The twister was only about ten feet down. He could make it if he got a running start.

"Cyrus!" Aurora cried.

"Guys, watch yourselves!" Cyrus said to Desmond, Rocco, and Luna as he ran back and took off into a run.

He jumped into the air and landed on the railing for a

split second before throwing himself down into the living room.

The smell of fetid, acrid smoke hit him hard. Electric power sent static electricity crackling all over his body.

He held out his hands in front of his face as he flew into the wall of demon eyes.

<hr>

CHAPTER FIFTY-TWO

<hr>

THE LAYERED, chocolatey intensity of a Sumatran blend stirred in Becca's nose.

Her eyes were closed and heavy with slumber.

A lamp shone against her closed eyelids. She sensed the warmth and light, but she adjusted her head, nestling it deeper into her arms.

"Are you going to wake up or what?" a voice asked.

Cristián.

Becca opened her eyes. She had fallen asleep, her head in her arms like a kid playing heads-up 7-Up. The lamp on her eyes was one of the mason jar lights hanging over the bar.

She was in the Wicked Cat. Soft morning light streamed through the windows. The place looked as if it had never been attacked. Patrons breakfasted in the booths. In the kitchen, the microwave dinged.

Cristián sat on a stool next to her. His gaunt frame had returned to how she remembered it, like he hadn't been shot in the abdomen. His creamy hair and handsome Spaniard looks were back.

"Long night?" he asked. "Couldn't even make it up to your apartment, huh?"

Becca wiped drool from her face. She remembered the fight at the barn. "I was…fighting."

"You mean with Garamanthus and those demon hunters?" Cristián asked. "You must've really been dreaming. Becca, that was six months ago."

Cristián held up his phone, which showed a date on the lock screen. It was May.

She yawned, and her eyes focused. Chicago spring was in full bloom outside. A woman in a short sleeve blouse and shorts passed by as if in a hurry to her job. A couple strolled down the sidewalk, walking a French terrier. Lakes of sunlight radiated off car fenders.

There wasn't a single snowflake. Across the street, Logan Square Park was an intense pop of green, rustling with its music of swaying trees and leaves.

"Six months?" Becca asked.

Cristián watched her sympathetically. "Becca, the demon's gone. Cyrus saved you."

Grog splashed around in her head as she tried to remember.

"The Regulators repaired the Wicked Cat too," Cristián said. "You can't even tell that this place was in a fight."

In the kitchen, the microwave dinged again. Becca got a nagging feeling to go check. She hopped off the stool and sleep-walked into the kitchen. There was no one there.

Above the cooking counter, the LED control panel on the microwave beeped with "Done" in a reptilian green flashing on the screen. Smoke emanated from the corners of the door.

"Guys, you're going to set this place on fire!" Becca cried, irritated.

She started toward the microwave, but as she got closer, something didn't smell right.

A mixture of burnt popcorn and rotting trash hit her. She almost retched at the smell.

She covered her nose with the crook of her arm as she

opened the microwave. Thick smoke clouded her eyes and sent her into a violent, chest-rattling cough.

"What the hell is this?" she asked.

The yellow lights of the microwave illuminated an oblong shape no bigger than a bag of popcorn. The smoke cleared, and when she saw the horned demon's head with its gold, chipped teeth, rotting cobalt-blue flesh, and a giant cavity where a nose should have been, she felt as if she had been punched in the gut.

"Did you think this was a game?" Garamanthus asked.

A hand sprouted from the microwave and latched onto her wrist. "I just wanted to give you a false sense of security because you seem to have forgotten all I've done for you."

"Let me go!" she cried.

Garamanthus's head emerged from the microwave. It elongated and ballooned to twice its size. His horns dripped lava and the microwave elongated into a metallic blue, malformed trunk that reminded her of an ox.

"I will never forget this!" Garamanthus cried. "I will never forgive you!"

Becca pulled away, but the demon's iron grip was too strong. Garamanthus pushed her down and twisted her arm as she fell to the kitchen floor.

"Before I came along, you were just a snotty little girl masquerading as a woman," Garamanthus said. "These last six months, I gave you every skill you needed to survive. I taught you how to fight. I taught you how to talk your way out of problems. I taught you that you can't live in the light without just a little bit of darkness. And this is how you repay me."

Becca strained against the demon's grip but looked up at him resolutely.

"You taught me some things, but those weren't real lessons," she said. "You taught me that I am always better off believing in myself than someone else."

Garamanthus pulled her toward the back of the kitchen. "Then I've taught you nothing and I've wasted my time," he said. "Get on your feet and come with me."

Becca resisted, but the demon was too strong. He dragged her toward the back door and looked back at the door frantically. "Keep fighting me and maybe I'll kill you for real."

"I don't care what happens," Becca said. She swiped a soup spoon off a nearby rack and slammed it into the demon's face. The impact barely fazed him and bent the spoon back upon itself.

"You've got to do better than that!" Garamanthus cried, laughing.

He glanced back toward the door and quickened his pace.

Two hands clapped around Becca's waist and pulled her back. She yelled in surprise.

"Let her go!" Cyrus cried.

She couldn't see him, but she knew his voice.

"Cy?"

"I've got you," Cyrus said. "I promise this isn't an illusion. Pull back." Becca threw her weight into Cyrus.

"You foolish boy!" Garamanthus said. "She is mine!"

"She's her own person!"

Cyrus pulled her harder and she threw herself into his weight harder, stopping Garamanthus. Together, they pulled the demon back a few inches.

Garamanthus grunted as he fought them.

"Your time is up," Cyrus said.

"You just want to piss me off, don't you?" Garamanthus said, pulling Becca harder than he had before.

Becca tumbled forward, followed by Cyrus. The demon dragged her a full foot toward the door.

With a hind leg, Garamanthus kicked the back door open. A wall of blood oozed out of the door and into the kitchen. A thousand almond-shaped white eyes blinked open in the dripping blood. Distant laughter erupted beyond the door.

The sight sent a chill through Becca. She didn't want to find out what was beyond that door.

"That's what's waiting for you!" Garamanthus said. "That's what's waiting for both of us. I should've done this a long time ago. I should've killed you and found another host. You were a waste of time!"

"Bec, we can't go through that door!" Cyrus cried. "Trust me!"

"Cy, he's too strong," Becca said.

"We have to work together," Cyrus said.

Another voice sounded behind Cyrus. "I've got you, Cyrus. Keep pulling, honey!"

Her mom.

"Becca, don't give up!" Aurora said.

Suddenly, Becca felt as if she had an army behind her. She dug her boots into the tile floor and pushed backward. Garamanthus's hooves scratched the floor as they dragged him away from the bloodied door.

"More help is here," another voice said.

Desmond.

"Don't forget us!" a cheery voice said.

Luna. And Rocco.

"Hands off my friend, demon!" a final voice said.

Gilberto.

Becca didn't know why, but she wept as everyone pulled her as hard as they could.

Garamanthus cried in protest. "I will gut each one of you!"

"That's kind compared to what I want to do to you," Cyrus said, groaning.

"You won't have me," Becca said, hardening. "I have too many people fighting for me."

Garamanthus's eyes widened with fear.

Becca channeled her inner martial arts and jumped into

the air, landing a hard kick on the underside of Garaman-thus's chin. The demon staggered back and let go of her.

Becca clapped her hand around the demon's swarthy wrist now.

"This is *my* life!" she cried.

She pushed against Cyrus's pull, changing the direction of the tug.

"Bec, what the hell are you doing?" Cyrus asked.

She pushed Garamanthus toward the door. "This ends now! Help me push!"

Garamanthus wriggled against her, but Becca and the team overpowered him.

"You will carry guilt with you for the rest of your life," Garamanthus said. "I curse your name, and I call upon my brothers and sisters to find you and make your life miserable in this life and in the next—"

Becca landed a kick to the demon's knees, sending his hindlegs into the wall of blood.

Garamanthus wailed in agony as the wall began to slurp him up like a vacuum. His entire body convulsed and his wrist shook wildly in Becca's hand.

Suddenly, Becca was airborne. She lifted off the ground as the wall of blood sucked Garamanthus in.

Cyrus tightened his grip around her. "Bec, let go!"

"I want to make sure he's extra dead!" Becca said.

"Bec, not a good idea!" Cyrus said. "Let it go!"

"This is my only chance," Becca said, her eyes narrowing. "It's my only—"

"You have to let go!" Aurora cried. "This isn't what you think it is."

The wall of blood was up to Garamanthus's waist now. Still, the demon screamed in excruciating pain. His screams rang in her ears and sent the kitchen utensils clanging off the walls.

"God, this feels so good," Becca said.

She wanted to see Garamanthus burn for what he'd done to her. She was finally getting her wish, and she wanted nothing more than to see him suffer.

She swelled with pride. She was finally doing it. Finally showing him what she was capable of. Finally…embracing her dark side.

Her dark side…

She realized what she was doing.

What the hell *was* she doing?

The blood was up to Garamanthus's neck now.

Becca let go just as the wall of blood swallowed the demon's head. His arms went limp and retracted into the wall like noodles being slurped.

An explosion rippled from the wall and sent her flying backward. The kitchen collapsed around her as if it were made of toothpicks. She fell and fell and fell.

Then her world went dark.

CHAPTER FIFTY-THREE

JoJo PULLED Garamanthus's demon body from Becca's body like a long, syrupy string of cobalt-blue supernatural goop.

He yanked the last bit of the demon from Becca and hurled it to the floor. The twister of electric eyes and laughing demons jerked across the barn.

A tangle of bodies landed on the floor: Mr. Doesn't Matter and his sister, and a few others he didn't recognize. They weren't dead—just knocked out.

JoJo hovered across the room and set his sights on Garamanthus's swirling, dying body. The demon was forming slowly into a mass of blood, broken cobalt skin, and bone. The demon said nothing as it lay on the floor in defeat.

"Well, well," JoJo said. "You are a fun way to spend the night."

Simone giggled. She crawled across the floor, the demon minks on her coat sniffing and salivating over Mr. Doesn't Matter, who lay unconscious.

"Can I do it?" she asked. "Baby, let me do it…"

"Not him," JoJo said. "I want him to know that I kept my end of the bargain. "

"Fine," Simone said curtly. "Then let me have the others."
She gestured across the span of unconscious people.

JoJo squinted at them, then at her. "Maybe you ought to
chill for a minute."

A gun cocked. Out of the corner of his eye, Catalina
aimed an assault rifle at him.

"The demon is mine," she said.

"Who would have imagined that a demon hunter and a
demonsharp would be fighting over the rights to kill a *demon*,"
JoJo said. "Awfully ironic, isn't it?"

"I said he's mine," Catalina said.

"It's a personal affair, then," JoJo said. Still floating in the
air, he folded his arms and stroked his chin. "From the sound
of your voice, *very* personal."

The only thing that lay between JoJo and the two women
was the dying demon.

"I suppose this is how it's destined to be forever. Worse
than a game of cat and mouse. Demon and demon hunter,
forced to fight again and again until the world ends. Either
you destroy it or I do. Crying shame, if you ask me."

He rose higher into the air. "That doesn't sound like the
kind of world that anyone wants to live in," he said. "None of
these people here certainly do."

Catalina didn't take her eyes off him.

"But maybe there's a way we can end this amicably," he
said, opening a palm in Dominica's direction.

Dominica's body seized up. Her arms flew backward, her
back arched, and she lifted into the air. Her eyes froze open.

"Leave her alone!" Catalina barked.

"Why would I do that?" JoJo asked.

He willed the twister of demon eyes toward Dominica.

"The only reason I didn't kill that kid, his sister, and their
gang of friends was because the kid was smart enough to
make a deal with me. I might be an evil kind of guy, but I
always keep my word."

He closed his palm. A low cry escaped Dominica's lips.

"Here's the deal," JoJo said. "You want to kill this Garamanthus the Coward for some reason or whatever. Maybe he killed your husband. Or maybe he stole some money from you. Or maybe you're in a century-long feud. For all I know. The hell if I care. But you need him. You need to hold his last moments of life in your hands so you can snuff them out and make you feel better about yourself because of some deficiency you have. All you demon hunters are deficient in some way. Don't act like I don't know you. But I'm not exactly a wholesome guy either, you follow?"

Catalina gritted her teeth.

"You *do* follow. Right on. I've got your sister in the palm of my hand, and in a few seconds, I'm going to begin extracting the demon I put in her a few days ago."

JoJo twirled a finger and Dominica's body contorted into a U shape as a demon screamed within her. Slowly, a silver skein emerged from her shoulder and JoJo willed it to him.

"Oh, your poor, poor sister. Haven't I heard that before? You see, if you had come to me like an honorable person, we could have worked out our differences. We would have gone to war, but we could've set a date and time like armies did when armies were armies. But no—I drove you demon hunters out of town, and you had to go and act like a hydra. I cut your heads off, and then you come back sneakier than before. That's not how things are done in *my* city."

He paused longer than usual. He couldn't quite tell, but Catalina's blood had to be pumping. He was loving every minute of this.

Meanwhile, Lord Traxus was curling out of Dominica's shoulder like tagliatelle in a pasta machine.

"Soon, I'll have my demon back, and your sister will be so weak that my girl will finish her off. They don't get along, if you didn't realize—but I can end all of this on one condition."

He grinned. "I'll let your sister off the hook if you agree to a permanent cease fire."

Catalina's eyes were so wild, they might as well have bugged out of her head.

"Cease fire!" she cried.

"Where I'm from, it means that I won't try to kill you, and you won't try to kill me. Again, an old army thing. But look at the flip side: you get the satisfaction of killing cowardly Garamanthus, who frankly did a wonderful job of handing himself to you on a golden platter, and I get my city back. Find yourself some other demonsharp to hunt."

"We exist to kill your kind," Catalina said.

"That sounds suspiciously like a declination," JoJo said. "You're going to let me kill your dear old sister over a demon who was already dying?"

He twirled his finger faster, accelerating Lord Traxus's exit from Dominica's body.

Simone approached Dominica, licking her lips. The minks in her coach shrieked with delight.

"Three seconds left to make your decision," JoJo said.

Catalina didn't budge. Her finger inched toward the trigger.

"Three. One!" JoJo cried. He grabbed the demon's skein and ripped it violently, throwing Dominica into Catalina just before she pulled the trigger. The two women toppled to the ground.

Simone was on top of Dominica in an instant. Then she was flying through the air with her hands across Dominica's neck. The two women crashed into the wall and there was a sickening crunch of bones. Simone stood, laughing. Dominica lay sputtering at her feet, then stopped moving.

A tear jumped into Catalina's eyes as she scrambled for the rifle.

"No!" she cried.

"A date with destiny!" JoJo said. "We're going to fight

forever, then. Deep down, I knew you would never turn away from a fight."

He grabbed a knife from the inside of his mink coat. He zoomed across the room and impaled the demon in the neck.

Garamanthus opened his mouth into a soundless scream. The demon's sinewy muscles twitched as JoJo twisted the blade. Then his body broke into a million black wisps that fluttered up into the ceiling like bats before shattering out of existence.

Catalina roared. She crawled feverishly toward the gun.

JoJo pointed at the gun. Lord Traxus, who was now an amorphous shadow with glowing red eyes, scooped the rifle off the ground and hurled it across the barn.

Catalina was on her knees now.

"No," she said softly.

"How do you want to do this, sweetheart?" JoJo asked, touching down on the floor. "You can go crying or you can go screaming."

A dark hand pulled Catalina up by her collar.

"I've got you," the necromancer said, huddling his body close to hers. He had come out of nowhere, like a snake hiding in the bushes.

"Big mistake," JoJo said, his anger rising.

Then, he saw that not everything was as it seemed.

The necromancer stared JoJo in the eye and put a finger to his mouth. Then he spoke to Catalina while surreptitiously slipping the necklace off her neck.

JoJo watched them curiously.

CHAPTER FIFTY-FOUR

"I'm at your command," Kirk said. Catalina was so close to him that he could smell the sunflower perfume on the nape of her neck.

A silver, legless spirit flew around the room, wailing and confused.

Dominica. Kirk knew a fresh spirit when he saw one. They were usually disoriented and shocked. Somewhere deep down, he felt just a little sorry for the woman. No one ever saw death coming. At least, not most.

Like his brother. There was a man who knew death. He eased into the next phase of existence like a seal into water.

He channeled his brother. Years ago, Aidan had taught him how to pick pockets. It was all about misdirection. Fooling the other person's brain to focus on something while you performed the act…

"We're in this together if you want your family back," Catalina said.

"And I'm here," Kirk said, jiggling the clasp on the skull necklace at the center of Catalina's neck. "You asked me what I was willing to do to get them back. You got your answer."

The clasp came undone.

"I'm starting to come around to your way of thinking," he said. He glanced up at JoJo. "Maybe you're right, Catalina: everyone in life gets their comeuppance, if it's not in this life."

Catalina puffed. "Sure took long enough to teach you."

The necklace slid off her neck silently and Kirk palmed the skeleton.

He backed away from her.

"I'll take JoJo and you take his girlfriend," Catalina said. "We'll fight on my mark."

Kirk said nothing, backing away further.

"Kirk?"

Kirk held up the necklace and jangled it between his fingers. Catalina spotted it instantly and clutched her bare neck.

"Damn it," she said under her breath.

"This is a beautiful piece of jewelry," Kirk said. He finally had the prison that contained his father and brother. He held their literal souls in his hand. The sharp edges of the skull's emerald eyes glowed with their spirits.

"On second thought, JoJo," Kirk said, eyeing the necklace. "She's all yours."

JoJo laughed uncontrollably. "Either this is the best act of all time or you just got bamboozled, demon hunter."

"You think you can save them?" Catalina asked Kirk. "That's a warded necklace, you idiot. Only my sister and I know the counterspell."

She tilted her head toward Dominica's dead body. "And if you haven't noticed, my sister's dead."

"Minor detail," Kirk said. "And not a big deal at all."

He pointed to Lord Traxus, who sat at JoJo's feet. The demon was a glowing, hulking mass of roiling shadows energy with horns.

"Hey, demon," Kirk said. "Want to have some fun?"

Lord Traxus stood.

JoJo started to protest, but Kirk said, "I know the game,

man. Don't worry. I'm not stealing him from you. Just give me a minute. You're a man of your word and I'm a man of mine. You and your girl aren't my enemies and I'm not yours."

JoJo watched him quietly, then motioned for him to continue.

"Two minutes," Kirk said, holding out a palm.

Lord Traxus obeyed and streamed into Kirk's body with the force of a hard punch. The impact made Kirk stagger backward.

He didn't feel so empty anymore.

He felt…normal. The demon swirled inside him and settled into his soul. He felt invincible.

"You know the woman's brain," Kirk said. "Tell me the counterspell."

"No!" Catalina cried.

Lord Traxus laughed. "A wise man. I was beginning to think that all of the knowledge I accumulated in her mind was useless."

The demon took control of Kirk's body and held the necklace up to his eyes. He said a quiet spell in French, and the necklace shimmered with light.

The emerald eyes flashed like green fire as two souls poured out.

"We're baaaaaaaack!" Bruce cried, zipping around the barn like a frenzied bird. His spirit was colorless, and Kirk could only made out the outlines of his father's legless form. No one else would have been able to hear him. "If I still had a body, I'd rip that crazy woman apart—I told you we were going to run into trouble—hey, what the hell's going on, son?"

"It's pretty clear, Dad," Aidan said. His soul circled Kirk. "Kirk saved us, and now he needs help."

"Bingo," Kirk said. "You always caught on quick, brother."

He smiled. "Glad to have you two back. I was starting to miss our banter."

"Starting?" Aidan asked.

Kirk pointed to JoJo. "Hey, man, don't let me hold you up."

JoJo nodded.

"I'll kill you all!" Catalina cried.

JoJo sent the twister of demons into Catalina. She roared as the demons devoured her.

Kirk looked away and put two fingers in his ears. Even that didn't muffle Catalina's cries and the sounds of bones cracking.

The demons laughed crazily as they ravaged Catalina's body. Then, the twister dissipated like fog on a sunny day.

All went quiet around the barn. Cyrus, Becca, and the others began to stir.

"One last thing," Kirk said. He held up the necklace and Lord Traxus spoke an incantation.

Catalina's and Dominica's spirits whirled around the barn, wailing. Death had taken them by surprise.

"Everybody gets their comeuppance," Lord Traxus said, speaking for Kirk.

The emerald necklace glowed. Catalina and Dominica's souls cried as they drifted toward the skull's emerald eyes. The necklace was like a magnet sucking them in. Soon, each soul entered an eye, and in a lightning flash, they disappeared. The emerald eyes glowed like dying embers with the last remnants of their souls, then went dark.

Kirk jingled the necklace. Lord Traxus streamed out of his body in a long, spaghetti-like fashion and back into JoJo, who accepted the demon with a snort like he had just taken a line of cocaine.

Kirk staggered backward.

"Thanks, brother," Kirk said.

JoJo saluted him. "I don't know you, but I'm glad we were on the same page."

"Baby, why can't I kill them?" Simone asked, pouting over Cyrus.

Joe just snapped his fingers. "I'm not going to go over this again, Simone. Get off the floor, swallow those mink, and let's ride."

JoJo pointed to Kirk.

"Do you know these people?" he asked.

"Depends on what you mean by the word 'know'," Kirk said.

"You let them know that I could have ended all of them, but I didn't because of the sign from the universe," JoJo said.

"Sign?" Kirk asked.

JoJo spread his hands out across the barn. "I've concluded that life is just a latticework of signals. It's no coincidence that you, me, those demon hunters, Mr. Doesn't Matter, and the rest of this crew all met over the last few days," JoJo said. "I happen to think it's a sign of something. Tell that kid the rest of our deal is off. I'm feeling benevolent tonight. He saved me from an all-out war. Tell him—may we never meet again."

Simone stood. She clasped the buttons on her mink coat and primped her hair. "There you go with those signs again," she said. "The only sign you should be following is mine, because I told you that Dominica was nothing but trouble."

JoJo put his arms around Simone and kissed her on the cheek. "Okay, I was wrong. There were two signs tonight. Yours, and the one I was thinking about."

"Which is?" Simone asked.

"How about you show me when we get to the limo?"

JoJo and Simone laughed as they walked out of the barn.

Cyrus opened his eyes. Uncle Marty's barn was in tatters. The place looked like a bomb exploded.

Oh boy. Uncle Marty was going to murder his mom.

He sat up and put a hand on his head.

His mind was swimming. If what he saw was correct, he had just been inside of his sister's mind. No—her spirit.

Holy crap…

He looked around immediately for Becca. She lay on the carpet. A giant bloody gash festered on her shoulder.

He ran to Gilberto and shook him awake. "Hey, we've got to heal Bec."

Gilberto startled. "Whoa, that was trippy," he said.

He spotted Becca and immediately ran to her, pulling out his leather healer's pouch.

"It's going to be okay, Becca," Gilberto said.

His mom, half straddling the couch, woke up.

He knelt in front of her. "We did it, Mom," he said, taking her by the shoulders. "We saved Becca."

Aurora's eyes went to Becca. "She's hurt," she said, concerned.

Cyrus grinned. "Nothing Gilberto can't handle."

He glanced around the barn.

"Where's JoJo? Where's Catalina?"

"I took care of them for you," a voice said. Kirk leaned against the wall, tossing Catalina's skull necklace from palm to palm. He grinned widely at Cyrus.

"You!" Cyrus said, balling his fists.

"Chill out," Kirk said. "Normally, I wouldn't stick around for tearful reunions, but I owe this one to your sister."

Cyrus relaxed a little. Something in the necromancer's body language told him that there wasn't going to be a fight. Kirk was relaxed. Almost euphoric.

"I want you to tell your sister something for me," Kirk said. "I want you to tell her that I'm sorry. I didn't mean to lie to her and get her blood pressure up. But I had no choice. Catalina was holding my dad and brother hostage, and I think you can relate to the fact that I had to do what I had to do to save my family."

Cyrus didn't know what to say.

Kirk pushed off from the wall. "Oh, and that weird guy—JoJo and his crazy girlfriend—he wanted me to give you a message, Cyrus. His girlfriend was hell-bent on killing you while you were still asleep. JoJo told her no. He wanted me to make sure that you knew that he spared your lives. He also told you that the deal is off. He said it was a thank you for helping him destroy those demon hunters. And he also said—what was the quote—oh, right. He also said that may the two of you never meet again."

Cyrus breathed a sigh of relief. He was prepared to give JoJo six months of his life. But if Kirk could be trusted, now he didn't have to.

"Thanks?" Cyrus asked, confused that the words were coming out of his mouth to Kirk MacLeod, of all people.

Kirk saluted Cyrus. "Sometimes, enemies can be allies. By the way, Bruce and Aiden say hi."

The ground shook.

"What's that?" Aurora asked.

Cyrus frowned at Kirk.

"I hope you weren't buttering me up," Cyrus said. "Because if you were—"

Kirk glanced around the barn, just as curious as Cyrus.

"I meant what I said," Kirk said. "No bullshit—"

Boom!

An impact threw Cyrus across the barn. A tornado of timber, glass, and furniture flew across Cyrus's vision and he covered his eyes.

Everyone screamed.

Then all went quiet again as the barn settled and groaned.

"What the hell?" Cyrus asked.

In the middle of the barn, Bart's L train with the drill on the front hung in suspension, tunneled up from the earth.

Smoke drifted off the lead car.

The doors slid open and Bart and Wendy jumped out with shovels at the ready in an attack stance.

"We had a heck of a time finding this place!" Bart cried. "We came as soon as you called. Mr. Grant, are you okay?"

Cyrus laughed. "I'm fine, and it's great to see you guys, but I didn't call you."

"We're so glad you're safe, dear," Wendy said, throwing her shovel aside. She threw herself into him and hugged his waist. Her soft, earthy smell was a welcome relief. He hugged her back.

"I'm glad you guys weren't here," Cyrus said. "Things got pretty dangerous for a while. But if I didn't call you, who did?"

"I called them," Desmond said. He held up a metal cone and pewter whistle.

"You called them?!!!" Cyrus cried. His face contorted like an anime character's, and his world turned into a pinwheel of yellow and red for a few seconds as he said the words and stared daggers at Desmond. "How the hell do you know them?!!"

Bart scratched his head. "Heh."

Wendy backed away from Cyrus cautiously. "I guess you spilled the beans, Bart."

"What do you mean spilled the beans?" Cyrus muttered.

Desmond put a hand on Cyrus's shoulder. "Cyrus, we've got a lot to talk about. But you didn't really think I would let you do all of this by yourself, did you?"

"You knew all along?" Cyrus asked. "You knew about JoJo?"

"JoJo was Desmond's idea," Rocco said.

"What?!!" Cyrus asked.

"No offense, Cyrus, but you have a big mouth," Desmond said. "And Becca had Garamanthus listening at all times. We had to engage JoJo secretly without Becca knowing. I'm sorry for the subterfuge. You did a helluva job."

Cyrus hung his head. "I'm just a puppet…"

"You saved your sister," Desmond said. "I wasn't the one who rescued her at the Montclair Hotel. I didn't negotiate with JoJo. You did that. I just made sure you had a little firepower."

Cyrus hooked a thumb at Wendy and Bart. "You mean firepower of the three-foot-tall variety?"

"We take offense to that," Bart said, standing tall. "We're three-and-a-half feet."

Cyrus screwed his face at Bart and Wendy. "So… You told me that you served Murgalen."

"And we did," Wendy said. "Terrible mistress."

"You said you knew me," Cyrus said.

"*After* Desmond told us about you," Wendy said. "And we were pleased to know about all your endeavors that helped us be free."

Cyrus shook his head. "Damn. I can't believe this."

Wendy took his hand. "I do hope we can still be friends, dear."

A pile of wooden timbers nearby shifted, and Kirk pulled himself out of the rubble.

"You guys sure know how to party," he said. He stopped, studying the gnomes.

"I didn't die and go to heaven, did I?" he asked.

"No, we're still alive," Cyrus said. "Though I might die of a heart attack in a minute."

"Gnomes," Kirk said. "I've always heard of you, but never met in person."

"Pleased to meet you," Wendy said.

"Hey, nice necklace!" Bart said.

"This?" Kirk asked, jingling the skull necklace. "I hate this thing. You can have it."

Kirk tossed the necklace to Bart.

"This would go great in the vault," Bart said. "Beautiful

emeralds. We'll take good care of this. This is right up our alley, mister! What do I owe ya?"

"Free of charge," Kirk said. He stood in the doorway, slipped on his sunglasses, nodded at Cyrus, then vanished into the night.

Bart slid the necklace around Wendy's neck. "Early Christmas present."

"Oh, Bart," Wendy said, blushing. She pulled him into a long kiss.

Cyrus took another look around the barn—at Gilberto healing Becca, his mom watching with concern, Desmond with his arms folded, Rocco and Luna straddling chairs in the kitchen, the gnomes waddling around the barn in awe, and Bart and Wendy kissing, and he exploded into laughter.

CHAPTER FIFTY-FIVE

One Week Later

JoJo lit up a joint, sucked in heady marijuana smoke, and leaned back in his executive chair. He tilted his head back at the ceiling and blew a ring of smoke.

He'd never noticed his ceiling before. Acoustic tiles. The tiles, normally beige, were almost orange from all the smoke. As his high kicked in, he could have sworn that one of the water spots on the tile looked like a galaxy.

He laughed to himself.

He'd destroyed those damned demon hunters. He'd made good with Simone and she was back to her usual mood, which was to say she was only just a little somber, but happy when they were together.

What a relief. If he'd learned anything, it was to keep his main squeeze his main squeeze.

He closed his eyes. The demons in his mind came alive.

"You were lucky to get out of that ordeal," the leader said.

"We're going over this again?" JoJo asked. "Let it go."

"At least you took our advice to hire someone to shore up the structural weaknesses around this place."

"No more rats," JoJo said. "This place is as secure as the Mona Lisa now."

"Good."

The demon's voice flickered away as someone knocked on the door.

Simone stood in the doorway in a frayed jean skirt and a white t-shirt.

"Someone's here to see you, baby," she said.

JoJo frowned. "If it's that vacuum guy, tell him to beat it."

"Not him," Simone said, sauntering over to the desk. She grabbed his blunt and took a puff. She ran her fingers along his chest and stood behind him. Her touch relaxed him and made him feel like he was an old Egyptian pharaoh being caressed by his queen.

A man appeared at the door. A middle-aged man. He held a baseball cap in his hands. His day-old stubble, frightened eyes, and a meek aura told JoJo all he needed to know.

"Right on," JoJo said.

"Mr. JoJo?" the man asked after a while.

"What can I do for you?" JoJo asked.

The man began to tell him a story. Some sob story about someone after his family or whatever. Something about needing protection. The man's voice droned on.

At least Simone was listening. She ran her hands along JoJo's neck. That was their new signal. Physical contact meant the asker was a keeper. Another servant in his army of demon holders.

JoJo separated from her and motioned for the man to continue as he headed for the door.

"…and I was hoping you could help me," the man said finally.

"Is that right?" JoJo asked.

The demons came alive in his mind again, laughing like jackals.

"For Pete's sake, contain yourselves," JoJo said.

"Excuse me?" the man asked.

Simone giggled.

"Don't worry, my man," JoJo said. "I talk to myself sometimes."

He shut the door and locked it.

"Sounds like you want to get into some trouble," he said, grinning.

Kirk lay shirtless on a beach chair in the blinding, merciless Mexican sun, reading the last pages of his space opera novel.

"Deep down inside our hearts, no matter how much pain we've endured, the love light is as bright as a star. Our hearts don't operate in zero magnitude, Devi. You just have to learn to embrace what's inside."

Devika entered new coordinates into the ship's navigation system and gripped the joystick tightly.

She pulled on the joystick hard, and in the column of hyperspace, the ship did a one-hundred-and-eighty-degree turn.

Then she blasted off into the endless stream of purple, toward another part of the galaxy, toward the fate of someone who she'd never met but who desperately needed her help.

TO BE CONTINUED…

Kirk stayed on the final words a moment. The roar of the ocean waves nearby swelled around him as a flock of seagulls flew over him. A little girl toddled by, followed by a mom in a bikini speaking German. This resort—a new one on the other side of the country—was just as lovely as the first one.

Kirk turned the page. There was…nothing. Not a thing. The book just ended.

The line about hearts in zero magnitude…Funny how the universe spoke to him sometimes.

And To Be Continued? He bought this book at an old bookstore, took all these years to read it, and To Be Continued was all he got?

Kirk expelled air and tossed the book aside. It landed in the sand. The author needed writing lessons.

"Ah, you've become an erudite man," Bruce said, hovering next to him. His father's spirit was almost invisible in the cool blue sky.

"Worst book I've read," Kirk said.

"*Only* book you've read," Aidan said, hovering next to him.

Kirk tipped his sunglasses at his brother. "Don't lecture me again about my lack of interest in women. You can see how that worked out."

"Ha!" Aidan said. "Catalina sure fooled me. I still love Mexico, though."

"We're grateful, son," Bruce said. "If you hadn't come to the rescue, we would have been stuck in that necklace forever. It was just awful!"

Kirk swiped a martini glass off the sandy concrete and downed the last of the bitter clear drink. It screamed down his throat, in a good way.

"What was it like in there, Dad?" Kirk asked.

"Like a genie stuck in a bottle," Bruce said. "In a lead bottle where the only thing you can hear is your own voice."

"I would have thought that was heaven for you, Dad," Kirk said, winking.

"Funny," Bruce said flatly.

"So what *did* you come all the way down here to do if you're not interested in dating?" Aidan asked.

"Haven't figured it out yet," Kirk said. "But without any demons, I'm so light, I could fly away."

"Shall we go on the hunt for one, then?" Bruce asked.

"Naw, Dad. I think I like it this way."

"That woman poisoned your brain," Bruce said.

"If she poisoned me, then I wouldn't have saved you. Ever thought about that?"

"You're making good points today, son."

"Just today, eh?" Kirk asked. "All right, I'll stop ribbing you."

He started down a long, paved path that wound down to a beach. People were speckled on the beach here and there, lying on towels and building sandcastles. He took in the salty breeze. His brother and father swirled around him.

"I was hoping maybe we could just enjoy each other's company," Kirk said. "Just chill and talk. Like we used to do in the old days."

"Now you're talking," Aidan said. "God, what I could do with a body again…"

"But tell me something, son," Bruce asked. "Is this it for you? Or will you continue the sacred family art of necromancy?"

"Sacred necromancy?" Aidan asked. "Dad, being inside that skull really did a number on you."

"Pshaw!" Bruce said. "Answer the question!"

Kirk made it to the sand. He waded into the waves and stared out at the vanishing point where the ocean met the sky and clouds.

"Is this the end of Kirk MacLeod, the necromancer?" Bruce asked again more forcefully.

"It's not the end," Kirk said, "It's just…To Be Continued."

"What the hell is that supposed to mean?" Bruce asked.

Kirk let himself fall back onto the sand. The waves enveloped him up to his chin.

"I have no idea," he said, "and that's exactly where I want to be right now."

"Becca, I'm speechless."

Becca lay on Carolyn Davidson's leather couch, comfortable as a baby in a womb. She had told the therapist everything while staring at the copper tin ceiling she loved so much. An essential oil diffuser threw gentle notes of eucalyptus and orange into the air.

Becca closed her eyes. "I'm free."

She swung up and adjusted her bandanna. Her shoulder gave off a flare of pain that quickly subsided. The gash was almost healed and looking better every day. It was going to leave a scar, but she could live with that.

For the first in a long time, she felt back to her normal self. No demon seizing her insides. No constant interruption of her thoughts. No tears. Just herself and her own thoughts. She had forgotten what that felt like.

"I am astounded by your progress," Carolyn said. "You're going to have me scribbling notes for days."

"I brought you something," Becca said, grabbing a gift bag from a tote bag she brought. She handed Carolyn a black bag of Costa Rican whole bean roasted coffee, one of her favorites that she served at the Wicked Cat.

"This is so sweet," Carolyn said.

"It's the least I can do," Becca said. She smiled. "Thanks for listening to me. I think I'm going to be okay now, Carolyn."

"I think so too, Becca Grant."

Becca rose. She hated that this was probably the last time she'd visit Carolyn. She was going to miss this homey greystone. She took another look at the Christmassy interior and told herself she would never forget this place.

Carolyn escorted her to the door, and Becca slid on her duffel coat.

"Can I ask you something?" Becca asked. "I know it might be rude, but I just have to know."

"Ask away," Carolyn said.

"What type of paranormal are you?"

A wide smile broke across Carolyn's face.

"I'm what you might call a hybrid," she said. "I'm part white witch, part psychic, and part dream mage."

"Whoa," Becca said. "Crazy."

Carolyn opened the door. "I wish you all the best, Becca."

It was unseasonably warm for the holidays. The sun was shining and melting the snow. Bits of grass poked through the yard. As soon as Becca unlatched the wrought-iron gate, she turned back to the home. Sure enough, the greystone was replaced with a simple two-story frame house. No one was home.

Becca shook her head, laughed to herself, then began the short walk back to the Wicked Cat.

The Wicked Cat was back to its regular wicked self. Desmond had pulled some strings and had the place magically repaired. You couldn't even tell that a battle had taken place there.

Becca stood on the corner and watched her shop. The patrons eating croissants and drinking coffee, the waiters buzzing around, and the steady stream of people coming in and out of the front door.

She had built this place.

The building was an empty space when she'd bought it. She had walked through it and envisioned what it could be. And here it was. One of the best coffee shops and bars in Logan Square, maybe Chicago. And *she* built it.

Why hadn't she ever thought about it before? Maybe because she was too busy doing.

It was good to slow down every once in a while. Maybe that was the real lesson Garamanthus had taught her. When it was all said and done, the most important thing was the people you loved and what you did for them.

The only reason she was standing on this corner, admiring what she had done, was because there was one person in particular inside the Wicked Cat who loved her and was willing to sacrifice his life, just as she would have done for him.

Her brother sat at one of the tables by the window. He saw her and waved.

"Hey, Becca's back!" Rocco said as Becca walked through the door.

Rocco, Luna, Cyrus, Desmond, Aurora, and Gilberto were sitting at a table.

Luna hooked an arm under Rocco's. "You look radiant, Becca."

"Thanks," Becca said.

"It's oozing off you," Cyrus said.

"Oozing?" Becca asked, staring at him flatly.

Cyrus made a sorry face and shrugged. "You know what I meant."

"Yep, bud, I follow ya," Rocco said. "But Luna's right. It's so good to see you back to normal. Luna, we'd better go. Desmond's got us on a flying mission."

Rocco downed the last of his scotch, fist-bumped Cyrus, and touched Becca on the shoulder gently.

"Good luck with the apartment tour," Luna said to Cyrus.

Becca slid into a chair across from Cyrus.

"Your wound's healing nicely," Gilberto said. "Your mobility is pretty good today. Remind me to give you some more of that blend I made you yesterday."

"Done," Becca said.

Desmond drank a glass of rum. "I was just educating everyone here on the virtue of peace and quiet. I hope we can enjoy it for the holidays."

"Amen to that," Becca said.

"There's always a chance of the world going south before Christmas," Cyrus said.

Becca balled up a nearby napkin and flicked it at him.

"Hey!"

"If that happens, find somebody else to be your partner in crime," she said. "I'm done."

Desmond checked his watch. "Gilberto, I'm headed to your side of town. Need a lift?"

Gilberto grabbed his coat. "That would be great. *Beverly Hills Cop* is on tonight and I don't want to miss it."

"I hope the repairs are to your liking, Becca," Desmond said, sliding on his leather trench.

"It's perfect, Desmond," she said.

Desmond winked at her. "We'll try to keep it this way from now on."

Desmond and Gilberto said goodbye and left, leaving Cyrus, Becca, and Aurora.

"So, how was therapy?" Cyrus asked.

"Do tell," Aurora said. "Was Carolyn just as flabbergasted as I expected?"

"More," Becca said.

She recapped the session as Cristián brought a fresh round of drinks and pretzels.

Her, her mom, and Cyrus. Just as it always should be.

Cyrus's watch beeped, pulling him from Becca's story.

He had found an apartment a few blocks away, and he had told the manager that he wanted a tour.

"Crap," he said. "I've gotta go."

"The tour?" Becca asked. "You sure you don't want us to come with you?"

"I wanna see it for myself first," he said.

"My son is growing up," Aurora said.

Cyrus kissed his mom and sister on the cheek, dashed upstairs to the apartment to grab his electric board, and he booked it to the address the apartment manager gave him.

"What do you think?" the apartment manager asked. She was a short Bosnian woman in a business suit and brown hair in a bun.

Cyrus stood in the middle of a studio apartment with exposed brick walls and creamy brown hardwood floors. The place sported a stainless steel fridge and dishwasher, a nice view of the street two stories down, and track lighting. The place was only three hundred square feet. Tiny, but big enough for him.

"The rent is *how much* again?" he asked.

The woman told him. He did the math in his head. With the paychecks from the Regulators, part-time work with Fontanelli, and occasional waiting tables at the Wicked Cat, the place was well within his budget. Sure, it wasn't the nicest building in the world, but it was nice enough.

"Holy crap, I think I can afford this place," he whispered to himself.

"What was that?" the manager asked.

"Nothing," he said. He shook her hand. "I'll take it."

As they walked out, the manager told him the rules. By the time they made it to the parking lot, she promised him he could move in next week.

She left him staring up at the giant brick tenement building with a massive courtyard.

There was one last thing he had to check.

He strolled down the alley behind the building and stopped at the dumpsters. Several brown shapes caught his eye.

Brown rats raced under a dumpster.

"No need to run," he said. He crouched down and

watched as the rats scampered across the ground, and away from him.

It wasn't an apartment in Chicago without rats in the alley. But he could use that to his advantage. He bet his rat self could find ways in and out of the building that no one even knew about. It would help if a villain ever paid him an unexpected visit.

He stood and stretched.

It was a good day for a ride. The roads were slightly wet from melting snow, but all the ice was gone. On the way here, he had gotten some serious speed and caught all the green lights too, leaning into his board and swerving between cars. He checked the battery level on his board. Plenty of juice left to cruise around Logan Square. His kind of day.

He threw his board down and hopped on. He crouched down and hit the acceleration button on his remote.

Then, a dazzle of green out of the corner of his eye. A woman crossing in front of him. She didn't see him.

"Crap!" he cried.

He swerved, struck a dumpster, and rolled across the ground.

"Ow!" he said, rubbing his arm. He had several scratches.

"Oh my God!" the woman cried, running to him. "Are you okay?"

He glanced up at her.

She was breathtaking. She was a Latina with a ponytail off to one side. She wore a green coat. Her big brown eyes studied him for broken bones.

"I'm sorry. I didn't see you."

"No worries," he said, standing up. "I should have been watching out."

The woman sighed with relief.

"Cool board," she said.

"I can't live without it," he said, patting it lovingly. He took off his helmet and ran a hand through his hair.

"Do you live here?" he asked.

She nodded.

"Wait, I think I recognize you," she said, tapping her chin. Cyrus stared in her brown eyes, and they were so beautiful, he almost lost his focus. "I know! I've seen you at the Wicked Cat."

Cyrus rubbed the back of his head. "Yeah. That's my sister's coffee shop and bar."

"A few of my friends have started going there recently," she said. "It's a good place for…you know…"

"Paranormals?" Cyrus asked, raising an eyebrow.

She smiled. "You said it, not me."

Now his mind was wild trying to figure out what type of paranormal she was. He was determined to find out.

"I'm moving in," he said. "And it's nice to meet a neighbor and—you know."

He extended a hand. She smiled and took it, then asked what it was like to ride on the board. He told her that it saved him on more than one occasion on supernatural missions. Her eyes widened with intrigue and she twirled a strand of kinky hair and bit her bottom lip.

What a crazy year, he told himself as they stood in the alley flirting. *I'm going to love living on my own!*

He waited for the perfect opening, then cracked a cheesy joke.

She laughed, and he laughed with her, grinning wide.

THE END.

AFTERWORD

So concludes Cyrus Grant's adventures (for now?)…

I had a blast writing *The Chicago Rat Shifter*. This afterword is a behind-the-scenes look at how this series came to be and some fun facts.

Inspiration for the Series

All of my series begin with a mix of weird, seemingly unrelated inspirations.

(1) A killer song lyric

A single song lyric inspired this entire series when I first heard it in 2019. It's from "Apartment", a song by The Free Nationals featuring Benny Sings on vocals, from the Free Nationals' self-titled debut album (which was my favorite R&B album of that year).

The opening lyric to the song is "It was a long and sad goodbye / but now it's time to pick up the pieces / I have to leave my sister's couch today…"

The song is about a guy who is looking for an apartment after a bad breakup, sleeping on his sister's couch, and wanting to rebuild his life. That describes Cyrus Grant exactly when we first meet him in *Dead Rat Walking.* (The final scene in *Year of the Rat* brings everything full circle. He finally finds that apartment, and it's everything he could have dreamed of. He's a lot more mature too.)

(2) frustration finding a book to read

The idea to make Cyrus a rat shifter came one day after I was looking for some urban fantasy to read, but I kept stumbling across shifter romance novels. I enjoy romance novels, but I've always thought the shifter stuff is a little over the top. Especially the book covers. I came up with the idea for a rat shifter as a tongue-in-cheek response to all the wolves, lions, tigers, and bear shifters out there. I wrote the book that would have interested me on that lazy afternoon: a non-romantic shifter story where the main character is not an alpha, and is a different kind of animal.

But…why rats?

(3) an unforgettable Chicago memory

Years ago, my wife and I visited a friend in Chicago. She lived in Bucktown, which is a trendy neighborhood on the north-west side, not too far from Logan Square. One night, we were walking to dinner at dusk and we had to pass through the alley behind her condo. The ground was crawling with rats. They swarmed the dumpsters for food, and there were so many of them that they didn't care about the humans passing by.

I had to give my wife a piggyback ride through alley. She was terrified of the rodents. I was fascinated.

A few years later, we traveled to New York City for the first time. My wife was nervous about seeing rats again, but we didn't see a single rat. In fact, we saw more rats in Chicago than we ever saw in New York City. That always stuck with me.

My stories always start with what-if questions. "What if there was such a thing as a rat shifter? How could something like that happen? Who in their right mind would *choose* to become a rat? What if they were turned into a rat against their will instead?"

After that, the story took care of itself. So, in summary, this series came into being because:

1. an old memory (2015)

2. a browsing session on Amazon that went nowhere, and (2018)

3. A song lyric that described a character that intrigued me (2019)

It's funny how ideas mix over time and become fully-fledged series. Once I heard "Apartment", everything fell into place.

Once I wrote Chapter 3 of *Dead Rat Walking* (the chapter where Becca sits Cyrus down, tells him to get a job, and that she's kicking him out of her apartment), the story and the characters became clear to me.

The City of Chicago

I have always believed that the city is a character in urban fantasy. I wanted to make Chicago feel real and lived in.

I've spent a decent amount in Chicago. It's only a few hours away from Des Moines, Iowa where I live, and I used to travel there extensively for work. I spent most of my time in northwest Chicago and downtown, so that's why I set the series there.

I also set each book in the series with excerpts from the wonderful poetry of Edgar Lee Masters' *Spoon River Anthology.* His poems embody America in the 1800s, and Masters lived in Chicago and set his poetry in Illinois.

Chicago is a city with an amazing history. It is an architectural wonder; the fact that it exists at all is something people don't often think about. The area is a low-lying swamp. Engineers raised the city between four and fourteen feet on jackscrews to avoid many of the issues living in a swamp creates (health problems, flooding, and so on). When you walk in downtown Chicago, there's an entire history below your feet that you can't see.

In the late 1800s, a company built underground freight tunnels to transport freight, supplies, and garbage between buildings downtown. Those tunnels fell out of use and flooded in 1992 during a construction accident, causing all sorts of hell in the city. So, if there were paranormals living underground, these freight tunnels would be a great place for them to inhabit—much like the Midwest Gnome Clan. They were directly inspired by stories of these tunnels.

There are so many great pieces of history in Chicago that are fodder for fiction. If you've never been to Chicago, I hope that this series will make you want to visit there someday.

I am especially grateful to a group of Chicago-native beta readers who gave me some pointers on how I portrayed the city, particularly Logan Square and the L system details. They helped me with a lot of the little everyday details that I hope helped the city feel lived-in.

Cyrus and Becca

Cyrus's story is a coming-of-age story. It's not a teenage coming of age story, but instead a journey into mature adulthood. Through a series of poor decisions, he ends up in the wrong place at the wrong time, and he gets turned into a rat. The series is about him adapting to life as a shifter and learning how to live his new life despite a permanent change in his life that he didn't ask for. And yet, he learns to thrive, with his best life ahead of him. That's such a great metaphor for life in general.

Becca's story is a story of trauma in *Rat City* and *Year of the Rat.* Unlike Cyrus, she's already got her life figured out, but through a series of bad decisions in *Rat City*, she ends up possessed by a demon. Becca's story for me was about learning how to live with trauma. Just before I wrote *Year of the*

Rat, my wife contracted COVID-19 and suffered a serious chronic complication as a result, one that has changed the course of her life forever. I tapped into those feelings of dread and sadness when I wrote this novel.

When I wrote this series, I knew that while it was Cyrus's story, that his relationship with his sister would be central to the plot. No matter what, they stick together.

Rats

Rats are fascinating animals, and I spent dozens of hours learning about them.

I consulted a rodent biologist when writing this series. He studied rats and spent a lot of time with them. He helped me get the rodent biology parts right. He helped me add a lot of little touches here and there that I hope made the rat scenes more memorable and vivid.

The final battle in *Dead Rat Walking* between Cyrus and Thurston as rats was inspired by a famous painting by John James Audubon called "Black Rat." It depicts two rats in a bird's nest fighting over an egg. Cyrus and Thurston are fighting on a tree branch as the fae world is collapsing around them.

The scene in *Rat City* where Cyrus shifts into a rat on top of Gilberto's church and ventures across a telephone wire and down the neighboring building to spy on Aidankirk but encounters Bruce MacLeod's spirit was another scene that drew from a lot of biological research and stories about rats.

Villains

This series differs from others that I have written in that the villains are very prominent. In fact, when I wrote this series, I considered it to be a study in villains. That's why every book features the main villain as a point-of-view character.

In *Dead Rat Walking*, I had a lot of fun with Atticus Thurston and exploring how someone so brilliant could be corrupted and seduced into evil. Murgalen was inspired by reading fae lore.

In *Rat City*, I spent time inside the head of Aidankirk, and how two brothers could be so evil and yet likable at the same time. In some ways, Kirk's story in *Year of the Rat* is similar to Cyrus's—he'd do anything to get his brother and father back. Some of the rules of necromancy are explored further in my other urban fantasy series *The Good Necromancer*. If you liked the necromancy in *The Chicago Rat Shifter*, you'll love it in *The Good Necromancer*.

In *Year of the Rat*, I had a blast with JoJo. The character was inspired by and takes his name from a song called "JoJo" by Boz Scaggs on his *Middle Man* album. If you read the lyrics of the song, you'll understand. The opening lyric in that song is "Look out behind you / JoJo's got his gun…" When JoJo draws his gun on Barry in the first chapter we meet him, that's an homage to the lyric. And of course, JoJo's mink coat is also a call back to that song.

I thought it would be fun to explore a character like JoJo. He's unique in my villain rogues gallery, and I haven't written a villain quite like him—a mink-wearing demon collector who stores his demons in the bodies of willing servants in exchange for favors. Yep, that's definitely a fun villain to explore.

JoJo's girlfriend Simone is named after another song on the *Middle Man* album.

Originally, JoJo and Simone were going to die, but as I made it further into the story, it was clear to me that they had to survive. JoJo is the kind of guy who goes bump in the night. If there is such a thing as a paranormal world with a seedy underbelly, it would be filled with hardscrabble types like JoJo and Simone. While Cyrus and Becca got the happy ending they deserved, JoJo and Simone are reminders that there is always evil in the world, and it always lives to laugh another day. And, whether we accept it or not, it is sometimes stronger than good.

Catalina Parva was inspired after observing a married couple in an airport while I was traveling just before I wrote this novel. I was sitting near this married couple in the airport who was not comfortable with each other. They were extremely formal, asking each other's permission for everything. ("Honey, is it okay if I leave my bag in this chair next to you while I go to the restroom?") There was something odd about that couple that I couldn't put my finger on.

Then I had a weird thought: what if they weren't actually married, and the whole thing was a ruse? Then, Catalina was born.

Final Thoughts

I wrote this entire series "into the dark", meaning I had no idea what would happen. When you first met Cyrus in the sewer, fighting for his life, that was the first time I met him too.

I wrote this entire series on the seat of my pants with only a small idea of what was to come. I don't write story outlines like most authors. I just make it up as I go. It's a lot more fun that way, and if I'm having fun, my hope is that you will be too.

Whatever life experiences I'm dealing with at the time make their way into my stories. For example, me being in the airport and encountering that awkward married couple happened only a few days before I wrote Kirk's first chapter in *Year of the Rat*. I had no idea who was going to be waiting for Kirk in his hotel room. Then I remembered that couple in the airport. A few minutes and mental gymnastics later, I wrote a beautiful woman with a gun and skull sitting in Kirk's room. I just followed my fingers and trusted my subconscious to do something intriguing.

This entire series (and my fiction writing) is filled with little examples like this. My novels are a chronicle of my everyday experiences in this regard.

I hope *The Chicago Rat Shifter* was as much of a roller-coaster ride for you as it was for me. It is an honor for me that you made it this far, and I would be honored if you turned the page and joined me in one of my other fictional worlds.

—Michael La Ronn
Des Moines, Iowa
August 15, 2022

9 798885 510615